Sphere of death

'I think we should do away with all this royalty lot. Pension them off, shoot the . . .' Detective Sergeant Joseph Bragg's expressed penchant for republicanism, that sunny spring morning is abruptly terminated by an almighty explosion which rocks the Old Jewry headquarters of the City of London Police. It sparks off an intricate and highly dangerous investigation into a plot which threatens the monarchy itself.

In 1894 London has become a sanctuary for political refugees from all over Europe. Known anarchists are being given safe haven. But for how long can they be kept inactive?

Forced by Special Branch into a desperately risky undercover operation, upper-crust Constable James Morton infiltrates the anarchists' cell in the guise of a Swiss nihilist. He has to assist in meticulous preparations to wreak carnage on the streets of London, in the name of Freedom from the Capitalist classes.

To Special Branch, Morton is expendable; to Catherine Marsden, the *City Press*'s feminist reporter, he is a rejected suitor who is nevertheless vital to her happiness; to Sergeant Bragg he is a close and respected colleague in mortal danger.

Bragg's efforts to control events and extricate his valued constable turn into a race to avert widespread bloodshed and to foil a plot against the Prince of Wales.

The pace is fast, the background authentic, the plot gripping. *Sphere of death*, Ray Harrison's ninth novel, will delight previous admirers and attract new ones to the redoubtable duo of Bragg and Morton.

Books by Ray Harrison

French ordinary murder (1983)
Death of an Honourable Member (1984)
Deathwatch (1985)
Death of a dancing lady (1985)
Counterfeit of murder (1986)
Season for death (1987)
Harvest of death (1988)
Tincture of death (1989)

SPHERE OF DEATH

Ray Harrison

Constable · London

First published in Great Britain 1990
by Constable & Company Ltd
3 The Lanchesters
162 Fulham Palace Road
London W6 9ER
Copyright © 1990 Ray Harrison
ISBN 0 09 470270 5
Set in Linotron 10pt Palatino
by CentraCet, Cambridge
Printed in Great Britain
by St Edmundsbury Press Ltd
Bury St Edmunds, Suffolk

A CIP catalogue record for this book
is available from the British Library

TO AUDREY AND ADU

1

'Did you see the bit in that Met circular, about the headless corpse, lad?'

Detective Sergeant Joseph Bragg and Detective Constable James Morton, of the City of London police, were strolling back to their Old Jewry headquarters, in the warm April sunshine.

'No, sir,' Morton said jauntily. 'I have not yet got round to it.'

'Well, you should. We have to know what is going on in their area, just as much as in our own.'

'Yes, sir. I am afraid that this hansom cab strike makes life rather involved.'

'Yours maybe,' Bragg said sourly. 'Most of us are too damned tired, when we get home, for involvements.'

'I presume it was murder.'

'What? . . . Oh yes, must have been. This middle-aged woman sent a large trunk to Charing Cross station, for despatch to Berlin. The carrier's men noticed some dampness at one end, and a bit of a ripe smell. So the railway police opened it, and found the body of a man – minus his head.'

'Some mild marital disagreement, no doubt!'

'She was picked up by Jock Simpson. I met him in the pub, last night. He said she came as quietly as a lamb . . . a little, mousy woman, he said.'

'And the head?'

'She had already sent it to Paris!'

'Never the twain should meet, eh?'

Bragg grimaced. 'I suppose that you won't have got round to the circular about the Queen's return, either,' he said.

7

'No. Are we to be honoured by an invitation to guard the royal person, on her arrival?'

'Victoria station, on the twenty-ninth.'

'Do we mingle with the crowd, as usual?'

'I expect so,' Bragg said grumpily. 'If you ask me, there are plenty of things should come before that.'

'Before protecting our gracious Queen?' Morton asked, in mock astonishment.

'Don't be so bloody naïve!' Bragg said irritably. 'She has been in Italy for the last six months. You can't say she has had any hand in running the country, from there! And, when she gets back, she will bugger off to the Isle of Wight; and nobody will see her till she's off to the Mediterranean for next winter.'

'She is quite old,' Morton said equably. 'I imagine that none of the royal palaces is comfortable, during the winter.'

'You could buy a couple of coal mines, for what it has cost to ship her and her hangers-on out to Florence. And you can bet it doesn't come out of her pocket. That lot has a mountain of money, but every time they stir, they hold out the begging bowl.'

'You seem rather jaundiced this afternoon, sir.'

'And why shouldn't I be? They have their hand in your pocket at every turn. I can't smoke a pipe or drink a pint, without I'm subsidizing their extravagances . . . I don't know why you are happy about it, lad. With all your money, they must cost you a fortune.'

'Ah, but I have not got your penchant for republicanism,' Morton said lightly.

'And what's wrong with it? The Americans manage very well without a royal family. I reckon we could take a leaf or two out of their book.'

Morton grinned. 'With an American mother and an English father, I could hardly take sides in that argument.'

They stopped at a road junction, while an omnibus turned across their path. It was crammed with people. Some were even standing precariously in the open, on the top deck, clinging to the slatted backs of the seats. On the other side of the junction, a group of women and children stood wearily, waiting until the crossing was clear. In a great city, like London, Morton reflected, you only had to take out one small component of the transport system, and chaos ensued with appalling rapidity.

'Come on, lad,' Bragg said, as a small gap opened up in the stream of carts and vans. They dodged across under the noses of the great cart-horses. As they approached the other side, the group of women began hesitantly to pull their children into the traffic.

'You know what I think, lad,' Bragg resumed belligerently. 'I think we should do away with all this royalty lot. Pension them off, shoot the buggers . . .'

There came a sudden explosion, practically beneath their feet; a dull bang and a blast that flung them against the wall of a building, yards away. Bragg's dazed body was pinned to the ground by Morton's. He shook his head to clear it.

'Christ Almighty!' he mumbled. 'What the hell was that?'

'Now you know what happens, when you traduce God's anointed!' Morton said, scrambling to his feet.

Women were screaming and children crying; horses reared and their drivers swore. A man was standing by the wall, with blood pouring down his face: another was peering distrustfully into a gaping hole in the pavement. Morton brushed the dust from his clothes and went over. It was a shallow brick manhole. The heavy sweated cables, in the bottom, showed that it was a junction-box for the electrical system.

Bragg appeared at his elbow, holding a large piece of jagged cast-iron. 'Look at this! It's a wonder no one was killed.'

'Is that a part of the manhole cover?'

'It is . . . I reckon if those women hadn't moved into the road, there would be some corpses around.'

'Are you all right, sir?' Morton asked solicitously.

'Apart from some bumps and grazes. And you?'

'I'm fine.'

'Come on, lad. We're going to get someone to answer for this.'

'Which electrical company is it?'

Bragg turned the piece of metal over. 'From the letters cast into this side, it looks like Edison & Swan United. They are in Holborn Viaduct, aren't they?'

'A mere hundred yards ahead.'

9

'Good. Everything seems to be under control here, so let's see what they have to say for themselves.'

They walked the short distance to the flamboyant new office building and climbed the stairs to the top floor. They found themselves at a polished oak counter, with a large office beyond. No doubt, this was where the public would come to pay their bills. By the looks of it, they could not yet have many customers, for the only clerk in the room was a youth with his feet on his desk, reading a book.

'Hey!' Bragg yelled.

The youth looked up. 'Yer?' he asked.

'Is this a part of one of your manhole covers?'

Reluctantly he slid his heels off his desk and strolled over. He took the piece of iron and turned it in his hands.

'Yer,' he said.

'This has come from a manhole that has just exploded.'

The youth looked at Bragg stolidly. 'Oh, yer?' he said. 'I 'spect I'd better get somebody down to mend it.'

'Never mind about that,' said Bragg wrathfully. 'I want to see the man in charge, and quick about it.'

'Oh, yer?'

'Yes, I bloody do!'

'Right, I'll see if he's in.'

The youth drifted to the back of the room and disappeared through a door. Soon afterwards, a smartly dressed man bounced into the office. He hurried across to the counter.

'Thank you so much for coming to tell us,' he said effusively. 'Where is the manhole in question?'

'On the corner of Brooke Street.'

'Ah, yes. John, tell our engineers to attend to it at once. Safety is our watchword in this company, sir, safety above all.'

'Safety?' Bragg exclaimed incredulously. 'The bloody thing exploded! It threw me and my constable damned near ten feet. You are lucky there weren't serious injuries, or worse!'

A cautious look had come over the man's face. 'You are police officers, then?' he asked.

'We are. And we want some answers.'

'Well, gentlemen,' he said reasonably, 'although I accept without question your assertion that there was an explosion in

10

our manhole, I cannot thereby accept your inference that it is our responsibility. It is not a characteristic of electricity, that it explodes. I would be the first to admit that, in the wrong hands, electrical power can be dangerous. You will recall that, last month, a horse was killed in Cannon Street by electrocution. That, of course, is in the area of the Consolidated Electric Company. We warned, at the time the tenders were being considered, that Consolidated had cut corners in safety to get their price down. And we have been proved right. If the insulation is inadequate, the power can leak out with dangerous consequences.'

'But it would not explode?'

'No. Electricity is not a substance, it is a force. Of itself, it cannot be explosive.'

'Look here, mate, I wasn't bloody imagining it!' Bragg growled.

'Of course not,' the man said in a placatory tone. 'And I am greatly relieved that you were not injured. However, I must point out that manhole covers are not secured. Anyone could raise one, and insert an explosive substance beneath it.'

'But they would have been seen!'

'Not necessarily. I believe that it is possible, nowadays, to trigger off an explosive by means of a clockwork device.'

'You mean, it could have been put in the manhole during the night?'

'Indeed. The anarchists blew up part of the Tsar's Winter Palace, some years ago, with just such a mechanism.'

'But we aren't in Russia!'

'True. Yet it is not much more than ten years since the Irish were exploding bombs in London. Perhaps the Fenians are becoming active again. And there are scores of foreign anarchists living here.'

'Hmn . . . Maybe we ought to go and have another look.'

'Indeed, gentlemen, and be assured that our company will be happy to give you every assistance.'

Bragg and Morton hurried back, to find that barriers had already been erected round the hole, and that the debris had been swept up. The injured and shocked passers-by had been spirited away; the street had returned to normal. A workman

11

was leaning against a hand-cart by the hole. In it were thick rubber mats and a jumble of plumber's paraphernalia.

'Are you mending this lot?' Bragg asked.

'Yes.' The man took a step and peered into the hole. 'We shall have to remake the joint, to be on the safe side. The gaffer has just gone to switch the current off.'

'Do you mean that it's still alive?'

The man grinned. 'Keep your hair on, mate. There is nothing to worry about with electricity, if you know what you are doing.'

'That is what everybody connected with it says. But how do I know you are not a bunch of lying sods?'

'If I were, I'd be six feet under before now.'

'Did you sweep the debris up?'

'No, the street orderly did.'

'Where are the sweepings?'

'He chucked them on to a passing dust-cart.'

Bragg sighed irritably. 'Did you see anything that might have been a bit of clockwork?' he asked.

The man shook his head. 'No, I didn't see nothing like that.'

Morton peered into the manhole. The bottom had been swept clean; only a few small chips of brick and some dust remained. He was about to rise to his feet, when he detected a faint odour of coal-gas. He beckoned to Bragg.

'There seems to be a gas escape,' he said. 'I wonder if that could have set off the explosion.'

Bragg knelt down by him and sniffed. 'Are you certain?' he asked.

'It is unmistakable, surely?'

'If you say so. Smoking thick twist has taken the edge off my smell, lad. Do you want to follow it up?'

'I feel that we ought, since public safety is involved.'

'The gas company is in Clement's Lane, isn't it?'

'Yes.'

'Oh, well, the exercise will do us good.'

The gas company was housed in modest premises, but seemed much more thriving than the electricity company. Bragg produced his warrant-card, and they were shown up to the manager's office.

12

'Why should you come to me, about an explosion in an electricity company manhole?' he asked with some asperity.

'We are trying to establish the cause,' said Bragg. 'People have been injured.'

'You have not answered my question, sergeant.'

'I take it that your gas mains run along that street, sir.'

'Yes.'

'Are they close to the electric power cable?'

'They should most certainly not be! The electricity people were required to leave ample clearance, when they were laying their cables.'

'The fact remains, there is a strong smell of gas at the site of the explosion.'

The manager looked at Bragg frostily. 'Since there has been an explosion of some magnitude in the electricity company's distribution system, it is hardly surprising! Now, if that is all, I will see that any defect in our pipes is speedily remedied.'

'Right,' Bragg grunted. 'Is that a classified directory of the telephone company there, sir?'

'It is.'

'May I borrow it for a moment?'

The manager reluctantly pushed it across his desk. Bragg flipped through the pages, then gave a murmur of satisfaction. He rose to his feet. 'Thank you for your courtesy, sir,' he said sardonically. 'We may want to see you again.'

'What were you looking for?' Morton asked, as they clumped down the stairs.

'Well, it is still early. If we go back to Old Jewry, the Commissioner will be chasing us for something or other. I thought we might take a short train ride, instead.'

'To where?'

'I would have expected someone with a Cambridge degree to say "whither?".'

Morton laughed. 'Then, if I were to get my priorities right, I should be asking "whence?".'

'Fenchurch Street station. I thought a jaunt to Stepney might be in order.'

'And who, pray, is of interest to us in Stepney?'

13

'There is a firm called Boland Kerr & Co, in Butcher Row. They are suppliers of explosives.'

'I see. Are you inclined to conclude that the explosion was caused by a bomb?'

'No, lad. I am still keeping an open mind. But we shall have to make a report, and I would like to have covered all the possibilities, before you start to write it!'

An hour later, they were standing at the trade counter of Boland Kerr & Co.

'You are not exactly run off your feet,' Bragg remarked to the grizzled storeman.

'No, sergeant. Most of our stuff is used in the excavations for the new underground railway. Since they haven't got anywhere proper to keep it, they draw what they need for the day, first thing in the morning.'

'Good. So you will have plenty of time to help us.'

'What is it? Has some explosive gone missing?'

'No. I want you to give us the benefit of your technical knowledge . . . There was an explosion in an electricity company's manhole, this afternoon. It has been suggested that someone might have blown it up with a bomb.'

'Someone like the gas company?' the storeman asked, with a smile.

'Well, they cannot be too pleased about the way electric lighting is taking over, in the main streets and the offices. Though, from what we have heard this afternoon, gas is still a sight safer . . . I have a bit of the manhole cover here. To shatter that thickness of cast-iron, there must have been quite a force.'

The storeman took the piece of metal over to the window, and scrutinized it carefully.

'Has it been wiped, at all?' he asked.

'No. It is just as I picked it up. Mind you, I have had it in my pocket all afternoon.'

'Another thing. Was there a burnt line along the pavement, by the manhole?'

'No. I am sure of that.'

'You see, if a charge had been fired by a safety fuse, there would have been a black mark where it had been.'

'Someone suggested that it could have been set off by clockwork,' Morton said.

'Well, one thing is certain sure. If there was a bomb, it was not charged with black powder. If it had been, there would be a film of black on the inside of the cover.'

'Of course there would,' Bragg muttered. 'Just like a black-powder cartridge, fired at close range.'

'What about other explosives?' Morton asked.

The storeman scratched his chin. 'You know,' he said, 'if the iron had not been clean, I would have thought it might be black powder. It's a fairly gentle sort of explosive.'

'Gentle?' Bragg asked in astonishment.

'As these things go, yes. That is why they use it in coal mines. A modern explosive like blasting oil or guncotton, or even dynamite, is too fierce. It shatters everything in reach. If someone had put a stick of dynamite in the manhole, you would never have found a piece of the cover as big as this.'

'You are of the opinion,' said Morton, 'that there was no explosive involved and, therefore, no bomb.'

The storeman frowned. 'No, I'm not saying that. But I'm no expert. You should really go to a chemist, if you want a proper opinion.'

'What about coal-gas?' Bragg asked.

'Well, you know, same as I do, that a gas explosion can bring a house down. I don't know how you would go about setting it off, though, short of a fuse.'

'Before long, we shall begin to think we imagined it,' Bragg said grumpily, as they took their leave.

They arrived back in Old Jewry, to find a note on Bragg's desk. He read it scowling.

'It's from Inspector Cotton,' he said. 'Apparently, some American gentleman has been mislaid by the Great Eastern Railway Hotel. I am asked to look into it. Well, coming from him, I think it will wait until tomorrow.'

Next morning, Bragg and Morton were at the Great Eastern by nine o'clock. They had to kick their heels, for a time, while the manager and his staff dealt with customers anxious to pay their bills, and be away. At last, the manager broke off and came over to them. Bragg showed his warrant-card.

'We have come about your missing American,' he said. 'Was it you who reported him missing?'

'Yes, sergeant.'

'Who is he?'

'A Mr L. McCafferty.'

'Can you give us a description of him?'

The manager pondered. 'I would suppose him to be around forty,' he said. 'He is well built – indeed, one might describe him as somewhat plump. He has red hair, blue eyes and a pale, freckled complexion.'

'How tall?'

'I suppose, approaching six feet.'

'What sort of man is he, would you say?'

'From what little contact I have had with him, he seemed a very pleasant, talkative person.'

'Not the type who might have thrown himself into the river, then?'

'By no means. He seemed to be very engaging and . . . well, happy.'

'Hmn . . . How long has he been here?'

'He arrived on the twenty-sixth of March, and booked a room for a week. That included last Sunday night.'

'So, he should have been leaving yesterday. What about his luggage?'

'It is in his room. We did not require it, so I felt it best to leave things as they were.'

'That was very helpful of you, sir. When did you last see him?'

'It is difficult to be precise, of course, but the concierge is of the opinion that he has not taken the key of his room, since Thursday.'

'And why did you report his absence to the police?' Bragg asked.

'Well . . . he has been missing, sergeant – for some days.'

'Lots of people go missing, sir, for a variety of reasons,' Bragg said dourly. 'We do not go chasing after them, in the ordinary course. Are you saying that there are suspicious circumstances attached to it?'

'I . . . It did not seem in character, somehow . . . Yes, I do think it suspicious,' the manager added defiantly.

'I see.' Bragg sighed. 'Can we see his room?'

'Of course.'

The manager led them to the rear of the foyer. Morton was amused to see Bragg's mood lighten, at the sight of the hydraulic lift. They soared to the third floor, and the manager took them to a small room at the rear of the hotel. Bragg peered out of the window, and saw that it overlooked the railway train-shed.

'Not one of your best rooms, then?' he remarked.

'Many gentlemen prefer these rooms,' the manager said defensively. 'They tend to be somewhat warmer than the larger ones.'

Bragg grunted and opened the door of the wardrobe. A lounging suit, in a large grey check, hung next to a black frock-coat. On the shelf above it was a brown derby hat. A quantity of soiled linen had been thrown in the bottom of the wardrobe. Morton opened the drawers of a tallboy. Apart from some handkerchiefs and ties, in the top drawer, it was empty. On a stand in the corner was a cabin-trunk. Bragg raised the lid. It was half full of clothes, jumbled as if someone had rummaged through them to find something, and had not bothered to refold the garments. On the wash-stand was a partly-used cake of soap and a dry flannel.

'Was he clean-shaven?' Bragg asked.

'Yes, indeed.'

'There is no shaving-brush or razor here. I wonder why.'

'I have no idea, sergeant.'

'There do not appear to be any personal papers, either. That seems strange, to me, if our friend McCafferty was mislaid involuntarily . . . Well, there is nothing much to go on. Can you have his things packed, and store them somewhere for a bit? No point in keeping one of your rooms out of circulation, is there?'

'Of course. I will see that it is done immediately,' the manager said in a relieved tone.

'We'll go and have a word with your . . . What did you call him?'

'Concierge?'

'Right. We will let you know, if we find anything.'

Even the lift seemed unable to cheer Bragg now. 'Why is it that the new hotels are going all Frenchified?' he asked grumpily.

'You forget that this is the station the royal family use when they go to Sandringham,' Morton said lightly. 'And you know how much the Prince of Wales admires the French nation.'

'The female half of it, anyway. But what difference does that make? Blast it! This is England. Why can't they call them porters, like they always have?'

The lift-attendant sat stolidly on his stool, as if he were an automaton, hearing nothing. As soon as the door was opened, Bragg launched himself towards the concierge's desk.

'I gather that you think Mr McCafferty has not been in since Thursday,' he said gruffly.

'That's right, sir.' The man was large and placid, accustomed to humouring irate customers.

'How do you know?'

'Why, there is only one key to each room. So it's easy enough to see when it has not been taken. Mind you, I did ask the night porter, when the manager got worried. He said the same as me. That key has never been off the board since Thursday.'

'Why so sure? Why should you remember this particular man?'

'Well, the gentleman was very chatty – and generous. I am sure all right.'

'Did you see him, that morning?'

'As a matter of fact, I did. I asked him if he would like a newspaper, but he said no. Then he asked me where he could change some dollars into pounds.'

'And where did you send him?'

'Well, we like to impress our foreign guests, you know . . . I sent him to the Bank of England!'

'Did you, now? Then we might as well have a chat with them. Thanks.'

'Since my rooms are just around the corner,' Morton said,

18

'would you like to indulge in a cup of coffee? Mrs Chambers would have it made in a jiffy.'

Bragg frowned. 'No, lad. We have work to do. And once you start nipping home for a drink, there's no knowing where it will end. It only takes some sod from the uniformed branch to see you coming out, and suddenly it's a disciplinary matter.'

Morton shrugged. 'Very well.'

They pushed their way along the crowded pavements and, before long, came to the windowless bulk of the Bank of England. The gate porter touched his cocked hat to Bragg, as they strolled into the Garden Court.

'I wonder if McCafferty was impressed with this lot, or not,' Bragg said. 'Now, let us see if we can find our friend Gibson.'

'I imagine that, by now, he feels he has repaid whatever debt he owed us,' Morton replied.

'Ah, but we are entitled to interest. That is what this place is all about!'

They went into the ornate Cashier's Office. Bragg scanned the line of clerks, behind the long mahogany counter.

'There he is! And disengaged, too . . . Good morning, Mr Gibson. It's good to see you again!'

'Ah . . . Sergeant Bragg,' Gibson said unenthusiastically. A couple of years ago, Bragg had protected his reputation over the matter of some counterfeit notes. Since then, the sergeant had extracted a series of favours involving confidential information, which would have ruined Gibson, had his superiors got to know.

'You have moved along one, I see,' said Bragg. 'Does it mean you've been promoted, now they have thrown May out?'

'Mr May's departure does mean that I am more senior in the department, certainly, but it is not a promotion.'

'Now, why did they not have the foresight to make you Chief Cashier, eh? Have a young man, for a change. Who did they pick?'

'A gentleman called Horace Bowen.'

'Never mind, you will get it next time.'

'I fear not,' Gibson said gloomily. 'Mr Bowen is a mere ten years older than I. When he retires, I may well be regarded as too old to succeed him.'

19

'Well, there are more important things in life than promotion, believe you me! . . . I was wondering if you could see your way to giving us a bit of information.'

'Oh, yes?' Gibson said unhappily.

'A man was sent here by the Great Eastern Hotel, last Thursday – an American gentleman, name of McCafferty. He told them he wanted to change some dollars.'

'A great number of Americans come here for that purpose.'

'I'm sure. But he should stand out. He is said to be tall and well built, with red hair and a freckled face – around forty.'

'That sounds like our millionaire,' Gibson said with the beginnings of a smile. 'I dealt with him myself. What is it that you wish to know?'

'Why, everything we can get. He has gone missing.'

'I am hardly surprised, in view of the rashness of his conduct.'

'How is that?'

'He came to me with a bundle of mainly thousand-dollar notes, and asked me to change them for sovereigns.'

'And did you?'

'Of course – once I had verified that the bills were genuine.'

Bragg grinned. 'How many did he change?' he asked.

Gibson consulted his ledger. 'Fifty-eight thousand, three hundred and twenty American dollars,' he said.

'What did that amount to, in sterling?'

'Twelve thousand pounds.'

Bragg whistled. 'That is a hell of a lot of money!'

'Indeed. And, in sovereigns, a considerable weight, also. As I did not have the quantity required in my till, I passed him on to the bullion section to satisfy his requirements.'

'Why did he not take paper money? It would have been a sight easier.'

'It would hardly have been proper for me to ask,' Gibson said stuffily, 'and he did not volunteer the information.'

'Hmn. Can I have a word with your bullion people, do you think?'

Gibson considered for a moment, then: 'I see no reason why not,' he said grudgingly.

He led the way down a series of corridors, until they came to a courtyard which, in Bragg's estimation, must have been at the furthest limits of the premises. They waited, under the suspicious gaze of a porter, while Gibson went into an office. After a few moments he came out, accompanied by another man.

'This is Mr Pearce,' he said. 'It was he who dealt with Mr McCafferty. He will give you all the information available.' Gibson turned on his heel and hurried away.

'What is it you wish to know?' Pearce asked with a smile.

'Really, anything you can tell us. McCafferty has disappeared, and the hotel has reported him missing. Mr Gibson didn't seem all that surprised.'

'It was certainly most extraordinary. I was given a chit, by Mr Gibson, to provide sovereigns to the value of twelve thousand pounds sterling. We make them up in bags of one hundred, which are packed ten to a sack. So that meant twelve sacks in all.'

'What weight would that be?'

'In troy weight, two hundred and fifty-six pounds.'

'What would it be in ordinary weight?' Morton interposed.

'Two hundred and eleven pounds avoirdupois.'

'Christ!' Bragg exclaimed. 'That's getting on for fifteen stone – the weight of a big man.'

'True. I said as much to Mr McCafferty, but he seemed unconcerned. He said that, in view of the cab strike, he had procured a conveyance, which was waiting at the front of the bank. At my suggestion, it was brought round to the Lothbury entrance . . .' Pearce's smile broadened.

'And?' Bragg prompted him.

'The conveyance proved to be a costermonger and his barrow! We loaded the sovereigns on to it, and Mr McCafferty covered them with empty potato sacks. Then off they went. I asked if he would like one of our porters to accompany them, but he declined the suggestion.'

'In which direction did they go?'

'To Whitechapel, I would say. The costermonger was pure East End. Certainly, they went down Bartholomew Lane.'

Bragg and Morton went back to Old Jewry. As Morton jotted down some notes, Bragg pulled out his pipe. He carefully cut slivers from a rope of twist, with his juice-stained knife, then rubbed the tobacco gently between his palms.

'It's a damned queer business, and no mistake,' he said, beginning to feed the shreds of tobacco into the bowl of his pipe. 'Twelve sacks of gold sovereigns. How heavy would each of them be?'

'Over seventeen pounds.'

'You wouldn't want to carry that far!'

'It is quite extraordinary that McCafferty preferred coins to paper money,' Morton said thoughtfully.

'There is something even more extraordinary, lad. McCafferty must have brought those dollars into Britain.'

'Is it safe to assume that?'

'I think so. Where would you get dollar bills in that quantity, over here? Nowhere but a big bank. Now, if he'd wanted to bring that quantity of funds over from America, you would expect him to have done it by a letter of credit. That would be the only sensible way. In that case, you would think he'd draw it down in sterling. Dollar notes are not a fat lot of use, over here – particularly bills of a thousand dollars.' Bragg struck a match and applied it to his pipe.

'Accepting that premise,' Morton said, 'a normal tourist would not need to encash dollars to the tune of twelve thousand pounds, all at one time.'

Bragg flicked the match towards his waste-paper basket, leaving a blue trail hanging in the air. 'I have a feeling that it's all to do with anonymity,' he said.

'In what way?'

'Well, if you had brought a letter of credit, it would be traceable back to the issuing bank in America and, presumably, to their customer . . . So far as this end is concerned, a Bank of England note is numbered, and they know who they issued it to. But no one can trace a sovereign.'

'Yet, why change them all at once?' Morton objected.

'Perhaps the money was intended for one big transaction.'

'A small box of uncut diamonds would have been easier to handle than the coins. After all, McCafferty was taking an enormous risk, ferrying all that money around London in a hand-cart!'

Bragg puffed contentedly on his pipe. 'Perhaps all the money

22

was needed at once . . . for the purchase of something a bit out of the ordinary.'

'Like a brothel?' Morton suggested with a grin.

'Something like that. If he were dealing with shady characters, he might even have taken his razor along as a weapon.'

'Whatever his purpose, with such a large amount of gold there must be a distinct possibility that he has been robbed and disposed of.'

'Silly bugger! I suppose we shall have to list him as missing. Get his description out to the Met, as well, will you, lad? But, first, we might see if our old friend Foxy Jock knows anything.'

They walked by back streets to Spitalfields Market, then into the run-down area north of Aldgate. It was a maze of narrow alleys and noisome courts, lined with decaying clapboard houses. Ragged children clustered around them, begging for pennies. Hard-faced women lounged in the doorways. As they passed a pub, the door crashed open and a man staggered out, his face streaming with blood.

'It's business as usual here, anyway,' Bragg said, taking some coins from his pocket, and scattering them for the children.

They came to the corner of Spelman Street. Jock McGregor's pawnshop was as dejected as the buildings around it. The three balls hung crookedly over the doorway, the windows were so grimy that they were virtually opaque. A bell jangled in the shop, as Bragg opened the door. After a moment, they could hear shuffling in the alcove behind the scarred counter. A face peered out from the limp curtain that screened it.

'Ah, Sergeant Bragg,' said Jock, in a hoarse, whining voice. His flaccid face was mottled pink, his bald head fringed with greasy, yellowish-white hair. He held out a hand ingrained with dirt, his eyes wary.

'This isn't a social call,' Bragg said roughly. 'I damned near brought a warrant with me.'

'Now, you know I never touch anything that's been prigged,' Jock protested piously.

'Not much, you don't! We've recovered the sapphire bracelet pinched from the Bensons' place. I know bloody well you fenced it, Jock. If I can only prove it, I'll see you spend the rest of your sodding life in the Scrubs!'

23

'I know nothing about it, Mr Bragg! I havenae even clapped eyes on it,' Jock wailed.

'I reckon I ought to arrest you on suspicion – do the world a good turn. We could fit you up with something.'

'No, Mr Bragg! You wouldnae do that. You're too much of a gentleman; not like them in the Metropolitan police!'

'Don't bank on it, Jock . . . I want some information.'

'I'll do anything I can to help – you know that.'

'Well, see you bloody do. The word is that a Whitechapel barrow-boy might have come into a bit of money. Nothing illicit . . . But I want to know who it is. Understand?'

'Yes, Mr Bragg. I'll put the word out.'

'Right. And don't take for ever!'

2

Morton closed the door of the brougham; there was the brief flutter of Catherine's hand, and the carriage moved off. He waited until it had turned the corner, then set off to walk home. Had the evening been a success, he wondered. For his part, it had begun too breathlessly for comfort. It had been late when he left Old Jewry, and he'd had to be content with a hasty snack while he dressed. Since he would have to walk to the West End, where he was picking up the carriage, he had decided against evening dress and settled for a frock-coat. He fancied that Mrs Marsden's eyebrows had lifted slightly, when he was shown into the drawing-room. Catherine, of course, had been too much in control of herself to show surprise.

He regretted the necessity of the carriage. In the past, when he had taken Catherine for dinner or to a theatre, a cab had sufficed. In their new situation, a smart brougham might have seemed to her provocative, a crude demonstration of his wealth. But there was no other way. He could hardly have exposed her to walking along Haymarket at night, with its pimps and prostitutes. He smiled to himself; she would immediately have repudiated such a protective attitude, as masculine condescension. Her parents, of course, would wonder why he had not escorted her home, as usual. But he had felt it would be unwise. The evening had passed off well. Catherine had looked elegant in a blue silk gown, and had conversed brightly during the interval. He was glad, however, that he had proposed the theatre, rather than their customary dinner at the Savoy. For all their determination to enjoy the occasion, there was a hint of restraint between them. How could it be otherwise? He wondered what Catherine would say, if her parents quizzed her about their relationship . . . But Mrs Marsden, vague and tolerant, probably looked on him as no more than an eccentric acquaintance of her daughter. Her father, one of the foremost society portraitists, was more worldly-wise. Because of that, his expectations would have been set by Catherine's triumphant introduction to society, last Season.

Morton glanced up at the moon above St Paul's – cool, detached, unknowable . . . Perhaps he had been wrong to send her home alone. What he had intended as tactfulness, now seemed graceless. But he would have had to go into the house. Catherine's parents would have casually withdrawn, leaving the drawing-room door open as a gesture to propriety, and then . . . After their last encounter in that room, there could have been nothing but awkwardness and tension. Catherine had looked serene at the theatre, almost happy to be with him. But she had seemed reluctant to allow a silence to develop between them, lest the shadow of discord should blight the evening. No, it was better to take several giant steps backwards, begin again. No more tête-à-têtes, which could degenerate into recrimination and final rupture. She was not wholly indifferent to him, or she would not have accepted his invitation. Best take the pressure off, let her run free, give her time to tire of her freedom and hope to draw her gently in. If he failed, there were always other fish in the lake . . .

He was surprised to see that he was almost home. Despite the late hour, there were lights in St Botolph's church. No doubt it was some kind of watch-night service. A group of men outside the White Hart began to break up as he approached, to drift in his direction. He turned down Alderman's Walk, towards his rooms. Several more men were lounging on the churchyard railings, near his door.

'Goodnight,' he called, searching for his key.

''Night, guv,' a voice answered.

As Morton put the key in the lock, there was a rush of boots. Suddenly, fierce hands grabbed his arms, dragging him down the alley. He jerked his right arm free and struck out. There was a sharp cry of pain, then the arm was seized and twisted behind his back. He lashed out with his foot, and heard the crack of a shin-bone, then someone struck him a vicious blow in the kidneys. He could feel a wave of agony spreading through his body, sapping his strength . . . There were more men now, no longer quiet, shouting drunkenly. Morton's legs would not support him. His attackers were holding him up . . . hitting his face, blow after blow, with manic ferocity. He could taste blood in his mouth, it was trickling down his chin . . . Now the blows had stopped. He could feel them dragging him towards the gas-lamp.

'Hold his head back,' someone ordered.

He felt his hair tugged, he could dimly see a mist of soft light.

'I reckon that will do,' the voice said. 'Let's get on.'

They were dragging him now, the toes of his boots catching between the paving stones . . . Now gravel . . . He tried to force his dazed mind to think. They must be taking him into the churchyard . . . But why? Had they battered him just for their amusement? Then, once in the churchyard, they might kill him for their amusement . . . At least, it would be a release from the lancing pain. His senses began to fail. A red swirl was sucking him into a vortex of nothingness. He fought against it . . . he must not let go. He felt himself dragged up steps and propped on a seat. The men crowded round him, silent now, their violence spent. There came the scrape of horses' hoofs – they were moving! An omnibus?. . . Now a lurch, as the vehicle went round a corner, the iron tyres harsh on sets. He tried to look about him, but his eyes were too swollen . . . What was that? Again he felt the vehicle jerk sideways, as it broke free of tramlines . . . Tramlines? Then, they were taking him out of the City. He tried to remember the routes . . . It must be east or north. The pain in his back was diminishing a little, no longer overwhelming his senses. He heard a shout of 'Whoa!' and the vehicle stopped. The door was opened and he felt himself lifted, the breeze cool on his battered face. There was a lamp above him as he was carried through a doorway. He could dimly hear a conversation.

'Is he to be charged?'

'No. The guv'nor will be round, in the morning.'

'But we can't just hold him.'

'Well, if you need to be covered, how about drunk and disorderly?'

'That'll do.'

He could see gas-jets, the walls of a corridor. There came the sound of a key in a lock. Hands lifted him on to a bunk and covered him with a blanket. The door closed, like the clang of doom, and he slipped into unconsciousness.

Morton awoke, shouting, from a nightmare. There was a throbbing ache in his back, his limbs were stiff and cold. His face was like a plaster mask, it was so swollen. He found that he could see out of one eye. Light was seeping through an aperture closed only with bars. No wonder he was cold. Bars? . . . A prison? No, he remembered now . . . A police station – a cell in a police station. He had been set upon by thugs . . . and brought by them to a police station! What could it mean? He had not provoked them. He had strolled home down Alderman's Walk, begun to unlock his door, and then he had been attacked . . . Inexplicable.

He crawled painfully off the bunk and limped over to the window. There was nothing but a yard, enclosed by a high wall. The bars of the window were firmly embedded in the brickwork; there was no way out. Shivering from shock and the early-morning cold, he climbed back under the blanket. He drifted into a light doze, which was shattered by the bang of the door.

'A cup of tea for you.'

It was a uniformed constable – from the Met!

'You were good and drunk, last night,' he said cheerfully. 'Taking on all comers, they said!' He caught sight of Morton's face. 'Blimey! You look as if you'd done ten rounds with James J. Corbett, the world heavyweight champion!'

Morton took the cup and sipped. The tea was strong and stewed, but it took the taste of blood away.

'May I have a wash?' he muttered.

'No, mate. There's a note to say you can't. "On no account", it says. So that's that.'

'But why?'

'Don't ask me. I've just come on. P'raps it's only the blood that's keeping your face together!' He turned on his heel, and the door banged behind him.

Morton rolled himself in the blanket and fell into a deep sleep. When he awoke, the sun was slanting through the bars of the cell. He clambered painfully down and stretched himself. The ache in his back was subsiding, and he was no longer shivering uncontrollably. Shortly afterwards, the policeman brought him some breakfast. He was surprised to find that he was quite hungry. Still, he had eaten virtually nothing since noon the previous day! When he had finished, he lay on his bunk again and attempted to make sense of what had happened. But, try as he might, the elements would not combine to make any sensible pattern.

Towards noon, the door was opened again. This time, the constable was accompanied by a burly man in civilian clothes.

'I am Sergeant Curtis,' he said brusquely. 'You are to come with me.'

Morton got to his feet, and limped after Curtis to the top floor of the building. The sergeant gestured to a half-open door.

'In there,' he said.

A man was standing at the window, gazing out. The close-cropped hair and bulky physique stirred a chord in Morton's memory.

'That will be all, sergeant.' The man turned, his flinty-grey eyes regarded Morton coldly.

'Major Redman!' Morton exclaimed.

'Perhaps an apology is in order,' Redman said in his bleak, incisive voice. 'But it was necessary to make an assumption, and logical to act accordingly.'

'What assumption?' Morton asked.

'That you would wish to serve your country.'

'If the logic of that led to my being half-killed, I would prefer to abstain.'

Redman's square jaw set determinedly.

'I would not readily accept that I was wrong in my judgement,' he said curtly. 'As for the beauty treatment, it was necessary; that cannot be simulated.'

'It seems a curious prelude to asking for my help – if that, indeed, is what you are about.'

Redman waved Morton to a chair by the desk. He sat behind it, and studied Morton coldly.

'I do not ask for you help,' he said, 'I require it of you, as your plain duty. Nor do I think that you will disappoint me – not merely because of your family's distinguished military tradition, for I suspect that you do not hold that in high regard.' A look of contempt crossed the heavy, florid features. 'But you are not entirely gutless. And the service I have selected you for needs more intelligence and sensitivity than one would find in the general run of men.'

'Sensitivity!' Morton exclaimed. 'That is a strange word for the head of Scotland Yard's Special Branch.'

Redman ignored him. 'I have to say that I neither could, nor would, compel you to undertake this task. But you are a trained police officer, and highly regarded – in some quarters, at least. Moreover, you speak French and German like a native.'

'I speak them fluently, even idiomatically,' Morton corrected him, 'but I could not quite claim to have the accent of a native.'

'No matter,' Redman brushed the objection aside. 'The accent of a French-speaking Swiss would not be pure . . . Tell me, do you talk in your sleep?'

Morton gave an incredulous snort. 'How do I know?' he asked. 'I have never slept with myself!'

Redman glared at him. 'We cannot eliminate all risk,' he said icily.

'For God's sake, let us stop this cat and mouse game,' Morton cried. 'I take it that you set your bludgers on me for some serious purpose.'

'To preserve the security of the kingdom, no less,' Redman said with a level stare. 'There can be no more serious purpose than that. Indeed, it is the *raison d'être* of my branch and, to that extent, my personal responsibility.'

'Then, why do you not call on your own subordinates to discharge it?'

'I am compelled to admit that I am taking what some would regard as an unacceptable gamble, in approaching you. However, you are the only person on our files who comes near to having the necessary qualities.'

'Which are?'

'If I outline the situation in which we find ourselves, you will readily identify them,' Redman replied. 'Ever since Napoleon Bonaparte was finally defeated, this country has lived in a cocoon of economic ascendancy and military superiority. Apart from minor colonial skirmishes and the aberrant folly of the Crimean War, we have enjoyed undisturbed peace. Indeed, there is not a politician on our national stage who has any conception of what it is like to struggle for the very existence of the nation. Britain has remained free of permanent alliances, while profiting from short-term co-operation with other states. The present Liberal government thinks that we can continue this policy indefinitely . . . But times are changing.'

'In what way?'

'Europe is in a state of flux. There are conflicting currents that could destroy us all.'

'I find that hard to believe,' Morton said sceptically.

'Hear me out. You shall be the judge . . . On the one hand, we have new nation-states emerging by the forcible coalescing of smaller ones. Virtually in your lifetime, the Kingdom of Italy and the German Empire have been created by the sword. On the other hand, the nation-states are being undermined by the disaffection of their peoples. Subversive movements of all kinds are springing up. Their ideologies vary in particulars, but their common aim is to sweep away society in its present form, and replace it by some millennial system that will put us all back in the Garden of Eden!'

'But surely that is mere airy-fairy nonsense?'

Redman looked steadily at him. 'Tsar Alexander of Russia did not think so. He became a virtual prisoner in his palaces, but it did not stop them assassinating him.'

'That could never happen here!'

'Never? . . . The politicians all too easily comfort themselves with such nostrums, with the result that Britain is endangered on all sides. They cling to outdated concepts of Britain's position in the world, and put at hazard our very nationhood.'

'Surely you exaggerate?' Morton protested.

'Not so. We still cast France in the role of villain on the

31

European stage. So Britain gives shelter to any revolutionist riff-raff that succeed in crossing the Channel. This provides our masters with a libertarian stick to beat the French with. In retaliation, the French have sheltered and supported the Fenians, in their campaign to free Ireland from British rule . . . But this is all outdated. The Germans are not building a fleet to give the Kaiser some warships to review. It could suit Germany very well, to keep France and Britain at loggerheads . . . But the threat from below could sweep us all into the maelstrom, before that matters.'

'I have travelled extensively on the Continent – though, I grant you, not in recent years. But I have not seen any evidence that ordinary people were dissatisfied to the point of rebellion.'

'We have no time to send you on a grand tour,' Redman said frostily. 'So you will have to take my word for it. If we ignore the Fenians, who are a special case, Britain is the only country in Europe without a revolutionist movement. Anarchists of various hues are active in Spain, France, Italy, Austria, Germany and Russia – even you will allow Russia. Their aspirations transcend national boundaries, their ideologies are held with all the fervour of a religion. Properly directed, nothing could stand in their way.'

'Even if you are right, I do not see how it is of immediate concern to me,' said Morton.

'Very well, we will come to the specific. The French government has been informed – I should say reliably informed – that anarchist cells in this country are plotting the assassination of prominent French politicians, including the President himself. They have made representations to the British government, to stop harbouring these subversives and arrest them. Our Liberal government has recently reiterated that it has no power to arrest these people, and does not propose to take such powers. So, what should be the response of the French? Obviously, they will seek to create conditions in which the British might be induced to change their minds.'

'That, at least, seems logical.'

'The Fenians have been quiet for some years, so there is no possibility of bargaining there. But an alternative stratagem could be to stir up civil disorder within Britain, which would compel the government here to enact draconian powers. They could hardly refuse to expel the French anarchists then.'

'This is all very interesting,' Morton said irritably, 'but it does not explain why I have been battered to a pulp.'

The flinty eyes gazed at him appraisingly.

'Last week,' Redman went on, 'we picked up a Frenchman in Harwich. The name he gave us was Marcel Corbin; he was straight off a boat from the Hook of Holland. When we questioned him, he claimed to be an anarchist refugee from France. We were not convinced of this, and we have detained him here. We are now satisfied that he is, in fact, an agent of French military intelligence. But we need to know the nature of his mission. It could be nothing more than the elimination of certain individuals who are particularly irksome to his masters. Let me say that, if such were the case, I should be unconcerned. However, as I have indicated, his instructions could be to foment revolutionist activity in Britain. I tell you frankly, Morton, the Special Branch is not going to stand idly by, while this inert government allows our way of life to be subverted.'

'And what do you want of me?'

'I want you to impersonate a Swiss anarchist. I will have you put in the same cell as Corbin; you will gain his confidence and discover his plans.'

'A French-speaking Swiss anarchist, I presume. Are there any such?'

'Indeed there are. You will assume the name and character of a real man – one Paul Grillon. He was taken after an attempt at murdering a Russian Grand Duke . . . He died under questioning.'

'I see . . . We are playing in a game with high stakes.'

'Yes. Here is a file of information about Grillon. We have been planning this for some time, against the day.'

'Around me?'

'Around you. As I said, you are the only person who could succeed. It is now your choice.'

Morton took a deep breath. 'Well,' he said, with a painful smile, 'it would be a pity if my drubbing had been all for nothing.'

Redman gave a satisfied grunt, and left him to his reading.

Paul Grillon was certainly about his age, but no details of his physical appearance were given. However, it was in the highest degree unlikely that he and Marcel Corbin had met. The file contained exhaustive detail about Grillon's family background and upbringing. He had been the only son in a comfortable middle-class family – Calvinist, as one would expect near Geneva. He had been good at languages and geography, which might be useful. His life had followed the predictable pattern, until he was eighteen. Then, instead of attending the Protestant University of Geneva, he had gone to Bern University. Why was that, Morton wondered. Perhaps he had already embraced the anarchist cause. According to the file, it was rife in the whole of the Rhône valley. However that might be, Grillon had certainly become an active convert soon after arriving at Bern. Subsequently, he had veered towards the nihilist faction – which explained his involvement in an assassination attempt within Russia. Did he ever finish his university course? The file was silent on the point. Not that it mattered: Corbin would hardly probe his background to that extent. Nor need the paucity of detail about Grillon's capture, and the manner of his death, concern Morton. 'He died under questioning.' Redman seemed unaware of the images that phrase conjured up – or indifferent to them. No doubt the hapless Grillon would have been executed anyway. But to die under torture . . . Morton dismissed it from his mind. He had a job to do, specific and uncomplicated – though not necessarily straightforward. The thoroughness of his preparation showed that. He touched his swollen face, and Redman's bleak voice came back to him. 'That cannot be simulated.' They were taking no chances; it had to be important.

The door opened and Redman strode in, followed by two uniformed constables and the Special Branch sergeant.

'Have you digested it?' Redman asked curtly.

'I think so.'

'Good. Corbin is in a cell, down below. You will now be put with him, hence the escort. Remember, you will have all the time you need. Gain his confidence gradually. Do not arouse his suspicions by questioning him directly. Stay at the task until you know what he is about. Right, sergeant.' He regarded

Morton narrowly. 'Oh, I think that some fresh claret is called for.'

Morton rose, and the constables moved to either side of him. They marched him down to the ground-floor cells, with Curtis bringing up the rear. Half-way down the corridor, Curtis ordered them to halt. He came round to the front and, at a nod from him, the constables grasped Morton's arms. The sergeant looked at his prisoner dispassionately.

'Are you ready?' he asked.

Morton smiled and nodded.

'Right.' Suddenly Curtis lashed out with his fist, every ounce of his weight behind it. It caught Morton full on the nose. Every nerve in his battered face was screaming in pain; he could feel blood dribbling down his chin. There came the grating of a lock. He felt a push in the small of his back. He staggered forwards, tripped and fell, as the door clanged shut behind him. He lay there stunned for a moment, then became aware of a hand on his shoulder and a voice murmuring to him in accented English . . . He tried to rally his faculties. This must be Corbin, the French spy. And he . . . he was supposed to be a Swiss anarchist. It was all so absurd . . . 'That cannot be simulated.' It had not been gratuitous violence; it was essential, a protection for him. He mumbled a remark in French, was dimly aware of being hauled to his feet and collapsing on to a bunk, before insensibility overtook him.

When Morton came to the surface again, the light was begining to fade. He surveyed the cell through half-closed lids. It was similar to the other one, except that he could hear the rumble of cartwheels and the clatter of hoofs. Obviously a major thoroughfare ran outside – but which? On the bunk opposite, a man was lying. He was about thirty-five years old, with clean-cut features and brown hair. He shifted his position on the bunk, and caught Morton watching him.

'Ah, my friend,' he said in French which had a distinct Parisian accent. 'My name is Marcel Corbin. I have been waiting for you to awake. The pigs have given you a bad time, eh?'

'I would not answer their questions, so they have beaten me,' Morton muttered, trying to invest his French accent with a regional intonation.

Corbin swung himself from the bed and crossed to the door. He put his ear to the metal and listened intently. Then he grunted in satisfaction.

'What part of France do you come from?' he asked, perching on the foot of Morton's bunk.

'I am from a French-speaking canton of Switzerland – Geneva.'

Corbin's face fell. 'Are you? Then, why are you here?'

Morton hoisted himself into a sitting position. 'Why should I answer your questions?' he asked suspiciously.

Corbin laughed and got to his feet. 'We seem to be in the same boat, you and I.' He was above medium height, well built and athletic. 'Let me wash some of the blood from your face, before the light goes.'

He brought a bucket of water from the corner and, soaking his handkerchief, began gently to swab the caked blood from Morton's face . . . 'Cannot be simulated' . . . Eventually Corbin straightened up.

'At least you look better now,' he said with a smile. 'As you were before, you would have given me bad dreams! What part of the canton do you come from?'

'How do I know you are not a police spy?' Morton asked querulously.

'Do you think the British pigs keep Frenchmen on their payroll, just in case they capture a Geneva Swiss? It seems to me that you must be a desperate man, to think in this way.'

'I am sorry . . . But I have had very bad experiences.'

'Worse even than that?' Corbin gestured towards Morton's face.

'These are nursemaids, compared to the Okhrana.'

'Okhrana? You have been to Russia?'

'I escaped from them in St. Petersburg, and managed to get to Sweden – then through Europe to England.'

'Why did the Okhrana arrest you?'

Morton looked suspiciously at him. 'I am a nihilist,' he said shortly.

'Ah! A Swiss nihilist in Russia . . .'

'We had made an attempt on the life of a Grand Duke which, unhappily, failed. I think that I alone escaped.'

'I do not understand why the British have arrested you.'

36

Morton looked at Corbin uneasily, noting the alertness of his bearing, the intelligent hazel eyes.

'It was necessary to have funds for the attempt . . . There is a Swiss extradition warrant, for a bank robbery in Bern. That is why the British try to compel me to give them my name.'

Corbin pondered. 'How long is the sentence, in Switzerland, for a bank robbery?' he asked.

'I would be a very old man, before I was released.'

'But, was it not foolish to come to London? You would have been safer in the countryside.'

'Perhaps. But I know that there are anarchists in London. Here they are tolerated by the authorities.'

'Provided that they have not robbed a bank!'

'I hoped to contact them, and ask for their help. But I was arrested at Victoria station.'

'Did the police know that you were coming?'

Morton shrugged his shoulders. 'Perhaps.' He slid down on to his bed again, and wrapped his blanket round him.

Corbin walked over to the window, and peered out into the darkened street for a time. Then he took off his boots, and Morton heard the creak of his bunk as he lay down. All was quiet. In the distance, Morton caught the whistle of a train; a faint light from a street-lamp seeped between the bars. At last, his bruised body was reasonably comfortable. He could feel himself drifting off to sleep.

'And what is your name?' Corbin asked softly.

'I am not so foolish as to tell you.'

In the darkness, Corbin laughed. 'Well, I will tell you something,' he said. 'You are right. There is a cell of anarchists in London. I know, because they have been in contact with me.'

Bragg was finishing his second pipe of the morning, when there was a knock on his door and a constable poked his head in.

'There's a man to see you, sir,' he said.

'Who is that?'

'Name of Chambers. Young Silver Morton's man, I think.'

'All right then, bring him up.'

Chambers's usual blend of fastidiousness and professional deference was overlaid with anxiety.

'I have really come in search of Master James, sergeant. But I gather from the gentleman at the desk that he has not reported for duty this morning.'

'I was wondering where he had got to, myself,' Bragg growled.

'It is most extraordinary. When my wife took in his early-morning tea, she found that he was not there. Indeed, his bed had not been slept in.'

'You expected him back, then?'

'Most certainly. He instructed me, before leaving last evening, to lay out his attire for morning.'

'You mean the scruffy clerk's clothes he wears to mix with the likes of us?'

'Yes, sir. His working clothes,' Chambers said in remonstrance.

'So, where has he got to?'

'I was wondering if you could tell me.'

'All I know is that he should have been here two hours ago.'

'I . . . I begin to fear that he may be the victim of some . . . occurrence.'

Bragg looked up sharply. 'Why should you think that?' he asked.

'I went out, a short time ago, to the shops. It was as I returned that I discovered his latchkey was in the lock.'

'Are you sure that it was his?'

'There are only three keys to the outer door. My wife and I still have our own.'

'I see. What do you think might have happened?'

'We have no idea. But, in the ordinary course, Master James keeps us informed of his movements. He did not mention that he might stay away overnight.'

'Hmn. Have any strangers called on him recently?'

'Not at home, certainly.'

'Nothing out of the ordinary?'

'Nothing . . . except . . . Well, my wife did remark on it – she is worried sick, as you can imagine.'

'What is it?' Bragg rapped out.

'Well, he went out last evening. But he asked me to put out a frock-coat, instead of his dress suit.'

'Is that unusual?'

'In the circumstances, yes.'

'Christ Almighty! Do I have to prise every bloody word out of you? Stop being so damned discreet, and tell me what you think!'

The look of a rejected spaniel settled on Chambers's face. 'Well,' he said reproachfully, 'it must have been an occasion of some importance, for he went to the lengths of hiring a carriage from Newman's of Regent Street.'

'Did he, indeed? But you don't know what occasion he was going to?'

'No, sir. Master James did not confide in me.'

'Is that exceptional in itself?'

'He will often tell me in general terms – say, dinner in the West End.'

'But not this time, eh? And what do you make of it?'

'Well,' Chambers began hesitantly, 'the frock-coat suggests informality, whereas the carriage would imply a grand society function.'

'It is not the Season yet, is it?'

'No, sir, not till the end of April. But I have heard of hostesses, perhaps a little unsure of themselves, holding a dance some weeks earlier.'

Bragg smiled. 'You ought to write a book on manners for social climbers!' he said.

'Thank you, sir . . . On the other hand, I would not expect Master James to hire a carriage for his own convenience only – even allowing for the cab strike.'

'Someone else was involved, eh? A woman, do you think?'

'It seems possible. But in that case, the frock-coat . . .'

'What, man?'

'It would appear to be an uncharacteristic social solecism.'

'You mean, his clothes and the carriage didn't go together? But suppose he was going on somewhere? He would have looked stupid in dress clothes, the next day.'

'Yes, I see . . . Certainly that would be true.'

'Have you any idea who the lady might be?'

'No, Mr Bragg.'

'Could it be Miss Marsden?'

'I suppose it is possible,' Chambers said hesitantly.

'They are not exactly strangers, dammit!'

'Well, Mrs Chambers has thought . . . No, I do not think you should ask me personal questions.'

'Then what the bloody hell have you come bothering me for? You are reporting him missing, aren't you?'

'I suppose I am.'

'Then I want all the information I can get. What was it your wife thought?'

'It is just that she felt he was a little out of sorts, recently. She wondered if something was making him unhappy.'

'Well, we can't send the police forces of the Home Counties searching for him because he is unhappy – and I'm damned if I have seen any sign of it. Has he gone to his parents' house, in Kent, do you think?'

'No, sir. I went down to the telephone call-room in Cannon Street and rang the Priory. I spoke to the butler – in a roundabout way, you understand. I am sure he is not there.'

'We can only do something officially, if he is missing in suspicious circumstances,' Bragg said. 'You realize that?'

'Yes, Mr Bragg. Normally, I would not dream of interfering in what he does. But the door key . . .'

'Ah, yes. It was in the door, you say. What kind of lock is it?'

'An ordinary spring lock. He would certainly not need a key to leave the house.'

'Suppose he had popped back for something, left the key in the lock by mistake, and slammed the door behind him when he went out again?'

'It could be possible,' Chambers said dubiously. 'However, I did not hear him return, and I was in his bedroom, brushing the clothes he had taken off.'

'But he could have done?'

'No, sergeant. I remember now. Mrs Chambers and I popped out later in the evening – for a little refreshment, you understand.'

'I see . . . Then let me ask you again. Are you reporting him missing in suspicious circumstances?'

'I would not presume to do that, sir,' Chambers said unhappily. 'But you understand our position. My wife and I have looked after him, ever since he joined the City police. That is over five years ago . . . It's as if he were our own son, Mr Bragg.'

'Don't you worry,' Bragg said gently. 'Let me know if anything fresh occurs to you; and I will have a good poke around, myself.'

Catherine Marsden picked up the Wednesday edition of the paper, hot off the press, and turned to her article. She had interviewed the architect and builders concerned with the half-finished Bishopsgate Institute. Then she had gone to see the old rector, who had been the motivating force behind the project. He had outlined various ideas for utilizing the building. To her, it seemed to embody the best aspects of charitable endeavour. There was to be a large library and reading-room, a small hall where workers' educational classes would be held, and a larger one for musical concerts and public meetings. For the first time, ordinary people in the City would have a place to meet which was away from the pubs and music-halls. Some people would scoff at it, as paternalistic. But she agreed with Canon Rodgers – what matter the motivation, if the use to which it was put benefited the needy? She glanced through the piece and smiled to herself. Mr Tranter, the editor, had printed it complete, without a single alteration!

When she had been accepted by the *City Press* as a junior reporter, almost three years ago, Catherine had been advised to confine herself to just such charitable and social matters. The hard news, financial and economic, was to be left to the men. She had soon found this irksome, and had embarked on a succession of articles which exposed corruption in high places. Not only had this development provoked nervous disapproval in Mr Tranter, it had brought her into physical danger on more than one occasion. But, on the credit side, it had led to her friendship with Sergeant Bragg and, of course, James . . . She frowned, and switched her mind back to the article. It was a minor coup to be able to tell her readers that the new hall was

41

to be opened by the Prime Minister, Lord Rosebery. She had heard it from the rector, that very morning, and had just had time to amend her copy. A voice inside her murmured that it was a very minor coup, but she suppressed it. Journalism was her chosen profession, she had a right to be a little self-satisfied. Certainly, she would not rise to the top by being as slapdash as some of the men on the staff. There came a knock on the door.

'Come in,' she said briskly. 'Good heavens! Sergeant Bragg!'

He smiled. 'You've not eloped, then.'

'Eloped?' she exclaimed. 'With whom? What are you talking about?'

'Young Morton, of course. He has not been seen since yesterday evening. He hired a carriage, and vanished. We thought you two might have sneaked off to be married by a blacksmith!'

'We thought?'

'Me and the Chamberses.'

Catherine felt a sense of outrage growing inside her. 'Well, you and the Chamberses are wrong!'

'So, you did not see him, last night. I wonder what he was up to.'

'In fact, I did see him,' Catherine said coldly. 'And I share in your perplexity at his antics.'

'How did he seem?'

'Much as usual, perhaps a little more off-hand than usual.'

'Off-hand?' Bragg echoed in surprise.

'He had invited me to the theatre. I should have realized that he would be in a sardonic mood, for the play he chose was *The New Woman* at the Comedy. As you can imagine, it was a trivial piece, which poked fun at women who try to succeed in a man's world.'

'He was pulling your leg!'

'By no means! It was, after all, a first night. And I had dressed for the occasion. But he had the bad taste to arrive in a frock-coat.'

'And that reflected on you, did it?'

'Inevitably,' Catherine said haughtily.

'But he did come for you in a carriage.'

'And packed me off home in it, alone.'

Bragg looked at her speculatively and tugged his ragged moustache. 'Do you think there was anything troubling him?' he asked.

'How would I know? I am not his *confidante*.'

'But . . .' Bragg frowned in perplexity.

'If you must know, sergeant, some weeks ago he proposed marriage to me, and I rejected him.'

'You what?! You rejected him? Christ Almighty! What's got into you, girl? The finest young man you are ever likely to meet, and you turn him down?'

'Stop shouting, sergeant! I will not be bullied.'

'You want your head examined, you do! Buggering about with this newspaper rubbish, when you could be settled down with a man who bloody worships you!'

'He showed scant signs of it last night!' Catherine retorted angrily.

'Good God! How old are you?'

'What has that to do with anything?'

'You sound like a spoilt child, that's what! Do you expect things to be the same, after you've turned him down? I would have seen you in hell before I'd ask you out again.'

'It could have been mere condescension,' Catherine said frostily. 'It was my birthday. He might have imagined that I would have no one else to celebrate it with.'

Bragg sighed irritably. 'Except for one thing,' he said, 'I'd think it likely enough he'd really gone to a new woman.'

Catherine bit back an angry retort. 'What thing is that?' she asked.

'His key was in the door this morning.'

'I do not understand.'

'Chambers found it. Now, he didn't need to unlock the door to get out. So he must have come home . . . but he never got inside.'

'Perhaps he left it in the door when he came in to change for the theatre,' Catherine suggested, in growing alarm.

'No. The Chambers went out to the pub, after he'd left.'

'Could he have gone to his parents' home?'

'He could have, but he didn't. We have checked . . . Can you tell me what he said, when he left you?'

43

'He told me that he would walk home.'

'Did he say why he was not coming back to Park Lane with you?'

'No.'

'He didn't tell you he was going anywhere else?'

'No.'

'Well,' Bragg said heavily, 'if he was going home, he got no further than the door . . . What time did he leave you?'

'The performance ended at eleven o'clock. I suppose that I was in the carriage, and away, by a quarter past eleven.'

'So, he should have been home before midnight.'

'Sergeant,' Catherine said, trying to keep the note of panic out of her voice, 'are you suggesting that some mishap has befallen him?'

'You ask yourself, miss. When he left the office, last night, he was as chirpy as a sparrow. We had arranged what we were going to do today; everything was normal. You were the only person he saw after that. If you don't know why he might have skedaddled, then he could be in trouble.'

Bragg left the *City Press* office still bursting with indignation. Those two would make an ideal pair, and they got on marvellously in the ordinary way. But this absurd social code the nobs had seemed to stop them getting any closer. In the Dorset countryside, where he had been brought up, they'd soon have known their own minds. A quick cuddle behind the haystack would have settled it, and to hell with benefit of clergy. This lot waltzed around each other, wondering about pedigree, worrying about social status . . . No, that was not fair. By such a yardstick, she would have accepted him like a shot. He, if anybody, had been born with a silver spoon in his mouth. Society matrons were fighting to grab him for their daughters – the son of the Lord Lieutenant of Kent, a millionaire by virtue of his American connections, and likely to inherit a baronetcy before too many years were up. No, it was in Miss Marsden's favour that she had not snapped him up: there must be more to her than he had given credit for . . . Perhaps he shouldn't have interfered – kept his mouth shut. People knew their own business best. And yet, they would make a perfect couple, blast it! He put the thought from him, and walked as briskly as he could along the crowded pavements. By the time he had reached Morton's rooms, his irritation had evaporated. He rang the bell. There came a bang from above and the sound of feet on the stairs. Perhaps he was back . . .

'Ah, sergeant.' Chambers looked even more doleful than when Bragg had seen him in the morning. 'Any news?' he asked.

'Then he has not returned?'

'No, sergeant. But there is one thing. The rector of St Botolph's has brought Master James's hat. He found it in the churchyard, this morning.'

'Are you sure it is Morton's?'

'Yes. It has his initials, stamped on the sweat-band.'

'Right. Let me know, if anything else turns up.'

Bragg went over to the church, and found the rector in the vestry.

'I gather that you found a hat in the churchyard,' he began.

The rector had a round pious face, fringed with a skimpy grey beard. 'Yes, yes,' he said with a smile. 'I knew, at once, to whom it belonged. Mr Morton is a regular attender at morning service, when his duties – and his cricket – allow!'

'Where did you find it, sir?'

'In the bushes, by the gravel path. I come that way from the rectory,' he explained.

'I see. I wonder if you can help me, sir.'

'In what way?'

'I am a policeman. I work with Constable Morton.'

'Ah, then you must be Sergeant Bragg. He has often spoken appreciatively of you.'

'I am afraid that he has gone missing, in what we must now assume to be suspicious circumstances.'

'Oh, dear! I am sorry to hear that.'

'We – know that he left the Haymarket around quarter-past eleven, so he should have been home before midnight. It seems certain that he reached here, because his servant found his key in the lock, and you have now produced his hat . . . But he never got up the stairs to his rooms.'

45

'Goodness gracious! Are you saying that he has met with foul play?'

'It is certainly possible.'

'And you are suggesting that it might have occurred around midnight . . . I wonder.'

'What is that, sir?'

'I was holding a rehearsal for a wedding, in the church. It was exceedingly late, because the groom had been unfortunately delayed. Shortly before twelve o'clock, there was a disturbance outside, and a great deal of drunken shouting . . . I am afraid that we have far too many ale-houses in this vicinity.'

'I see, sir. Anything else?'

'Well, sergeant, on my way to the church I did notice a most unusual conveyance in the churchyard.'

'What was it like?'

'It was a two-horse van and, in the lamp-light, it seemed of very sturdy construction. There was a door in the rear, with steps beneath it. In each side were two windows, which had stout bars across them.'

'Sounds like a prison van,' Bragg remarked. 'Was it still there when you went home?'

'No, sergeant. Indeed, when the disturbance outside had subsided, I distinctly remember hearing the sound of its going.'

'You are sure of that, sir?'

'Oh, yes. There was little other traffic, at that time of night.'

Bragg left the rector and walked along the crowded pavement to Bishopsgate police station.

'Hello, Jack,' he greeted the sergeant on the desk. 'Tell me, were you moving any prisoners last night?'

'Prisoners? Us? No! We only get drunk and disorderlies here. Up before the beak and bail, that's our lot. Why?'

'There was a Black Maria standing behind St Botolph's church, around eleven, last night. By midnight it had gone.'

'Sorry, mate, I can't help you.'

'Who was on that beat, last night?'

'Just a minute.' He thumbed through the book on his desk. 'It was Constable Jenkins . . . I see that he's on three days' leave.'

'Where does he live?'

'In the section house. But I think he has gone home to Wales. He's only a youngster.'

'Right, thanks.'

Bragg decided to continue up the street. It might be worth asking the Met station, at Shoreditch, if they'd had anything on last night. It seemed the only other possibility. He mounted the steps and went over to the counter.

'My name's Bragg,' he said, showing his warrant-card to the duty-sergeant.

'Oh, yes?' the man said laconically. 'And what do the swell mob want of me?'

'Just a bit of information.'

The sergeant looked suspiciously at Bragg. 'And what's that?' he asked.

'Were you moving any prisoners last night?'

'No,' said the sergeant firmly.

'Had you anything on – a snatch operation, or something?'

'No, sorry.'

Bragg went dispiritedly back to Old Jewry, and then home. There was nothing further he could do, and he was getting jaded. It was different when a case involved someone you knew, whom you worked with. Perhaps he ought to pass it over to somebody else, somebody who could be objective . . . But they'd only poke about a bit, shrug their shoulders and give up. No, this was his . . . He opened the front door of his lodgings, and went down the back stairs to the basement kitchen. Mrs Jenks, his landlady, looked up from the stove.

'There's a young lady to see you,' she said in her sharp voice. 'I put her in your sitting-room.'

'Did she give a name?'

'No need. It's that Miss Marsden.'

Bragg groaned inwardly. An unproductive day, and now faced with eating humble pie for his boorishness. It was no use, he would have to get her off his back. He climbed the three flights of stairs to his rooms at the top of the house. Miss Marsden was standing at the window, gazing out.

'Ah, sergeant, you have come.'

'Yes.'

Bragg went over to the fireplace, and picked up his favourite

47

pipe from beside the clock. He was determined not to lose his temper, this time.

'Have you discovered anything?' she asked anxiously.

'Nothing good.' He undid his tie and began to take off his collar.

'What is it?'

'All right, nothing at all . . . Look, miss, James Morton is an adult male, with all the money in the world. He's been playing at policemen to impress a young woman who's playing at journalists: if he decides to go off with some society tart, because she has turned him down, that's his affair. It certainly isn't police business . . . But I'll have a thing or two to say to him, if he ever shows up.'

3

The next morning was cold and showery. A gusty wind blew straight through the bars of the cell. Morton rolled himself in his blanket, and lay on his bunk for most of the time. Nor was his weakness wholly simulated. His face felt like a pumpkin, his body was stiff and sore. Corbin, on the other hand, tramped up and down the cell, his face thoughtful. Morton could well believe that he was a trained leader of men. His determination and aura of purpose were almost palpable. From time to time he would suspend his pacing, and sit on Morton's bed. He would chat in a friendly way, building confidence, probing Grillon's background. Then, before it became obvious, he would resume his march. It ought to be the other way round, Morton thought. It was he who was supposed to surreptitiously quiz Corbin! Still, if the bridge between them was built, it did not matter from which side.

After a constable had brought their meagre meal, at noon, Morton began to feel more lively. He would never achieve his purpose, if he were content merely to listen to what Corbin intended him to hear. He would have to extend the boundaries of their conversation, probe and analyse. He was fortunate in knowing much of France well, though that did not extend to the Jura – the *département* nearest his supposed place of birth. He would have to be careful. But, so far as he could tell, Corbin was as ignorant of that area as he, and had certainly not been to Switzerland.

As they chatted, Morton found himself warming to Corbin. He was naturally attracted to outgoing, incisive people. But, even though he enjoyed their conversation, he was aware that

Corbin gave no definite information about himself. Yes, he had been to so-and-so; yes, he knew the cathedral – but never a hint of what he had been doing there. In return, Morton gave snippets from the file on Grillon. He had embarked on a largely fictional account of the raid on the Bern bank, and had begun to realize that he was giving unnecessary hostages to fortune, when the key rattled in the lock and the door opened.

'Corbin, come with me.' A sergeant beckoned, an escort of two constables stood waiting in the corridor.

Corbin smiled and shrugged his shoulders. '*A bientôt*,' he said, and went out.

Morton went over to the window. There was a wide road beneath, the pavement a mere eight feet below him. The buildings opposite were old and nondescript. He had been right in his suspicion that he had not been brought far from the City. He was peering to make out the destination board of a tram, when the door opened again and Redman entered.

'Are you making progress?' he asked with an effort at geniality.

'Only generally,' Morton said. 'I think that Corbin is beginning to trust me, within limits. From what I have observed, you could be right in thinking that he is a military intelligence officer. He is certainly not my idea of an anarchist. His mind is very disciplined; certainly he manages to converse convincingly, without giving any real information.'

'Good, you are doing well. But we need to know, in some detail, what he is up to. You will understand that we would not be able seriously to embarrass the French government unless we could demonstrate a significant breach of neighbourly behaviour.'

'I will try to find out,' Morton said thoughtfully. 'But it may take some time. I have been dribbling out bits of information about Grillon but, if I do it in too obvious a way, Corbin will become suspicious.'

'Take all the time you need. Stick at it. I cannot express too forcibly the importance we attach to this matter.' Redman walked across to the window and stood there some moments in silence.

'One piece of information he did let slip,' Morton said with satisfaction. 'He has apparently been contacted by an anarchist group, since he came to England.'

'Ah.' Redman's face showed no surprise and little interest.

'He did not say more, and I was loath to question him further.'

'Perhaps you should have done so. After all he is a French agent posing as an anarchist.'

'And I,' Morton added with a smile, 'in the best traditions of a Feydeau farce, am an English agent posing as a Swiss anarchist. Perhaps there are no revolutionists in England at all, merely foreign spies masquerading as such!'

Redman glowered at him. 'That would not cause me to sleep easier at night, I can tell you . . . There is one thing, though. Corbin might be glad to get close to a real anarchist, like Grillon. It would give him a measure of protection, in a way.' He took out his watch and grunted. 'Well, I must be off. Remember – stick at it.' He walked to the door and locked it behind him.

It was dusk when Corbin was pushed into the cell again. There was blood spattered across his face, and one eye was puffy.

'The pigs!' he exclaimed angrily. 'They questioned me for hours, over and over the same ground. Then the old one came in, and they began to strike me about the head. They no longer asked questions, they contented themselves with beating me.'

Morton took the bloodied handkerchief and dabbed Corbin's face. He had not been seriously injured – nothing like the beating he had himself received – but was beside himself with fury.

'Have they beaten you before?' Morton asked.

'No, never!'

'Once they begin, it goes on and on – more violently each time, until they break you.'

'They will not break me,' Corbin said angrily, 'for I shall not be here!'

'You propose to fly out of the window?' Morton asked sardonically.

Corbin's head jerked round suspiciously, then he relaxed. 'Yes, my friend, I shall perform that feat – you also.'

'If only it were possible!'

Corbin strode over to the door and put his ear against it. Then he straightened up and beckoned Morton over to the window.

'When it is dusk, in about an hour, we shall remove the two centre bars, and escape.'

Morton snorted in disbelief.

'It is true,' Corbin insisted. 'Did I not say that I had been contacted by anarchists? One night, a week ago, they pushed a disgusting English *baguette* through the window. I went over and saw two men, who waved to me and hurried away. Inside the bread I discovered a hack-saw blade!'

'Incredible!'

'Nevertheless, true.' He lifted one corner of the palliasse on his bunk, and took out the blade. It looked worn and blunt, its protective paint scored with prolonged use.

'You will not cut through the bars with that!' Morton said scornfully.

'But it is already done! Look!' He crossed to the window, and poked gently with the blade at the top of the right-hand bar. Miraculously, a gap appeared – it had been completely severed!

'I concealed the cut with a paste of dirt and butter,' Corbin said triumphantly. 'See, the other bar is free at the top, also. I have been sawing every night. Whenever a vehicle went by I would saw, while the horse's hoofs concealed the noise. I only completed the work two nights ago.'

'What about the bottom?' Morton asked.

'There is a small sliver of metal uncut, on each. It should not take long to saw through it.'

This was a new situation, Morton realized. With Corbin gone, Redman's plans would be balked . . . Should he try to prevent it? But on what possible pretext? And, if he did, Corbin would never again confide in him. On the other hand, Corbin seemed to expect him to go also. 'Stick at it,' Redman had said. Suddenly, that was being transformed into 'Stick with him'. Well, it was the only way he was going to get any information.

Corbin finished cleaning out the saw-cuts at the bottom of the bars, and stood back.

'You see?' he asked.

'I think we could crack the remaining iron by bending the

bars to and fro,' Morton said. 'It would make no noise, and we would not need to wait for passing traffic.'

'Excellent! Let us lift your bunk under the window, it makes a serviceable platform. I think that it is already dark enough.'

'What will we do when we get out?'

'I have an address. Come, we must begin.'

Within ten minutes, they had snapped off the bars and wormed their way, feet first, through the aperture. The street was deserted, the gas-lamps well away from them.

Morton looked quickly about him, as they dived into a side-street. Shoreditch! They had been in Shoreditch nick! Once in the shadows, they crept to the bottom of the street and began to run. Eventually they pulled up, panting, at a major thorough-fare. It was well lit, and Morton had no doubt that it was City Road.

'Where are we going?' he asked.

'Hammersmith. It is to the west of London. I think that we have been coming in the right direction. It is a long walk, perhaps two hours. One could take an underground railway train, but I did not have time to get English money, before the pigs arrested me.'

Morton felt in his pocket. 'I have some,' he said.

'Then, let us go towards the brighter lights. That should be the best way.'

They walked south, towards the City. Of course! It all fitted . . . That was why only his pocket-book and gold hunter were missing, thought Morton. Either of them would have revealed that he was not Grillon, the student turned revolutionist. He had wondered why he had not been relieved of his other possessions, when it was plainly contrary to regulations to leave them with him, but they were innocuous . . . And that was why Redman had peered at the window. He knew!

'Look!' Corbin was pointing towards Moorgate station. 'There is a railway!' He bustled over to the booking office, and consulted the list of stations.

'Hammersmith! You see? And, as it is the final station, we shall not miss our destination.'

Morton passed over a florin, like a dutiful subordinate, and Corbin bought the tickets. It would be a dreary journey, Morton

53

thought. He wished he could have suggested going to Mansion House station; the trains to Hammersmith went much more frequently from there. They walked down to the deserted platform and waited. Corbin was not a natural criminal, Morton thought – or spy for that matter. He strolled about the platform, confident, full of elation. Well, if Redman had allowed the escape to take place, he was secure enough – for the moment.

After twenty minutes they heard a wheezing clank in the tunnel, and a squat engine eased its way to the platform. The air was suddenly filled with steam and acrid smoke. Passengers stumbled out of the carriages, handkerchiefs to their faces. Morton followed Corbin to the rear of the train, away from the fumes. They were not alone in this. A group of belated clerks followed them into their compartment. Then, just as the train was about to leave, a prim, middle-aged woman flung open the door and hauled herself inside. She sat down in the corner, opposite Morton, and began arranging her belongings around her. Then she caught sight of Morton's face, and gave a small cry of alarm. She made to open the door, but the train was already moving. Instead, she pressed herself into the corner, her bag clutched protectively to her bosom.

Silly old biddy, Morton thought uncharitably. He would have liked to reassure her, but a Gallic accent would have confirmed her worst suspicions! Every time he moved, she flinched back. Eventually, he decided to close his eyes, as the only way of assuaging her fears . . . The swaying of the train was soothing, the rhythmical click of the wheels mesmeric . . . the hissing of the gas lights . . . He awoke to find Corbin shaking his shoulder.

'Come on, my friend, it is Hammersmith.' The prim lady was gone, the city clerks departed. There was a foul taste in Morton's mouth and his body felt stiff. He pulled himself to his feet and followed Corbin into the fresh air. The Frenchman clearly knew not only the address of their destination, but also how to get there. He set off briskly, turning from the main road into an area of substantial villas hedged about with box and privet. He stopped before a handsome house, with gothic turrets and a semicircular driveway.

'This is where we shall get help,' he whispered.

They went to an imposing doorway, and Corbin pulled the bell. Instead of the usual brass plate behind the bell-pull, there was an intricate casting. In the dim light from the street-lamp, Morton could see that its border was an elaborate pattern of foliage and ribbons. Above the bell-pull itself appeared the name WILLIAM and beneath it MORRIS. It was well that the maid appeared then, thought Morton, or he might have betrayed his astonishment.

'Yes, gentlemen?' she asked unperturbed.

'We would like to see your master,' Corbin said.

The girl smiled tolerantly. 'Who shall I say?'

'Tell him that we are two foreign gentlemen, who have not the honour of his acquaintance.'

The maid disappeared, leaving the door ajar. Shortly afterwards, a tall man of about sixty appeared. His pointed ginger beard was speckled with grey; a quiff of unruly hair stood above the domed forehead and long nose. He looked like a retired sea-captain rather than a famous artist, Morton thought. He stared at his visitors for a moment, then beckoned them to follow. He led them to a study at the back of the house, where a log fire burned in a wide stone fireplace. Without a word, he motioned them to deep armchairs, and gave them each a glass of whisky.

'Well, now,' he said in a strong, deep voice, 'I take it that you do not come wholly in peace!'

Corbin glanced warily at Morton.

'Thank you for receiving us,' he said in slow English, as if enunciating a prepared speech. 'I am a French citizen, my name is Marcel Corbin. This is a Genevois, with whom I escaped from police custody.'

Morris lifted his eyebrows. 'And why do you come to me?' he asked.

'It is well known, in France, that you are sympathetic to our cause.'

'Which is?'

'The overthrow of a social system where the poor are oppressed, so that the idle rich can grow ever richer.'

'Ah.' Morris turned his deep brown eyes on Morton. 'And you?' he asked. 'Do you also work for that end?'

'Indeed,' Morton said firmly. 'I have risked my life to prove it.'

'And do you have a name?'

'Paul Grillon.'

Morris raised his bushy eyebrows. 'I have heard of you,' he said warmly. 'I only wish that there were young people idealistic enough to put their freedom at hazard for the cause, in this country also.' He sighed. 'But the industrious classes in Britain are too supine. We had an incident, some years ago, when striking dock workers were marching towards Trafalgar Square. They were set upon by the police and military. There were some deaths and many injuries. We thought that it was the flash-point, that insurrection would spread to sweep away the whole capitalist system . . . But no. The government made placatory noises, the trade unions drew back, and the chance was lost.'

'Such unions are part of the conspiracy against the proletariat,' Corbin declared. 'They must be destroyed also.'

Morris sighed. 'And yet,' he said plaintively, 'the artisans ought to be the natural leaders – innocent of the taint of wealth, creating beautiful things with their hands, working together in harmony for the good of their own little community . . . Ruskin did try to achieve it, you know, years ago. He set up a socialist community, on a farm near Sheffield. "The St George's Guild", he called it. It should have been a perfect example of the communes we talk about today. All the crafts were included, to make the guild self-sufficient and self-supporting. The families were well, if modestly, housed; the governance of the guild was entirely in the hands of its members. It ought to have succeeded – but it did not . . . Perhaps it was the lure of the towns and cities around them, the spurious excitement they generate. I suppose that we ought to try the experiment again, in a remote place such as the north of Scotland.'

Morton looked round the opulent room, situated on the fringe of the nation's capital city, and smiled sardonically to himself.

'I very much fear,' said Morris, suddenly wrathful, 'that Britain is a lost cause to us. The factory workers and artisans, who would be the natural leaders of the lower classes, are too prosperous. There is resentment amongst unskilled, labouring workers, I grant you. But it is directed against the immigrant Irish, who are prepared to work harder than they, for lower wages.'

'But it is political change that we should seek first,' Corbin said emphatically. 'All things will flow from that!'

'I agree. But the government has, for the most part involuntarily, succeeded in creating an impression of political advance. Britain has now virtually universal manhood suffrage. The only demonstrably oppressed section of society is the women – and no one has ever succeeded in making a violent revolution out of women . . . I have to confess that I am wavering, myself. All my life, I have advocated catastrophe – a bloody uprising, if you will – to purge society of tyranny and bring a return to a simpler life; where co-operation, not exploitation, would be its hallmark. But now I seem to be crying in the wilderness, alone. With the establishing of the Independent Labour Party, even Engels has gone over to supporting change through democratic, parliamentary action.'

A silence fell, while Morris sipped despondently at his whisky. A half-burnt log slipped from the firedog into the embers, sending a shower of sparks up the chimney. Then Corbin put down his glass.

'Can you introduce us to someone who might help us?' he asked. 'It is well known that there are anarchists living openly, in London.'

'Indeed there are, Kropotkin, for one! Yes . . . I would advise you to go to him. He would know what you should do. But you shall stay here tonight. And I will give you clean shirts and collars, to replace those bloodstained ones. Both of you seem to be about my size.'

He rose and took an elaborately engraved calling-card from an escritoire. He wrote a short note on the back of it, and passed it to Corbin.

'Give my regards to Kropotkin,' he said. 'Now, I will ask Mary to show you to your rooms. No doubt, you would like a bath also.'

*

Next morning, after a leisurely breakfast, Corbin and Morton took their leave of William Morris. Corbin seemed to know precisely how to get to Kropotkin, and Morton had observed that Morris had not written an address on the card. It all went to confirm Redman's suspicions. An agent would have been fully briefed, would know the whereabouts of the principal anarchists in Britain, who could be manipulated to serve his ends. Corbin marched back to the railway station, and bought tickets for Paddington. Once there, they headed for Maida Vale. Morton admired the Frenchman's grasp of the topography. If he had not been to London before, he had an amazing ability to find his way through the maze of streets. It was as if he had pored over a street plan until its details were imprinted on his brain. Had they gone one station further, to Edgware Road, he could have taken a more direct route. But it was an impressive performance; Corbin would be a dangerous adversary. Eventually they turned down a side-street and stopped at a large Georgian house. A uniformed maid answered Corbin's ring. She took the card that Morris had given him and disappeared inside. After a moment, she reappeared and ushered them into an elegant sitting-room on the next floor. A tall, spare man rose from a chair in the window bay. He was about fifty, with fine aristocratic features and greying hair.

'Which of you is Grillon?' he asked, in immaculate French.

'I am,' said Morton.

Kropotkin shook his hand warmly. 'We old men have to give place to such as you, if the struggle is to be successful . . . But we heard that you were taken.'

'I was, Beck and Stavisky also. I alone managed to escape.'

Kropotkin sat down, suddenly gloomy. 'Tsar Alexander and his troops are a formidable force,' he said. 'We harry them, we foment discontent among the peasantry, and score the occasional triumph; but all this seems scarcely to dent the complacency of the aristocracy. I was one of them, you know, before renouncing my nobility to become an anarchist. They are like a great cancer in the body of Russia. They are alien. They do not speak the language of the people, they treat them like animals, and yet the proletariat do not rise up.'

'One day they will do so,' said Corbin.

'Yes . . . One day I shall go back to Russia.' Kropotkin's face brightened. 'They are ripe for revolution, they will sweep away these parasites . . . Let it be in my lifetime!' he said fervently.

'It will come,' Morton said quietly.

'Yes, but I must be there! I shall be needed. In one sense, cutting out the cancer is less important than the healing measures we take thereafter. There is no point in ridding ourselves of one oppressive system, to fashion another in its place. The Marxians advocate replacing the monarchy with a "dictatorship of the proletariat", which would wither away when the classless, collectivist society we advocate has been established . . . Have you ever heard of a centralized, governmental authority voluntarily abolishing itself? Marxism is a creed alien to Russia; its creator German. No . . . Authoritarianism is the besetting sin of all Germans; the authoritarianism would be sure to triumph over the communism.'

'You will be there, sir,' Corbin said with conviction.

'Yes, yes.' Kropotkin smiled expansively. 'And of what service can I be to you?'

'William Morris said that you would be able to introduce us to an anarchist cell over here in London.'

Kropotkin stroked his nose with his slim fingers. 'Yes,' he murmured. 'You understand that we anarchists are not active in Britain; nor must we become so. We are guests in this country, remember that. I do not wish to be compelled to wander the world again, my writing is too important.'

'We will remember.'

'Then I will send you to Halder. He is a German social democrat, and a fugitive from the Kaiser's vengeance. He had enough warning, and was able to escape with his personal fortune. He now uses his wealth to assist our common cause. I sent two other French anarchists to him, a few weeks ago. Perhaps you know them – Martial Bourdin and Monique Laloux.'

Corbin shook his head. 'No, but I shall be glad to make their acquaintance.'

'Good! The address is 23, Mansell Street. It is in Aldgate, on

59

the eastern fringes of the City of London . . . And good luck to you!'

Bragg followed the porter along the lofty corridor in King's College, and went through the door indicated. He found himself in a long laboratory, with rows of solid-looking benches equipped with sinks and bunsen burners. At the far end, a man was sitting at a table. He was modishly dressed in a lounging suit, dux collar and silk cravat. He was checking some papers, a dead pipe clenched between his teeth. He could not have been more than thirty-five, Bragg thought doubtfully.

'Excuse me, sir.'

The man looked up in surprise. 'Yes?'

'I am told that you are Dr Porteus, the Professor of Chemistry.'

Porteus smiled. 'I have that somewhat doubtful pleasure.'

'Detective Sergeant Bragg, City police.'

Porteus raised an eyebrow. 'And how can I be of service?'

Bragg took a chair, with a sigh. 'I'm hoping you can solve a conundrum for us, sir. A couple of days back, we had an explosion in an electricity junction-box. No serious injuries, but that was sheer good fortune. The electricity company said that it couldn't be their fault, and suggested a terrorist bomb. But there was a smell of gas after it. We went to the gas company, but they said that their main must have been fractured by the explosion. Nobody wants to accept the blame.'

Porteus grinned. 'That can hardly have come as a surprise.'

'No, I'll grant you that. Then we went to an explosives company, with a piece of the iron manhole cover. The storeman looked at it, but couldn't decide whether it had been a bomb or not. I tell you, I was walking along the pavement, at the time. It exploded practically under my feet. It looked bloody like a bomb to me.'

'How do you think I can help?'

'Well . . . Nobody set it off, that's certain. But I believe that explosives can be triggered by clockwork fuses, nowadays. I wondered if you had any ideas.'

'The notion of terrorists putting bombs in manholes gives one the shivers, does it not?' Porteus pondered for a moment. 'Nevertheless, I could argue a case for its having been somewhat more mundane than that. After all, the commercial application of scientific discoveries can be fraught with peril. Take coal-gas, for example. You are well aware of its explosive properties, from lighting your gas fire.'

'I don't have one, sir. I stay with the old coal.'

Porteus laughed. 'Stout fellow! Well, I think I could rig up a demonstration for you.' He searched in his waste-paper basket and pulled out a circular toffee-tin. 'Eating humbugs is one of my grosser habits,' he said. He prised off the lid and made two small holes in it, at opposite sides of the rim. He then put a rubber tube on to a gas-tap and inserted the end into the tin. There came the hiss of the gas, and Bragg started back.

'There is no need to concern yourself,' Porteus said. 'The proportional admixture of coal-gas and air is the critical factor in the situation I am postulating.' He rammed the lid tightly on to the tin.

'Now, let us consider what we have,' he said didactically. 'Here is a vessel filled, to all intents and purposes, with coal-gas. It has not exploded, so we can presume that it is not in a dangerous state. Agreed?'

'Yes.'

Porteus struck a match. 'If I apply a light to one of the holes in the lid, so, you will see that there is a flame above the aperture. Since air is not, in itself, combustible, we can safely assume that the gas within the tin is being consumed. Now watch.'

The little flame above the lid continued to burn, and Bragg shifted impatiently in the silence. Suddenly there was the crack of an explosion. The toffee-tin whistled by Bragg's ear and shattered a glass cabinet behind him.

'Christ!' he exclaimed. 'I could have been killed!'

Porteus grinned boyishly. 'There can be no scientific advance without risk, sergeant. Well, there you have your explosion. Now, let us consider why. We said that the coal-gas in the tin was being consumed; in fact it was burning at the level of the aperture, as a Bunsen-burner does. In the process, air was being drawn into the tin through the other hole, to replace the gas

61

that was being used up. Then there was an explosion. Why was that? This experiment demonstrates that, at a certain point, a mixture of gas and air becomes explosive. Then the external flame is able to flash back through the hole, and ignite the contents of the tin. Now, we filled the container with gas, and introduced air in order to reach the critical level. But there is no reason why it should not apply to the converse situation. Let us visualize an electricity manhole, the cover virtually sealed with dirt. Let us further suppose a, perhaps small, escape of gas from an adjacent main. Over a period, the mixture of air and coal-gas in the manhole could become potentially explosive.'

'All right,' Bragg said irritably, 'I give you that. But there was no flame to set it off.'

'No. But into our hypothetical situation we could introduce faulty insulation of the electricity cables, so that there is sparking. Then you could certainly get your explosion.'

'You seem to be having to make a lot of assumptions,' Bragg said grumpily.

'It is the privilege of the theorist, sergeant!'

'Are you saying that I can forget all about terrorists and their bombs?'

'By no means! I was merely constructing an alternative explanation. If you will let me have your piece of the manhole cover, I can carry out some tests on it. Unfortunately, the University authorities have decreed that I must levy a charge for such work.'

Bragg laughed. 'I can't see the Commissioner agreeing to pay for that! Anyway, I threw my bit of iron out of the train window. It's somewhere on the track, between Stepney and Fenchurch Street.'

Catherine paused half-way up the great, curving staircase of Lanesborough House, and tried to still the turbulence of her thoughts. Was she being precipitate? Ever since Sergeant Bragg's visit, the previous afternoon, she had been smarting from his tirade. Yet she could no longer suppress the growing acknowledgement that he could be right, that she might have reacted differently to James's proposal, had she been given time to consider . . . Men said that women were not mentally robust enough to cope with difficult problems, hold down a proper job. Was it true, after all? Was the pressure of life clouding her judgement, warping her sense of proportion? She thrust the thought from her contemptuously . . . And yet . . . The frock-coat had been a small thing: did she really want James to be just another man-about-town? Of course not! Anyway, she had behaved immaculately herself. She would wager that James had not for a moment detected her inevitable sense of deflation . . . But suppose he had? Suppose he thought that she had accepted his theatre invitation merely for the opportunity to display herself in society? The idea was absurd! He should know her better than that . . . Yet why had she accepted? After her rejection of his proposal, it was the last thing she should have expected – even wanted. But, truth to tell, she had been relieved to get it. She liked his company; he was amusing, attentive – a gentleman. And it was obvious, from his persistence, that he admired her. Then, why had they got into this impasse? The fact was that she had begun to think in stereotypes, to react like one. His proposal of marriage had been made in grotesquely inappropriate circumstances, but that did not mean that it was any the less sincere. What did she want? Camellias in a conservatory, and an orchestra playing Viennese waltzes? No, the truth lay much deeper than that, on both counts. She had a very warm regard for James, not because he was a stereotype of a gentleman, but because he was a considerate, affectionate, trustworthy man. And herself? She had become a caricature of a feminist, strident, defensive, prickly; and now she might have to make the best of it . . . But she had to know! He was too kind ever to let his actions reflect upon her, but she must be prepared. She swept up the remaining flight of stairs and went into the grand drawing-room.

Her godmother was sitting in the window alone, save for her crony, Mrs Gerald de Trafford.

'Come in, child.' Lady Lanesborough beckoned her. 'You are almost a stranger! Would you like some tea?'

'No, thank you.' Catherine subsided gracefully into a chair.

'And how is Harriet?'

Catherine laughed. 'Mamma is her usual vague, charming, irritating self!'

'Goodness! How censorious the younger generation is, nowadays,' Mrs de Trafford said.

'Are you looking forward to the Season?' Lady Lanesborough asked. 'I hope that you are not going to opt out of it again.'

'The question hardly arises, until I have received invitations,' Catherine said lightly.

'You will, I shall see to that. I trust that you are not still set on your policeman. You could do far better than him.'

'Who is that?' Mrs de Trafford asked.

'You know, the second son of Sir Henry Morton – the Lord Lieutenant of Kent. With his elder brother so sick, I expect he will inherit the title,' she said thoughtfully. 'I suppose a baronetcy is something.'

Catherine laughed. 'You need have no fear, I have given the *coup de grâce* to any hopes he might have had.'

'Good, good! You could make a much better match. Let us see . . . I would think that Lord Brandon might be brought to the point of settling down. He is forty, after all. He has large estates in Norfolk, and interests in Midlands coal-mines, so I believe. He might do . . . Then there is Lord William St Charles. He is only a second son – but he comes from a wealthy family, even though the title is recent.'

'Stop! Stop!' Catherine held up her hands in mock horror. 'My ambitions go far beyond the convenience of a society marriage. I intend to devote my energies to becoming the premier journalist in Britain. After all, someone must carry the fight into the enemy's citadel.'

A stricken look crossed Lady Lanesborough's face. 'That is all very well, when you are young,' she said cautiously. 'But, take my word for it, in twenty years you will want security. Where will you look for it then?'

'I would prefer to do without it,' Catherine said loftily, 'if it meant that I had to put up with the usual philandering husband.'

'Is it really such an imposition? After all, you can have a good time in your turn. Believe me, my dear, by the time you are my age, it does not matter, either way.'

Catherine laughed. 'To be debauched by my own godmother was the last thing that I expected! Why, at the font you renounced, on my behalf, the vain pomp and glory of the world, coupled with the carnal desires of the flesh. Now you reproach me for spurning them!'

'You are a provoking child!' Lady Lanesborough retorted. 'Whatever words were put into my mouth at your christening, inside I was merely promising to advise you as to what was best for your own good. And that I am continuing to do.'

'Nor would I wish to dissuade you,' said Catherine. 'It is stimulating to have so eloquent a counterpoint to one's chosen theme. But I must not tease you. I have really come to gossip.'

The two ladies' faces brightened, and they leaned forward eagerly.

'What have you heard?' Mrs de Trafford asked.

'Nothing at all definite,' said Catherine conspiratorially. 'Just the merest whisper of a rumour.'

'What about?' said Lady Lanesborough urgently.

'An elopement.'

'Ah! How thrilling! What a start to the Season! Who is it?'

'You have heard nothing?' Catherine asked.

'Nothing. What about you, Molly?'

'I have not heard a word,' said Mrs de Trafford, in a voice charged with excitement.

'Oh,' said Catherine disappointedly. 'That makes it difficult for me . . . You must see that, as a journalist, I cannot be seen to breach a confidence or my sources would dry up. In any case, if you are not already aware of it, then it cannot have happened.'

'Perhaps it is merely in contemplation,' suggested Lady Lanesborough.

'Yes . . . I suppose that is possible,' Catherine said thoughtfully.

To avoid the risks attached to walking through the City in broad daylight, Morton suggested that he and Corbin should wait until dusk, before approaching Mansell Street. They therefore strolled over to Regent's Park, and spent the rest of the morning in the zoo. Having lunched on pork pies and beer, they went down Regent Street and on to the Embankment. Morton's swollen left eye was now a shiny purple, and drew many inquisitive glances. It would be easier to loiter inconspicuously by the river. Corbin seemed to have a less detailed knowledge of the streets here, and kept to the main thoroughfares. Morton wished that he had claimed to have been in London for some time, before his arrest. At least, then, he would have been able to show some familiarity with the back streets. It would be ironic if the plan were wrecked by an acquaintance, hailing him from the other side of the road. When the Embankment ran out, at Blackfriars, he had to insist on plunging into the mean alleys bordering the river. They lurked there till dusk fell, then found their way to the Tower. This gave Corbin his bearings again, and they turned north to Aldgate. Mansell Street was lined with old soot-blackened terraces. In the middle of the west side, however, a pair of rather grander houses had been erected. They were set back from the pavement, and there was a flight of steps to each front door.

'The house we seek is the first of those two,' Corbin said with satisfaction.

Morton suddenly felt a strong sense of foreboding. He seemed to have won Corbin's confidence; but, as Redman had said, this was partly because Corbin needed to believe in him. Now he would be meeting someone in touch with real anarchists. He wished that the Special Branch file had contained more information about anarchism as a philosophy – if one could call it that. Certainly, he was in no position to debate its finer points; that meant he was vulnerable. Perhaps his best defence was to adopt a kind of truculent reticence, a moody modesty.

The door was opened by a German maid, who was past her first youth. 'Yes?' she said.

'We have been sent to your master by Kropotkin,' Corbin replied.

'Wait here, and I will tell him.'

She reappeared, moments later, and ushered them into a long room at the front of the house. It was over-furnished with heavy pieces. The walls were covered with pictures in ornate gilded frames. The end overlooking the street had been made into a sitting-room, with *chaises longues* and armchairs on a large Persian carpet. The other end was evidently used as a study. There was a big roll-top desk, and a table overflowing with books and papers. A man was seated at the desk, holding up an admonitory hand. He finished writing, put down his pen and turned to them.

'You come from Kropotkin?' he said in English. He rose and walked over to them, hand outstretched. He was of medium height and somewhat corpulent. He had a round cherubic face and twinkling eyes. His expression seemed set in a permanent smile.

'Yes. I am Marcel Corbin, from France. I regret that I do not speak German.'

'And I am Franz Halder. I am charmed by your *politesse*. However, English has become the lingua franca among us, and it serves . . . Perhaps I should tell you something of myself,' he said, leading them to the armchairs. 'I was a professor of philosophy in Munich, and a prominent member of the Social Democratic party. Once Bavaria had been absorbed into the German empire, however, I found myself in a position of considerable danger. Even the friendship of Ludwig II of Bavaria would not have sufficed to protect me, in the face of the anti-socialist laws brought in by the Prussians. So, I abandoned my post and fled to England. Here I can still be of service to the party, by writing pamphlets and so on. Inevitably – and I am sure that this is of more interest to you – I have met other *émigrés* who have made London their home . . . Now, tell me about yourselves. Monsieur Corbin, perhaps you would begin.' The beaming smile invited confidences.

Morton could see Corbin relax by an effort of will. He smiled at Halder. 'I am an unashamed anarchist,' he said. 'I joined them in Dijon, when I was working in the area. We were planning a bombing in Lyon, but we were betrayed. I fled to Holland and took a boat to England. But I was arrested on landing and brought to London, where I was imprisoned for many days, until I escaped.'

'Really?' Halder gave a giggle. 'You should have waited. They would have released you. There are no laws here under which you could be brought to trial for being an anarchist.'

'I do not trust them,' Corbin said shortly.

'And you, sir?' Halder's twinkling eyes swung round to Morton.

'I am Paul Grillon,' Morton said in an accented voice. 'I was born near Geneva, at a village called Vernier, where my father was the schoolmaster. When I went to university in Bern, I became attracted to the nihilist cause. I left university, and joined an active cell. I and two others travelled to Russia, to make an attempt on the life of Grand Duke Michael. We were almost successful – it was merely that we did not understand enough about animals.'

'What do you mean?' Halder asked, his smile broadening.

'We knew that he and his entourage were coming to St Petersburg. We placed a large bomb in a culvert, on the road he must use. It was open country, so we were confident that we would hear the noise of his escort in ample time.'

'But he took another road?'

'No, no! All went according to plan. We led a large cart on to the road beyond the culvert, so that the carriage would be forced to stop above it . . . But, at a certain time, we had to leave the horse to its own devices. Unfortunately, it became unsettled by the noise of the approaching cavalcade, and began to move away. There was little we could do . . . We tried to detonate the mine when the carriage was going over it, but only succeeded in killing two of the rear-guard. There was, of course, a hue and cry. All three of us were taken, and I alone escaped . . . I also was arrested on my arrival here in London.'

'The English police seem to have, at the moment, an unexpected enthusiasm for arresting people.' Halder's face still beamed, but the voice was sceptical.

'In my case,' Morton said, 'it can readily be explained. The Swiss police were seeking me, all over Europe, for a bank robbery in Bern – we had to have funds for our attempt.'

Halder laughed. 'I see! Well, as it happens, I have a kind of hostel for political refugees, in the next house. I see no reason why you should not have temporary accommodation there. Have you dined?'

'No.'

68

'Then come down into my basement, where they eat, and you shall meet them.'

'We gather that Martial Bourdin and Monique Laloux were sent to you by Kropotkin,' Corbin said.

Halder seemed perceptibly to relax. 'Indeed! They are still here. Follow me.'

He led them down a back staircase into what must once have been the kitchen of the house. The centre of the room was occupied by a long table at which two men and a woman were sitting. They were coming to the end of a cold supper.

'My friends,' Halder said in a bantering tone, 'I would like to introduce two more foundlings – Marcel Corbin, who is French, and Paul Grillon, from Geneva.'

He turned to the newcomers. 'The gentleman at the end is Caserio Santo. He comes from Milan, and his civic pride leads him to sing opera constantly, in an atrocious tenor.'

Santo was in his early thirties, slight, with an olive skin and black beard. He did not smile at Halder's sally.

'I might describe him as our contradiction,' Halder continued. 'He claims to be a Bakuninist – which should incline him to widespread carnage, as a means of spreading the anarchist gospel. He has, however, a strong impulse towards martyrdom, a compulsion to make his personal statement of dissent in one supreme moment of glory. His days here are spent in planning the perfect propaganda deed.'

Halder turned towards the other man.

'Martial Bourdin is our enigma,' he said with a broad smile. 'He is a French intellectual, who ought to be a pamphleteer but hankers to be an activist. He subscribes to the theory of revolution, yet eschews extreme violence!'

Bourdin received Halder's remarks less passively. 'I am not convinced of the value of isolated acts of terrorism,' he said irritably. 'They certainly do not win over ordinary people. Once I threw a bomb into the foyer of a grand apartment block, in Paris. What happened? The concierge threw it out again. When it exploded, it killed a passing priest, two children and a dog. That gained us no sympathizers.'

'That was because you were afraid, and set too long a fuse,' the woman said contemptuously.

Bourdin flushed, and his delicate hands clenched.

'Now, now, my children,' Halder said genially, 'let us not quarrel amongst ourselves.' His gaze was transferred to the young woman. She had dark brown hair and a somewhat sallow skin. Nevertheless, she was good-looking, by dint of her small build and regular features. Her dress was plain, and a cigarette drooped from the corner of her mouth.

'Monique Laloux is from Paris. I might describe her as *terra incognita*,' Halder went on. 'She subscribes to an extreme form of nihilism, and thus should be a soul-mate for you, Grillon. However, I suspect that her passion for liberating the Russian peasant serves merely to transmute her anger at the subordination of her sex by men.'

Monique scowled at his beaming face.

'Now, my children. I will leave you to make friends. The arrival of our Swiss comrade has given me a happy thought for an article I am writing.' He disappeared up the stairs.

Morton took some food, and went to sit next to Monique.

'What is Halder's position here?' Corbin asked, relapsing into French. 'Is he your leader?'

'Leader?' exclaimed Monique, in a cold incisive voice. 'What have anarchists to do with leaders? We want no leaders!'

'Halder is our philosopher, if not our guide,' Bourdin said calmly. 'In return, we allow him to amuse himself a little, at our expense.' He was clean-shaven, his hair cut short. He also was in his thirties, and his fine features gave an impression of fastidiousness.

'You too are an anarchist?' he asked.

'Yes.' Corbin sat down beside him. 'I joined a cell at Dijon, while I was living in Beaune.'

'Why did you come to England?' Monique asked sharply.

'For the same reason as you, I suppose,' Corbin said. 'One of our operations went wrong. We suspect that we were informed on. However that may be, I am a wanted man in France.'

'You do not sound like a Burgundian,' Bourdin said. 'I was brought up there myself.'

'I am not.' Corbin casually lifted his glass and sipped. 'I come from a village near Bordeaux, and I worked as a buyer of wine. Then my employer decided to extend his business to Beaune, and asked me to go there. I was unencumbered with a wife, so . . .' Corbin shrugged.

Monique shot him a venomous look.

'Who was your employer?' Bourdin asked.

'Ginestet et Cie, the wine merchants. It was strange. I had been accustomed to wine-growing communes in Bordeaux, of course, but it had not occurred to me that such an organization could be a model for the fundamental unit of society. Our comrades in Dijon opened my eyes.'

Monique ground out her cigarette on the edge of her plate, and took another. 'And you, Grillon?' she said. 'What about you?'

'I?' Morton smiled modestly. 'There is little to tell. I became a nihilist when I was at the University of Bern. I abandoned my studies and joined an active unit. We mounted an attempt against the life of a Russian Grand Duke, and came within a hair's breadth of assassinating him.'

Santo suddenly launched into an aria from *The Barber of Seville*, and was angrily silenced by Monique. He got to his feet and stalked out.

'What happened then?' she asked.

'There was no cover, so we were taken,' Morton said simply. 'We were handed over to the Okhrana, in St Petersburg, and separated. One night, when the gaoler came on his rounds, I feigned illness. As he bent over me, I seized him by the throat and strangled him. Then I escaped in his uniform.'

Monique's eyes were wide, her lips parted. 'I have never before met someone who has actually struck a blow inside Russia itself,' she exclaimed. 'That was splendid!'

'It was almost splendid,' Morton said with a rueful smile. 'But I shall try again. I must avenge my comrades.'

There was a clatter of feet on the stairs, and two more men entered.

'Well, folks,' said the first, in English, 'what's to eat? I'm starving. Hans and I have been scouring the stores of this great city, and it kinda gives you an appetite. Say, you two must be the new boys Franz mentioned!' He bustled over to the table and filled a plate with food.

'This is Lee McCafferty,' Bourdin said, switching to English.

71

'He comes from America, and is suspicious of other tongues. He insists that we converse in English – and since he is our new paymaster, we comply.'

'Hey, no need to get sore!' McCafferty said exuberantly. 'We can all get by in it. That way, nobody feels shut out. It's important!' He wagged an admonitory finger. 'Come on Hans, get some food inside you.'

The second man had been looking at the newcomers appraisingly. He now came over, hand outstretched.

'Hans Schelling,' he said abruptly. He was enormous, thought Morton, about six feet six tall, and built like an ox. You could feel the fearsome strength of the man in his handshake. He had blond hair and moustache, and heavy features. A puckered scar slashed across his left cheek. He took his plate to the seat vacated by Santo. From there, Morton noted, he would be able to observe everyone.

'You folks anarchists too?' McCafferty asked, looking from Corbin to Morton.

'We are,' Morton replied, wondering if he was overdoing the foreign accent. 'And you?'

'No, not me,' said McCafferty, his mouth full. 'I'm kinda freeloading, except that I'm paying for the privilege!'

'I do not understand.'

'No reason why you should, son.'

He was in his forties, tall and well-built, with reddish hair and pale freckled skin. His violet blue eyes gave him the innocent look of an overgrown schoolboy.

'Have you been a member of this cell for long?' Morton asked.

'You're Paul Grillon, are you son?'

'Yes.'

'Right. I like to get my bearings . . . First off, Paul, I ain't a proper member of this cell; I'm just usin' the facilities. Second, I just walked in here, barely a week ago.'

'Walked in?'

McCafferty laughed loudly. 'I wanted to find some folks who'd help me with my logistics. I reckoned someone like this would be my best bet. But how to find them? I could hardly go up to a policeman and say, "Excuse me, officer, can you direct me to the nearest mob of revolutionists?" Then I realized that there were anarchist newspapers here! How 'bout that! So I went into the office of *Freedom,* and asked for the top man. After we'd stalked around each other like a couple of cats, for a time, he finally sent me here. Great!'

So this was Gibson's American millionaire. Well, well!

'But you yourself are not an anarchist, Mr McCafferty?'

'No, Paul. I've come over as a representative of the Fenian Brotherhood, in New York. We are going to give the government here one hell of a reminder that there is no place for the British in Ireland.'

'That is good!' Morton said warmly. 'If I can help you, I will. It was the English police that beat me like this.'

'You sure ain't no oil painting at the moment, son! As to helping, why not? Your English is pretty good!'

'It was my favourite subject at school. Once, I had an ambition to emigrate to America.'

'You couldn't do better. That's where it's all happening! A strappin' young feller, like you, could make a fortune. I wish I had my time over.'

'When we have gained our freedom in the old world.'

'Sure, sure . . . Well, now, Hans and I are working on the explosives problem at the moment. But, later on, maybe you could help. Have you guys got money? Everybody over here seems down to their last nickel!'

'None,' said Corbin.

McCafferty plunged his hand into his pocket and pulled out a handful of sovereigns.

'Here you are.' He trickled out a pile in front of Corbin and gave the rest to Morton. 'Now, why don't you bunk in with me, Paul? I'm in the first-floor room, next door, and there's a spare bed.'

'Thank you.'

Morton followed McCafferty into what had been the pantry. A door had been cut in the wall dividing the two properties. The next door basement held a well-equipped workshop and a variety of stores. Spilling out of a sack in the corner were several cast-iron spheres, with an external diameter of about five inches. Each had a small protuberance, with an aperture in it. Good God! This was not comic opera after all; it was in deadly earnest. They were bombs!

73

4

Morton woke up with a start, next morning, and glanced around to get his bearings. The room was large, like the comparable room in the other house. But this contained no comfortable furniture. His camp-bed was against the party wall, while McCafferty's was opposite, near the door. At the back of the room was a cheap wash-stand, and a few bentwood chairs were scattered haphazardly around.

McCafferty was on his back, breathing shallowly through a slack mouth. Morton wondered what to do about him. So this was the man who had changed dollar notes for sovereigns, at the Bank of England; who had been audacious enough to hire a costermonger to transport a fortune on his barrow, and walk into the *Freedom* office asking for anarchists. It was incredibly naïve and trusting . . . But perhaps it was the British who were naïve and trusting. Here was a nest of anarchists, on the fringe of the City of London itself. He had seen bomb cases with his own eyes. Well, Redman knew about the problem, so there was no call for Morton to act precipitately. His instructions were to find out what Corbin was up to, and that he was determined to do. But did Redman know what McCafferty was about? Probably not. The Irish nationalists had been quiet for some time. Parnell's disgrace, over the O'Shea divorce, had robbed them of their most effective leader, and it was years since their last outrage. From what McCafferty had said, he was planning another bombing campaign – or, at least, one big explosion which would encourage the native Fenians to follow suit. Morton supposed that he must have a responsibility to warn the authorities. At the very least, he could advise Bragg to stop trailing around London, looking for McCafferty! Apart from that, what could he tell them? It was a fair assumption that the outrage was to take place in the London area, or McCafferty would not have come here. But how much good did that do them? Morton knew neither the time nor the place of the intended explosion. Yet sending any message to Bragg was fraught with danger for him. It was pointless to risk the entire mission for the sake of giving only a vague warning.

It was Saturday. Had he not been shanghaied into this crazy situation, he would have been playing real tennis this afternoon. Well, there was no chance of Arthur Thomson's being perturbed by his absence. He would wait half an hour, then go off in search of another partner – or a young actress . . . That must have been one of the important factors to Redman, he thought. As a single man, he could disappear without anyone raising a hue and cry. Even the City police would shrug their shoulders. They still regarded him as an amiable outsider – content, for the moment, to be a constable, but not tied to the job as they were. It was unfair, he thought, in a flash of petulance. He had set his face against the life of aimless self-indulgence led by his peers; yet no one thought that he was serious about it, even after five years. They would say that he had reverted to type, write him off. In a sense it was justified. No real policeman would have been ensnared by Redman, he would have played it by the book. To that extent, they were right. He could afford to be flattered, to go along with Redman's assertion that he was the man for the job, the only man. It was his besetting weakness; Bragg had played on it time and time again – his relish of a challenge, his immature disregard of danger . . . Well, it was not going to come to that, this time. As soon as Corbin's plan of action became apparent, he would pull out and leave Redman to pursue whatever course he chose.

McCafferty awoke with a snort. He fumbled under his pillow, and brought out a packet of cigarettes and a box of matches. Eyes still closed, he extracted a cigarette and stuck it in his mouth. Only as he actually struck the match, did he open them. He inhaled deeply.

'Ah, that's better,' he said, coughing and spluttering. 'God, I hate the mornings!'

He rolled on to his side and gazed at Morton.

'It's good to have you here, Paul,' he said. 'It's kinda creepy, waking up on your own in this joint.'

'It is more comfortable than the prison cell I was in.'

'Yeah, I guess so. Your English is pretty good, son. That's why I wanted you to bunk in with me. I got pretty tired of not being able to talk easy to anybody.'

'I had the impression that Schelling speaks it well,' said Morton.

'Hell, yes. But his only interest is in guns and bombs. Maybe they are all like that in Holland. Wouldn't like to cross him; he's a real tough cookie, I reckon . . . What part of France is Geneva in, Paul?'

Morton laughed. 'It is in Switzerland, just over the French border. We gained our independence many years ago.'

'Thank Christ! I hate the bloody French . . . The Swiss make clocks, don't they?'

'As the French make brandy!'

'Huh! My drink is sour mash whiskey. Haven't had a drop since I came over. They've never heard of it here.'

'You are enduring much privation, for the sake of your cause.'

McCafferty leaned over, and ground out his cigarette on the floorboards. 'Hell, it's in the blood,' he said. 'We feel as much Irish as American. We'll go on helping the Fenians, till the British get the hell out o' there.'

'Helping with money, presumably.'

'Not just with money, no siree! With blood, if needs be. My father came over to fight, once the Civil War was lost. And by "over", I mean right here, in London. He wasn't like some of them sons of bitches, layin' low in France – your so-called Irish patriots, like Stephens, sashayin' round Europe, livin' high off the hog at the expense of the Brotherhood. No, sir, my daddy rotted seven years in a Limey jail for his part in it.'

'That seems unjust,' Morton said earnestly.

'Hell, he couldn't help himself. He was a natural hero, my Paw, a real Southern gentleman. As soon as the Civil War broke out, he joined Morgan's guerrillas. The pick of the cavalry, they were. Once, he took his men behind the Union lines, and captured a whole lot of ammunition and stores. Then he found there weren't no wagons around. So what does he do? He commandeers some Mississippi steamboats, loads them up with the ammunition and sails down river to the Confederate lines, with the Union batteries trying their damnedest to blow them out of the water! That was my Paw!'

'And are you, also, a Southern gentleman?'

'No, son. I can't say that I am. After the war, they had what they called the "Reconstruction", which meant that the Yankees came down and took all the best jobs. When my Paw came here to lead the Fenian revolt, Maw took me north – about as far as you can go, and still stay under Uncle Sam's coat-tails.'

'Where was that?'

'Toledo, in Ohio – that's near Lake Erie. There were people of Irish blood there, too. They were good to us, particularly after my father died.'

'How did that happen?' Morton asked sympathetically.

'Hell, I told you he was a hero, didn't I? I guess the failure of the uprising in Ireland got to him; and maybe his time in jail . . . Do you know? All that the Limeys give their prisoners is two pints of oatmeal gruel and a pound of bread a day. How 'bout that! Well, my Paw got feeling real sore about things. So he teamed up with a Captain Mackey, who'd been helping in the Irish rising, too. They got funds from the Fenian Brotherhood, in New York, and came to England to strike a blow for the cause.'

'As you have done now.'

'That's right, Paul. They set a charge of dynamite under one of the arches of London Bridge. But something went wrong, and they were both killed in the explosion.'

'*Mon Dieu!* But it was a glorious death.'

'So Maw said . . . Well, nothing's going to go wrong, this time.'

'We must make certain of that.'

'Do you feel like a stroll, after breakfast, son? I'd rather not be around in London, on my own. I kinda vanished from my hotel. The cops might be feeling a mite uneasy on my behalf!'

'To where do we go?'

'Ever heard of Karl Marx?'

'Of course.'

77

'Well, his daughter Eleanor is shacked up in Bloomsbury, with some guy named Aveling. Our friend Halder says she'll be able to fix me up with a logistics expert. Want to stretch your legs?'

After a breakfast of coffee, bread and cheese, which seemed to leave McCafferty more disgruntled than ever, they set off. At Morton's suggestion, they skirted the north side of the City, and came to Bloomsbury by way of Clerkenwell. McCafferty was in no hurry; indeed, he seemed somewhat out of condition.

'Have I met all the members of the cell?' Morton asked casually, as they strolled along.

'I guess so.'

'Do they stay all in the one house? It seems rather small.'

'It's OK. Schelling has the attic to himself . . . Now, that's a guy I can't cotton to. I get along just fine with most people, but not him. I don't know why. The guy never seems to unwind. You should be glad you're in with me, Paul. Don't get me wrong! What he don't know about explosives ain't worth knowing – but it don't make him easy.'

'There must be a couple of rooms on the floor above us,' Morton prompted him.

'Sure. Monique Laloux and Bourdin are in the back one; so I guess your friend Corbin must have bunked in with Santo, at the front.'

'Monique and Bourdin? I thought that they hated one another.'

'Yeah. I guess that Monique is one hell of a mixed-up lady. They came over together from Paris, France. Maybe they were shacked up together before. She seems a mite disappointed in him, and ain't chary of lettin' him know. That kinda gets to a man . . . Now the house we want is in Gordon Square, over there.'

It was a substantial terrace house, with wrought-iron railings around minuscule upper balconies. If Morton understood revolutionary propaganda aright, these were the very people who would be swept away in a river of blood! Once again, the door was opened by a maid in a starched apron and cap. After the customary interval, they were shown to a morning room at the back, overlooking the garden.

Eleanor Marx rose from her chair to greet them. She was of middle height, with a high forehead and determined chin. Her brown hair was pulled back in a bun at the nape of her neck.

'Mr McCafferty?' she asked, with a slight German accent.

'The same, ma'am.' He nodded a bow.

'Mr Halder begged that I should help you, if it were in my power.'

'I think that it is, ma'am. I know that you are a strong supporter of the Fenians.'

A shadow crossed her brow. 'That is so.'

'I have been sent to England by the Fenian Brotherhood, in New York. If I am to carry out my mission, I need assistance.'

'What kind of assistance?' she said unenthusiastically.

'The help of one man who knows his way around, who has been an active Fenian in Britain.'

'I see . . .' She stared out into the garden, deep in thought. 'It would not be politic,' she began eventually, 'for it to be known that I was helping you. In Britain, we are on the crest of a wave that will sweep the working people to total control of Parliament. I am prominently involved in the new Independent Labour Party. Our foes would seize on the slightest suggestion that we were linked to revolutionist movements, and exploit it to our detriment. I dare not risk that.'

'I see,' McCafferty said glumly.

'However, the same cannot be said of Engels. Although he now lives in London, he spent many years in Manchester. I know that he had links with the Fenians, in those days. I will ask him to prevail on them to send a representative down from the north.'

'Thank you, ma'am.'

'When do you require him?'

'As soon as possible. Get him to come to Halder's place.'

'Of course.' She smiled distantly. 'I will speak to Engels today.'

Bragg went into Bishopsgate police station early, on that Saturday morning.

'Well now,' he greeted the desk-sergeant. 'Has young Jenkins got back from the Celtic fringes?'

'Yes, Joe, he has. Popped in not half an hour ago. It seems he has a girl up here; he's taking her out this afternoon.'

'Where will I find him?'

'At the section house, I shouldn't wonder.'

'Right, thanks.'

Bragg plunged into the narrow streets behind the police station. It was a poor area for the men to live in, he thought. Mind you, the section house was as good as, or better than, the barrack-rooms most of them had been used to. And these courts and alleys were not as squalid as the ones over the City boundary, in Spitalfields. Even so, the men would feel better about themselves, be more effective, if they lived in pleasanter surroundings. But they had to live within the City boundaries; that was the rule. So there was really no way out. He climbed the stairs to the top floor and knocked on Jenkins's door.

'Come in!' a voice called.

Bragg found himself in a narrow room, not much bigger than a police-cell. Most of the space was taken up by an iron bed. There were rough wooden shelves on one side of the fireplace, and an old swivel chair was near the window. Jenkins was lying on the bed, reading a newspaper.

'Don't get up, lad,' Bragg said, 'I just wanted a quick word.'

'Yes, sir.' Jenkins levered himself into a sitting position. He was fresh-faced and spotty. He didn't look old enough to be taking out girls!

'You are on permanent nights, of course.'

'Yes, sir.'

'Last Tuesday, you were on the St Botolph's beat.'

'Yes.'

'I want to talk to you about that night – if you can remember anything, after all those Welsh cakes and laver bread!'

The lad grinned. 'It was a quiet night, sergeant. I didn't have anything to report.'

'Yes . . . Perhaps it was. But did you see anything unusual?'

'Unusual? Not that I know of.'

'Think, lad. There's a cab strike, the streets are quiet, quieter

80

even than normal. Not many vehicles at all; and, at that time of night, no tradesmen's carts or vans . . .'

'There was something struck me as peculiar, sir. There was a Black Maria drawn up in St Botolph's churchyard. It didn't worry me; after all, only the prisons or the police would use one of them.'

'How long was it there, lad?'

'I saw it when I first went down there. I suppose that was about quarter-past ten. It stayed there, because I saw it a couple more times. The last time I saw it was about midnight. I was late on my beat, because there was a bit of an argument outside an ale-house, and I'd stopped to sort it out. As I got near St Botolph's, I saw the Black Maria driving away.'

'In which direction?'

'North, up Bishopsgate Street Without.'

'Did you, now? Why would it be going that way, do you think? There are no prisons up there.'

'I dunno . . . There's Pentonville and Holloway.'

'Yes, but they are to the west. You wouldn't go to them through Shoreditch. You'd strike off towards City Road and the Angel.'

'I suppose so.'

'Anyway, well done, lad. If anything comes of this I might be able to get you off nights.'

'Ta, sergeant, but I wouldn't want split duties! Nights suits me – I can spend most of the evening with my girl.'

'Maybe. But a bright young chap, like you, should be looking ahead. You will never get on, if you're content with permanent nights.'

The lad looked abashed. 'Yes, sir; I'll remember.'

Bragg left the section house with a wholly unwarranted sense of well-being. But it was nice to see an alert youngster joining the force, instead of the usual ex-soldiers – their initiative dulled by years of regimentation. It took him back to his own start. Mind you, he'd worked in the City as a clerk in a shipping office, for some years. So he'd known his way about. Even so, the opportunities a couple of years on the beat gave you to acquire knowledge, enquire into how things were done, had been invaluable . . . Not that it had stood him in much stead.

81

Here he was, still a sergeant, never going to rise higher. He wondered what would have happened had his wife not died in childbirth, had his son lived. Would he have buckled down to it more, touched the forelock a bit? . . . No, it wasn't in his nature. In his book, merit was all that mattered; toadying to the likes of Chief Inspector Forbes should get you nowhere. He'd got where he was in the face of opposition from Forbes and Inspector Cotton. They'd washed their hands of him, said he was too headstrong, virtually uncontrollable. Of course, they'd been trying to manoeuvre the Commissioner into dismissing him. That was one instance where it had paid dividends for the head of the force to have come from the army. Lieutenant-Colonel Sir William Sumner knew a conspiracy when he saw one; and his penchant for interfering in the work of the lower ranks meant that he had a good idea of their worth. So, instead of being thrown out on his ear, Bragg had been condemned to work on his own! Almost a free-lance! Reporting through Cotton, but not really under his operational control. Indeed, Sir William seemed to use him, from time to time, for jobs dear to his own heart – jobs he would have liked to investigate himself, if he'd had the skills. This outcome left Bragg with no way ahead, but what did that matter? He'd preserved his integrity, he could use his own methods, ruffle a few feathers in the City if he had to – but get results. Things had even improved, when they'd put young Morton with him – as big a misfit as Bragg was himself. With his background and education, he clearly needn't care a toss. There had once been a rumour that he was being groomed to succeed Sir William, when he retired. There might have been some truth in it – still might be. After the Trafalgar Square riots, seven years ago, the military were out of favour; police forces were being expected to produce their own top brass . . . Well, if young Morton was ever to become Commissioner, he'd better set about finding him. Bragg took out his battered watch. It was still only nine o'clock. There would just about be time.

He walked quickly to London Bridge station, and caught an express train to Maidstone by the skin of his teeth. A stopping train to Hollingbourne was waiting there, for the arrival of the express. There was even a carrier with a trap, at Hollingbourne station, who was prepared to drop Bragg at the gates of the Priory, for a shilling. It couldn't have gone better if he'd planned it all! It was only eleven, and he was at the door of Morton's parents' home. His ring was answered by the butler.

'Why, Mr Bragg!' he exclaimed in pleasure. 'It's nice to see you, sir.'

'I don't suppose young Morton is at home?' Bragg asked gruffly.

'Master James? No. He has not been here for some weeks. Did you expect him to be?'

'No. Is Sir Henry in?'

'Yes, sir. I think he is in the gun room. Would you like to come in?'

As Bragg was being relieved of his hat, there came steps in the corridor, and Morton's sister caught sight of him.

'Sergeant Bragg!' she exclaimed excitedly. 'How nice! You shall be the first outside the family to hear my news!'

'What is that, Miss Emily?'

'Promise you will not mention it to a soul!'

Bragg smiled. 'I promise.'

'Mamma and Papa have at last agreed that my engagement to Reuben can be announced. It will be in *The Times* on the twenty-first of April, for the start of the Season!'

'This is Reuben Smith, the banker, is it?'

'Yes! We shall be married in August, I hope, and you must come to the wedding!'

'Well, miss, I'm a pretty rough sort of chap, as you know. I doubt if I would fit in at a society wedding.'

'Nonsense! My day would be spoiled, if you were not there.'

'We can't have that, can we?' Bragg laughed. 'All right, I'll come . . . And I'm very pleased, I want you to know that. From what little I've had to do with him, he seems a good solid chap. I'm sure you will be happy with him.'

'I know I will! Come along! Mamma is in the snuggery. I expect Parker will find Papa.'

She took him by the hand and hustled him down the corridor, to the small sitting-room which the family used when there were no guests. In that splendid mansion, Bragg thought, it was good to feel that they preferred to relax in a comfortable, rather shabby room, in front of a log fire.

Lady Morton greeted him with a bright smile. 'Sergeant Bragg! It is good to see you. I can see that you have heard Emily's news.' Her soft, New England voice was warm and welcoming.

'Yes, ma'am. He's a grand lad.'

'Ah, Bragg, there you are!' Sir Henry Morton came in. 'This is a surprise. James did not say that you would be dropping in. Where is he?'

'Well, sir, I was hoping that you could tell me.'

'Did you expect him to be here already?'

'Let's say, I was hoping he would be.'

'I don't understand you, Bragg. So far as we know, he is on duty, in London.'

'I have not seen him since Tuesday afternoon, sir. He did not come in on Wednesday morning.'

'But you expected that he would?' Lady Morton asked, puzzled.

'Yes, ma'am. We had already arranged what we would be doing, as usual.'

'Strange,' she said. 'It does not sound like James, to be so unreliable. And you have had no communication whatever from him?'

'None, milady.'

'Could he be working on a case, unbeknown to you?' Sir Henry asked.

'I wouldn't think so, sir. Nobody seems to know where he could be . . . Anyway, the only thing of note, at the moment, is the disappearance of an American tourist – and he seems to have gone voluntarily.'

'Are you implying that James might have gone somewhere involuntarily?' Lady Morton asked in a troubled voice.

'Hardly that, but Chambers found his latchkey in the door. It looks as if he went somewhere on the spur of the moment . . . In case you are worried, I have made enquiries – no bodies of young men have been found, since he disappeared.'

A look of concern crossed Lady Morton's face.

'Perhaps he has been kidnapped,' Emily suggested brightly.

'It is happening all over the place, in America. It might be that your missing tourist has grabbed James, and is holding him for ransom!'

Sir Henry gave a short bark of a laugh. 'That is hardly likely to happen over here, child. In any case, it is not commonly known that he is wealthy in his own right. And we have not had any demands for ransom.'

'But they might have been sent to Alderman's Walk,' Emily said. 'That was where he was snatched from.'

'I don't think we should let our imaginations run away with us, miss,' Bragg said quietly.

'I thoroughly agree,' said Sir Henry. 'However, as his next of kin, I authorize you to open any post at his rooms, in case Emily is right.'

Lady Morton shivered. 'I do wish that you two would stop speaking in such alarming terms. I am sure that the sergeant is right, and there is nothing to worry about.'

'What do you think happened, sergeant?' Emily demanded.

'I can't rightly say what I think, miss. The last person he was with, to our knowledge, was Miss Marsden.'

'Catherine? And does she not know where he is?'

'No, miss. He took her to a theatre, then sent her home alone, in a carriage.'

'What strange conduct!' Lady Morton exclaimed. 'I hope that he does not often behave so discourteously.'

'Can you think of anywhere he might have gone, ma'am? To get away from things for a while?'

'Why should he wish to get away from things?'

'Is there, say, a particular young lady that he is fond of?' Bragg persisted.

Lady Morton frowned. 'I would have thought that Miss Marsden was the person most nearly in that category,' she said after a pause.

'Not any more, it seems.'

'How can that be?' Emily exclaimed. 'He was devoted to her, anyone could see that. Had she not been so set on a career, they would have been married by now.'

'Do not exaggerate so,' Lady Morton reproved her. 'They are

85

good friends, but nothing more. I am sure that James will settle on someone more suitable . . . less city-orientated.'

Bragg sighed. 'I think Miss Emily is nearer the mark, ma'am. He did ask Miss Marsden to marry him; she turned him down.'

'Turned him down?' Sir Henry echoed. 'Good God!'

'When did this happen?' Emily asked.

'In the middle of March, it seems.'

'Last month? Ah, that was at the time there was that business over Louisa Sommers.'

'Does that explain Miss Marsden's rejection of him?' Sir Henry asked.

Emily cocked her head. 'It might,' she said. 'One never knows, with a man . . . But I know that she holds him in the highest regard. I expect that it is nothing more than a tiff. I had one with Reuben, last week!'

'Thank goodness that you did not reject him, because of it,' Lady Morton said fondly.

'I was wondering,' said Bragg, 'whether he might have gone off with somebody else – on the rebound, as you might say – someone, perhaps, not at all suitable.'

'Sergeant!' Lady Morton exclaimed. 'James would never do such a thing. He is far too much of a gentleman.'

'Yes, ma'am,' Bragg said drily.

Sir Henry cleared his throat. 'What enquiries have you made so far?' he asked.

'Only limited ones, sir. He is not at his rooms, or here. But with the ordinary nob of his age, you wouldn't think twice if he disappeared for a bit. I can't do more, unless you press for an investigation. He is a grown man, and just as likely as any other to do something unexpected.'

'That is not quite true, Bragg. He is answerable to you. I would have expected, at the very least, the courtesy of his informing you.'

'Then, are you reporting him missing?'

Sir Henry considered for a moment. 'No, sergeant, I would not wish to go so far. Young men are sometimes thoughtless. I take it that, despite the exaggerated fantasies of my daughter, there is no evidence to suggest that he went away other than voluntarily.'

'That's true enough. He could have easily left his key in the door accidentally.'

'In that case, I do not think that we should act precipitately. He is twenty-seven, and master of his own affairs. If he has had his proposal of marriage refused, he might well wish to reassess his future. I think that we ought to let him get on with it. Now, Bragg, I hope that you will stay to lunch.'

That night, Morton went down to the basement before supper. Bourdin and McCafferty were watching Schelling, who was mixing some dirty-yellow powder in a large metal bowl.

'What is that?' he asked.

Schelling smiled wolfishly. 'It is a little surprise,' he said.

'For whom?'

'Who knows? But it is important that we should be prepared.' He abandoned his stirring and went over to the corner, where he picked up one of the bomb cases.

'See,' he said. 'Halder has obtained these from a government arsenal at Woolwich. Some workers there are sympathetic to our cause.'

Morton took the metal sphere and examined it. 'But it is empty,' he said.

'Yes, but we will fill it. Unfortunately, I used the only explosive I brought with me, to test a clockwork detonating device.'

'Did it function well?'

Schelling scowled. 'No. We placed it under a manhole cover, in a street some distance from here. Then we hid ourselves and waited. Nothing happened.'

So Schelling had come near to killing him already, Morton thought. 'Why did it not explode?' he asked.

'I do not know. By then there were many people about, so we had to leave it there. It is of no matter; clockwork fuses are for cowards only.'

'But, if you have used all your explosive, with what will you fill the bombs?'

Schelling's teeth flashed in a grin. 'I am even now making more. Thanks to our friend McCafferty, and his money, we no longer need to be impotent.'

'Surely you are not mixing explosive in a metal bowl, with a metal spoon?' Morton exclaimed.

'Take it easy, Paul,' McCafferty said. 'There is nothing explosive about that – or so our expert says.'

'We are making black powder,' Schelling explained. 'Its composition has been the same for six hundred years. But it is not easy to buy the ingredients, in Britain, without people becoming suspicious. Would you like to take a turn at the mixing?'

Morton took hold of the spoon.

'The black substance is charcoal,' Schelling said. 'A manufactory would use a purer form of carbon, but charcoal has served for centuries. Try to break down those small lumps, it is important.'

Morton ground a piece of charcoal against the side of the bowl, till it disintegrated. 'What is the yellow powder?' he asked.

'Sulphur. When I have added twelve English pounds of potassium nitrate to the bowl, we shall have eight kilos of black powder. That stage of the mixing has to be done with great care. Then it really could explode!'

'Jeez! Now he tells us!' McCafferty said. 'Maybe it's a good thing that this stuff is hard to come by.'

'I do not understand,' Morton said.

'It's simple, son. The sulphur and the charcoal you can buy by the ton. But the potassium nitrate's a mite elusive. You understand, we have got to be real careful; we've been going to small drug-stores. At first I'd go in, ask for it in my best Limey accent, and nine times out o' ten, they look like I'm crazy – never heard of the stuff. Not that it's precious. You could buy a sack for a sovereign. But they only ever have it in small packets. Maybe it's poison, or something. Anyways, it'll take us till Thanksgiving before we have enough.'

That was something to be grateful for, Morton thought.

'How will you explode it?' he asked.

Schelling looked at him with a respectful smile. 'It is, indeed, a problem,' he said. 'In the olden times, they would cut goose quills and fill them with powder. But it is a poor substitute for a modern safety fuse. A goose quill might begin to burn, then go out. Or it might flash over and ignite the powder, before you have thrown the bomb.'

'Then, count me out, pal,' McCafferty said with a grin. 'I aim to live for ever! This guy Hans speaks English just dandy, don't he, Paul? He does the buying now. When you hear him talking in a store, he sounds like he's a visiting professor, or something, gettin' stuff for an experiment!'

'In the French Foreign Legion, you soon learn to speak the languages of the men,' Schelling said proudly. 'I was a sergeant. The men under my command were German, British, Italian – and the officers spoke French. It was better than Leyden University, I can tell you!'

Bourdin had been following the conversation closely, cocking his head like a bird at each new speaker. Now he broke in.

'I have said that it would be better to steal some fuse. In France there are quarries, where they keep explosives in a small building. Fuses also, I think.'

'Why not steal the powder too?' Morton asked.

'They use dynamite, mostly,' Schelling said. 'That is of no use to us; we need a powder.'

'Hans and I have been exploring the country to the south-east from here,' Bourdin went on. 'But we have been unable to find such a quarry.'

Morton laughed. 'You have been wasting your time. The hardest thing in Kent is chalk!'

'How do you know that?' Schelling asked suspiciously.

Morton cursed his indiscretion. 'I studied the geography of England, at school,' he said. 'For the first time, it seems that it will be of use.'

There came the sound of Monique's voice, calling them to supper, and the dangerous moment was gone. They trooped through the hole in the wall, and took their places round the table. This time there was a bowl of vegetable soup, thick slices of bread, and a roasted loin of pork.

'This looks good,' Morton said. 'Who does the cooking?'

'Halder's cook,' Monique replied. 'She has a new kitchen on the floor above.' She pointedly sat by Morton, and Bourdin scowled.

Santo and Corbin came down, as the soup tureen was pushed

around the table. Morton had half-expected Monique to serve the soup – but, of course, that would have placed her in a subordinate position. He had to be constantly on his guard. A rash remark could bring nemesis down on his head . . . The soup disposed of, the roast was passed round the table likewise, each hacking off a slice. It was hardly surprising that the anarchists had so little success, Morton thought. They were absurdly concerned not to acknowledge any superior authority, which might diminish their freedom as individuals. It was small wonder that they found it difficult to execute a coherent operation.

During the meal, Monique made a succession of cutting remarks at the expense of Bourdin, while edging ever closer to Morton. He could hear Bourdin muttering threats in French, which clearly carried to Monique also. Her face was cold, scornful, but clearly she was enjoying the game.

'Grillon says that there is no rock in Kent,' Schelling intervened, after a particularly cruel gibe from Monique. 'So we could have saved our efforts in searching for a quarry.'

'Then where look?' Santo asked, waking from his habitual introspection.

'Yeah, you got any notion, son?' McCafferty said. 'Damned if I wanna try fillin' goose quills with explosive. Sounds like one hell of a risk, to me.'

Morton smiled. 'It is some years since I saw a geological map of England,' he said. 'But I think you would have to go beyond Oxford, to the Cotswold Hills. They are of a stone from which many famous buildings have been constructed.'

'How far is that?' Schelling asked.

'I do not know, perhaps one hundred miles.'

'That is nothing, I will go,' Bourdin said eagerly.

'You would be useless,' Monique said contemptuously. 'You cannot speak English well enough. You would be conspicuous in a peasant area. People would be suspicious. Lee would be safer, and Paul.'

'Hey! Don't go volunteering me for that, little lady,' McCafferty exclaimed. 'I may know the lingo, but I guess it don't sound quite the same.'

'Ah, children, you have finished dinner!' Halder stood at the doorway with four bottles in his hands. He walked over to the table and poured wine into fresh glasses.

'I have a toast for you,' he said, waiting till the glasses had been passed round. 'Let us stand.'

With a scrape of chairs they all stood and lifted their glasses.

'To the black flag of anarchism,' Halder cried.

The toast was repeated in a self-conscious mumble, and the wine sipped. Morton sensed that it was unexpected, redolent of the old order which had to be swept away. Was Halder playing a game in his turn? Certainly, he was nodding his head with an inner satisfaction, like a smiling clockwork manikin.

'I hope that you will enjoy the wine,' Halder remarked, as he took a chair at the end of the table. There was a subdued murmur of approval, a general air of watchfulness.

'They were my last bottles of pre-phylloxera Château Talbot – a noble wine, as I hope you agree.' His smiling eyes swung round to Morton. 'I do not know much about the wines of Switzerland, Grillon. Are vines cultivated around your village?'

Morton felt his mouth go dry; the others were gazing at him like a hostile jury. He tried to focus his mind on the jumble of facts from the file, and his recollections of a holiday in Lausanne, years ago.

'Not in the immediate area,' he said, in as conversational a tone as he could muster. 'There are some vines on the south side of Geneva; but the main vineyards start at Commugny, to the east of Vernier, and stretch round the northern shore of Lac Leman to the upper Rhône valley.'

'Do they produce good wines?'

'I would not wish to venture an opinion,' Morton said with a smile. 'My parents are strict Calvinists. As you can imagine, every indulgence of the flesh was prohibited to me!'

Morton could see Monique eyeing him speculatively.

'Are the wines red or white, dry or sweet?' Halder persisted.

'The grapes in La Côte, which is the area I know best, are almost all black, but I have not heard of a red wine being made there. I did try some white wine from the Vaud, once, at the house of a friend. As I recollect, it was a little like a Moselle – perhaps more dry, but having not much alcohol! I fear you will think your Bordeaux wasted on me.'

'Ah, but Corbin makes up for your failings. He is an expert! What do you think of the wine, Marcel?'

Corbin took a sip and savoured it like a connoisseur. 'Excellent!' he pronounced. 'It has matured to perfection.'

Halder beamed in gratification. 'A great tragedy,' he murmured. 'Do you know, phylloxera has already cost France twice the amount of the reparations she had to make to Germany for starting the 1870 war? How is it to be stopped?'

All eyes were fixed on Corbin.

'Well,' he said uncomfortably, 'they have had some success by treating the ground with carbon disulphide. It is not pleasant! You can smell the odour from ten kilometres away.'

'And, of course, they are now using resistant root-stocks,' Halder said casually. 'Who would think that the variety which produces a wine so vile as retsina would come to the rescue of Château Lafite, or a Burgundy as great as Romanée Conti.'

Corbin nodded. 'Indeed,' he said.

Halder appeared to relax. 'Of course,' he said, 'there is nothing immutable in the taste of wine. We shall merely have to educate our palates to accept the new. Future generations will be just as content with their wines, as we were before the aphid struck. It is we, alone, who are to be pitied.'

'It is absurd that so much of France's resources should go into making wines that only the rich can afford,' Bourdin said abrasively. 'The wine which the peasants drink is little better than vinegar!'

'Yes, Martial,' Halder said gently. 'But you must allow me my little indulgences. A certain opprobrium is the burden I must bear for being a mere socialist. Come now, Santo! You, if anyone, can act as my confessor. How do you judge me?'

Santo shifted impatiently in his chair. 'I have no time for things of little importance.'

'Well said!' Halder beamed around the table. 'How are your plans maturing for the *ne plus ultra* of assassination?' he asked.

'I do not know who it shall be,' Santo replied, with a frown. 'I think, perhaps, it shall be Kaiser Wilhelm of Germany.'

Halder laughed scornfully. 'I think that you lower your sights, my friend! The Kaiser is not worthy to be the object of your great endeavour. He is a contemptible, strutting princeling.

Germany is not a nation, it is an uneasy coalition of fissiparous states. Nothing could hold Prussia and Bavaria together. No, Germany will crumble, when the time comes.'

'Who, then?'

Halder's face took on the benign, self-satisfied look of a scholar. 'I would do no more than suggest what pointers should guide you in your choice. It seems to me that the greatest impact of a single deed would be the removal of the head of a historic state which appears impregnable.'

'Russia, then?'

'No, Caserio. Already Alexander II has been assassinated. Every day, there are attempts on the nobility. A deed in Russia would carry little *éclat*. But that would not be so in the case of the Emperor of Austria, the President of France, or the President of the United States.'

'Hey!' McCafferty exclaimed. 'You leave America out of this! Keep your lousy quarrels in Europe.'

'But there are oppressed people in America,' Monique said sharply.

'Like hell, there are! Everybody has the same chance, back home. I could walk into the Waldorf in New York, and have a whiskey sour next to a Vanderbilt, if I had the money.'

'Then why are you not the President?' Monique retorted.

McCafferty smiled. 'I guess I'm a mite lazy . . . Anyway, what good would it do? If you killed the President, the Vice-President would step into his shoes. You would have achieved nothing.'

'You do not understand, my friend,' Schelling said. 'It would not be the intention to topple governments or conquer territory. Such a deed would cause a panic in the ruling classes every-where. If President Cleveland can be assassinated, who is safe?'

'Then, why not the Queen of England?' McCafferty asked angrily.

'Yes, why not?' Monique cried. 'She is at present in Florence. Caserio would be at home, in Italy.'

'No!' Santo thumped the table. 'She is a sick old woman. What glory would there be in killing her?'

'She is the head of the greatest empire in the world,' Corbin asserted.

93

'So? You do it!' Santo said scornfully.

Halder intervened with a bland smile. 'Let me remind you that it would be impolitic to assassinate the Queen of England or, indeed, to carry out any outrage here in Britain. This is our haven. The government here has resisted pressure, from almost every foreign power, to expel us. One might say that in this, as in many other respects, Britannia waives the rules. I beg you to be restrained. We must not foul our own nest.'

5

The bells jangled loudly, as Bragg burst through the door of Jock McGregor's pawnshop. A scrawny woman was at the far end of the counter, picking over a heap of shabby clothes, and haggling about their value.

'You gave me seven an' six before, uncle. Why not now?' she screeched.

'Times is bad, Mrs Nobbs,' Jock said plaintively. 'I'm robbing myself, to advance you six shillings.'

'I'll redeem 'em next week. My old man is comin' back from Lowestoft. He's been with the 'erring fleet. Made a lot o' money, he says. Goin' to set us up in the country, he says.'

'Why doesnae he send you money, then? Save you frae coming to me?'

The woman bridled. 'Don't you want my custom, then?' she asked sharply. 'I can easy go somewhere else.'

'If you did, I'd be a rich man, Mrs Nobbs.'

She looked at him shrewdly. 'Seven bob,' she said, 'or I go down the road.'

Jock sighed and shook his greasy locks. 'Six and sixpence,' he said, 'and that's the best I can do.'

'Right!' She looked round triumphantly at Bragg, as Jock wrote an entry in his pledge book. He handed her a ticket and a few coins, and she hurried from the shop.

'I'm my own worst enemy, Mr Bragg,' he said unctuously. 'I cannae bear to see little children starve.'

'Not when they could be prigging watches for you,' Bragg said roughly. 'One day, someone will string you up to your own brass balls.'

'Oh, no! I'm well respected in this neighbourhood. I am the poor man's banker, Mr Bragg. Many people couldnae carry on without me.'

'We might give them the chance to try, one day,' Bragg said shortly. 'What have you got for me?'

Jock gazed mistrustfully at him, from rheumy bloodshot eyes. 'Would that be about the gentleman in Whitechapel?' he asked.

'Of course it bloody would!'

Bragg took a menacing step forward, and Jock flinched away.

'I did hear a whisper.' He leaned towards Bragg confidingly, and Bragg caught the smell of his rank breath.

'What, then?'

'Nothing very big, Mr Bragg. But Alf Clancy seems tae have come into a bit o' money, unexpected like.'

'Alf Clancy? Where will I find him?'

'Whitechapel market. He has a whelk stall.'

Bragg glared at him belligerently. 'Right, Jock. And if you have been pulling my pisser, I'll come back and knock your bloody head off!'

Bragg banged out of the shop, and tramped the quarter mile to Whitechapel Road. For a hundred yards, on the north side, the street was lined with stalls and barrows. Here was a stall piled with poor-quality fabrics; next, one selling second-hand clothes. In the middle of the row, a crowd had collected. Bragg could hear the racy patter of a trader in crockery and pans. Now he was coming to the food stalls. He savoured the yeasty smell of the fresh cottage-loaves and currant buns. Here was a pile of glazed mutton pies, to remind him that it was almost lunchtime. In this dead season, the vegetable stall looked melancholy, with its mounds of potatoes, swedes and Savoy cabbages. Ah! This was it. The barrow had a painted sign above it, proclaiming the virtues of Alf Clancy, fishmonger. But if the wares were second to none, the clientele was well down the social ladder. The barrow displayed oysters, whelks, jellied eels – all food for the poor. A little colour was provided by the yellow glow of Finnan haddock, and a few sleek sides of kippered salmon for wealthy Jews. Behind the stall was a chubby man in a white shop-coat and straw boater. He was chewing a half-smoked cheroot, and smiling to himself.

'Mr Clancy?' Bragg asked, showing his warrant-card.

'That's me, mate,' he said cockily. 'What's up?'

'Nothing's up,' Bragg said reassuringly. 'I thought you might help me.'

'What, me? Help the rozzers? That's a laugh!' he chuckled. 'No, I was only joking!'

'They say you have come into some money recently.'

'Who says?' Clancy asked sceptically.

'Friends of yours.'

'They're no friends of mine, spreading lies.'

'Suddenly flush, they say. And looking at you, all ponced up, I reckon they're right. But I'm not saying there is anything illegal about it. I just want to know how you came by it.'

Clancy looked at him suspiciously. 'Honest?' he asked.

'Absolutely.'

'You're not trying to fit me up, or anything?'

'No. I already know where it came from, and you are in the clear. I just want to hear it from your own mouth.'

'I see . . . All right, then. There was this bloke, see. He come up to the stall last . . .' He took off his boater and scratched his head. 'Last Thursday morning. American gent, he was.'

'Big, red hair, freckled face?'

'That's him.' Clancy looked at Bragg warily.

'So, what happened?'

'He said he wanted to move some stuff, but he was in trouble 'cause of the cab strike. He asked me if I'd do it for him, on my barrow. To start with, I wasn't all that keen. I mean, I'd set it all out, hadn't I? Then he said what he'd give me, and I thought blimey! I could take three months off!'

'Did he tell you what the job was?'

'No. He was right cagey, but he said it wasn't far. So I unloads the barrow and off we goes.'

'Where did he take you?'

Clancy looked at Bragg suspiciously. 'Are you sure this ain't a put on?'

'Quite sure.'

'Straight up?'

'You can have it in writing, if you want.'

'Right, then. We goes up Aldgate, see, down Cornhill, and

stops right outside the bleedin' Bank of England! Blimey! He tells me to wait, and goes inside. After twenty minutes, this bloke in the posh uniform comes up and takes me round the back, into Lothbury. I sticks the barrow by some big iron doors, and he taps on them with his stick. They opens, and these blokes start loading me up with little sacks. Then my gent comes out, and covers them over with some old sacks I'd brought. Then we was off.'

'Where did you go to?'

'Back to Aldgate. He stops me on the corner of Mansell Street. He takes two of the potato sacks and we packs the little sacks into 'em.'

'How many were there?'

'Six in each.'

'What did you think was in them?'

'Think? I daren't flamin' think! I tell you, mate, I was sweatin' blood!'

'So, what happened then?'

'He pays me off, and says I can go. And he stands on the corner and watches me, till I can't see him no more.'

'So, you don't know where he went from there.'

'No.'

'What did he pay you for it?'

'Fifty quid.'

Bragg whistled. 'That is a hell of a lot of money!'

'S'right. But I'll tell you what, mate, if he came again, I'd tell him to sod off! I bloody nearly shit my trousers, coming back up Aldgate.'

Bragg laughed. 'Well, enjoy your fifty quid, and keep away from the fancy girls!'

He strolled back to Old Jewry, turning the story over in his mind. It was easy enough to be suspicious, the facts were bizarre. Yet everything had been done above board. Neither Gibson nor Pearce had suspected the *bona fides* of McCafferty. It was not for the police to shove their noses in, merely because it was out of the ordinary.

As he reached the top of the stairs, Inspector Cotton came along the landing.

'I've been looking for you, Bragg,' he said brusquely.

'I was in Whitechapel, sir, following up the McCafferty business.'

'Oh, yes? You know, Bragg, that name rings a bell . . . I think it's from way back, when I'd just been promoted Inspector.'

'I cannot see there is anything for us in the case, sir. Whatever he was up to, McCafferty went voluntarily.'

'Then that's one we can close down.'

'Yet I can't help wondering why,' Bragg said musingly.

'Forget that! Get on with the doing and dying. Have you heard from your lad yet?'

'Constable Morton?'

'Who else?' Cotton's lip curled unpleasantly.

'No, I haven't. There is no sign of him.'

'Huh! I always said he would never last. I was against it, right from the start; but the Commissioner would insist. Perhaps he will admit he was wrong, now.'

'He lasted over five years,' Bragg protested.

'What is that worth? Get him off the muster roll, Bragg. Then we can recruit someone who might be a bit of use to us.'

Bragg watched Cotton's retreating figure gloomily. It wasn't Morton they were after. It was just a way of getting at him. Well, if they wanted Morton off muster, they would have to do it themselves.

Morton lay on his bed and tried to evaluate his progress. His main purpose was to discover the nature of Corbin's mission, and already there were indications. When McCafferty had suggested Queen Victoria as a target for Santo, last night, Corbin had seized the opportunity to support the idea. But, as yet, there was no specific operation planned; nothing which could be used by the British to embarrass the French government. Nor was he any further forward with McCafferty. There was the clear intention to perpetrate an outrage, but no detailed plan. He picked up a pamphlet from a chair. It had been written by Halder, and was in German. Morton skimmed through it. The general drift of it was hostile to the German empire, advocating a decentralization of power back to the constituent states. No doubt Kaiser Wilhelm would regard it as seditious,

99

but it was hardly revolutionary. It proposed nothing stronger than strikes, to bring pressure on the government.

Why, then, was Halder involved with revolutionists in England, Morton wondered; giving them shelter and sustenance . . . No doubt, he was playing a deeper game. Politicians were adept at promising something, and imposing the opposite when they gained power. One thing was certain; Morton could not afford to probe deeper. So far, he had been accepted as Grillon, on the strength of the attempt on Grand Duke Michael. But if he began to venture into political matters, he would immediately be on thin ice . . . And there was another worry, which he had shoved to the back of his mind. He had been accepted readily, because people here knew of Grillon. But what if he encountered someone who had actually met Grillon? Amongst people like this, he could be given very short shrift indeed! He heard steps in the hall outside, and lay down again with his pamphlet. The door opened . . . It was Monique Laloux. God! He would have to watch his accent now!

'Paul,' she said in her hard incisive voice, 'I have a favour to ask of you.'

'A favour?'

She frowned. 'Very well, I do not ask it as a favour, I demand it as my right.'

'I see.'

'When you go back to Russia, I wish to go with you.'

'Why?'

'I intend to kill the Grand Duke Alexander Michaelovitch.'

'Do you?'

'He is to be married to Grand Duchess Alexandrovna, the daughter of the Tsar. If we could assassinate them both, as they drive from the church after the wedding, it would be perfect!'

'A splendid blow, indeed.'

'But more than that,' she said eagerly. 'It would be truly symbolic.'

'Of what?' Morton asked cautiously.

'It would strike at the State and the Church simultaneously. That is the curse which centuries have laid on Russia; an oppressive monarchy supported by the corrupt minions of a non-existent god – a nullity . . . Two evil parasites, bleeding the peasants white!'

'Ah, yes.'

She looked so naïve and vulnerable in her earnestness. Morton had an impulse to put his arm round her, to protect her from the dire effects of her fantasies.

'It will not be easy,' he said.

She took a cigarette from her bag and lit it. 'I know,' she replied. 'But with you, I could at least make the attempt . . . I chose wrongly. Martial does not live up to his name. He would like to carry out daring deeds, but his resolution fails him. Now, you have the courage and capacity to strike – you have already done so.'

'I am known by the Okhrana. Why do you not go alone? You could be supplied with *matériel* once you were there.'

'Would that I could! But, in this perverted world, there are many things a woman cannot do on her own.'

'What is it that you are proposing?' Morton asked, with a libidinous grin.

She crossed over and perched on the edge of his bed. 'That we should go together as man and wife.'

'It would involve great intimacy, over many months . . .'

Monique shrugged. At that moment she looked anything but seductive, with her lank hair and one eye closed against the smoke from her cigarette. 'That is of no significance,' she said. 'We are merely animals, after all.'

Morton lifted his hand and cupped her breast. She brushed it away indifferently.

'You must understand,' she said, 'that I will not allow you to use sex to exert dominance over me. It will be recreational, nothing more.'

'Of course.'

'Then it is agreed?'

'It is agreed.'

Monique stood up excitedly. 'If you could achieve one good for society, Paul,' she exclaimed, 'what would it be?'

Damn the woman! Morton thought. Love-making was fairly safe – at least it didn't get you into philosophical deep water. 'I

101

have not thought in those terms,' he replied. 'What would you choose?'

'Freedom from authority!'

'Before freedom from hunger?'

'Oh yes! One can starve with dignity; it is insufferable to live without it . . . It is the acceptance of authority that stunts the mind, that enables the many to be enslaved for the benefit of the few. We must have a bloody revolution to sweep away all authority.'

'But that is what you had, in France, not a hundred years ago.'

'Pah! For all the fine words, the revolution was seduced by the bourgeoisie. *Liberté, Egalité, Fraternité* exist solely for the town-dwelling, middle-class male.'

'Hmn . . . And which aspect of authority would you banish first?'

Monique tossed her head. 'The family, of course!'

'You have been oppressed by your family?'

'Most grievously! As a girl, I was fascinated by science, and my parents indulged me. I studied chemistry, physics, and mathematics; and I far outstripped the boys of my age. I formed a burning ambition to be an engineer, to make a career for myself. I applied for an engineering course at the Sorbonne – and I was refused. Nowhere could I read for a degree . . . My parents would not fight for me, they shrugged their shoulders, accepted the inevitable. When I protested, they said that I should forget science, get married, that was where a woman's future lay. When I refused they turned against me, tried to compel me to acquiesce.'

'You rebelled against that, of course.'

'Yes. Then I could no longer stay there. You see, families are ultimately against the individual. No one can attain maturity in so authoritarian an atmosphere.'

'You are absolutely right,' Morton said with conviction. 'I had a somewhat similar experience. My family was not so hostile as yours, but they were strict Calvinists – and I was unable to subscribe to their beliefs. Nevertheless, there were many advantages to my upbringing. My father encouraged me to study the English language, and the geography of England. He wanted me to go into international trade. He argued that the Queen of England ruled over two-thirds of the globe, so my future lay there.'

'Pah!' Monique dropped the glowing end of her cigarette on the floor, and ground it out with her foot. 'The Malayan coolie, up to his knees in a paddy field, has doubtless some grasp of English, but that does not make him the less downtrodden!'

'Exactly. That was why I abandoned my family.'

'But you did go to a university. What was it that caused you to break with your class?'

Morton pondered. 'I suppose it was meeting Beck and Stavisky. For the first time, I could feel altruistic. What do you think drives the other people in this cell?'

Monique frowned. 'Martial Bourdin has elevated the feeling of guilt to the dimensions of a religion. He disgusts me! Of the others I have little knowledge – except for Schelling. You must realize that one is admitted to this cell on probation. Halder satisfies himself as to one's background subsequently. That was why he questioned you about the wines of Switzerland.'

Morton gave a careless shrug of the shoulders. 'I have nothing to hide,' he said.

'Of course not.' Monique smiled warmly. 'But, when he probed Schelling's past, he found that he had been expelled from the Foreign Legion.'

'That must be a rare event,' Morton said. 'They have the reputation of being the most ruthless soldiers in the world.'

'Yes. Hans Schelling was in charge of the sergeants' mess, and there had been some petty pilfering. He identified the native orderly responsible, and elected to punish the man himself . . . He whipped him to death.'

'Good God!'

'Schelling is only an anarchist for convenience – he is driven by blood-lust.'

When lunch-time came, Morton took a chair beside Corbin. In him lay the reason for his sojourn amongst this bunch of self-deluding cut-throats. Anyway, they had arrived together, and it would not be in character for him to ignore Corbin. Having made her proposition, Monique sat with Santo, discussing the rival merits of Verdi and Bizet. Bourdin sat in the corner, staring broodily at Monique. Finally, the meal was over and they began to disperse. Corbin seemed disposed to linger, however. He brought glasses and a bottle of beer back to the table.

'Are you going back to Russia?' he asked.

Morton laughed. 'Indeed I am! And in the company of a fair assassin, no less!'

'Monique said as much, before you came in. But I wondered if it was merely a new gambit to provoke Bourdin.'

'It may be. We shall discover that, as the day approaches. In the meantime, there is no harm in planning on the basis that she is sincere. If she comes, I shall have a hot-blooded wife for some weeks. Who knows, perhaps I shall die happy as well as fulfilled!'

'Russia is a great distance away; you will be taking needless risks, since you are known to the Okhrana.'

'I do not understand you.'

'Surely there are just as worthy targets nearer at hand. You can find oppression and degradation everywhere – at the end of this very street.'

Morton pretended to consider. Redman had been right. Corbin was an *agent provocateur*. So, wherein lay his duty? Clearly this information itself would not suffice; he should try to find out all he could about Corbin's plans. Yet, given Grillon's obsession with Russia, it would be dangerous to change tack abruptly.

'Would you have me deny myself the delights of Monique's company?' he asked with a grin.

'I would rather sleep with a sea-urchin! No, my friend. It is just that someone of your talents and experience should not be wasted. You should be used to strike a fresh blow, ignite conflagrations in other states where society is rotten and tinder-dry.'

'But I have sworn to revenge my comrades.'

'And so you shall. But would they be any the less avenged if the deed were done thousands of miles away? We are not fighting one particular government, but the whole class system of Europe. It would be prodigality indeed to squander your ability in a sterile gesture.'

'But, what about Monique?'

Corbin snorted contemptuously. 'She is little more than an intellectual camp-follower. Russia, to her, is an unattainable fantasy. If she ever arrived there, through someone else's efforts, she would be useless!'

'Hmn . . . Then what do you have in mind?'

'Why not an act which will create havoc here, in London?'

'Halder would object to that,' Morton said.

'And why should we concern ourselves with him? He is not our leader.'

'Nevertheless, he gives us shelter.'

'Pah! England turns anarchists into craven effeminates. McCafferty takes no heed of Halder's bleatings. He is planning an outrage here.'

'But McCafferty has funds of his own. He is not dependent on the *émigrés*, as we are.'

'Have no fear, my friend. When the time is right, there will be money enough. Will you help me to plan an explosion?'

Morton pondered. So, Grillon's role in the affair would be as scapegoat; a genuine anarchist to be arrested, while Corbin escaped back to France.

Corbin's voice broke into his thoughts. 'This McCafferty is a nuisance to us. We would not wish to have our explosion mistaken for some deed of the Fenians. The propaganda value would then be lost.'

'Yes,' Morton said thoughtfully. 'But Lee is friendly towards me; perhaps I can discover their plans.'

'Good . . . Then you will join me?'

Morton smiled. 'Of course.'

When he got up and went back to his room, he found that McCafferty had not yet returned from his shopping; so Morton sat on his bed, trying to assess the situation. Then he heard cautious steps creeping down the hallway. There was a pause, and the front door was opened softly. Morton tiptoed over to the window. Corbin was slinking down the path to the road. On reaching the pavement, he turned right towards the Tower. Morton grabbed his hat and hurried in pursuit. As he reached the street, he saw Corbin turn right towards Tower Hill. He sprinted down Mansell Street. Corbin was now picking his way through the traffic, a mere hundred yards ahead. Morton hung back and watched. Now Corbin had reached the opposite pavement, and was approaching the gate leading to the gardens which surrounded the dry moat of the Tower. As he disappeared through the gate, Morton dodged across after him. Which way had he gone? The path went round the Tower, and, for much of its length, was straight. It would be foolhardy to try to tail him. On the other hand, it was possible to look down on the gardens, from the road running on the north side. Morton ran along Postern Row and lurked behind two old ladies, seated on a bench overlooking the Tower. If he had judged right, he would be able to see Corbin without much risk of being seen. If, however, the man had gone clockwise towards the river, he would have eluded pursuit. Morton waited impatiently . . . Three minutes . . . five minutes. Suddenly Corbin was in sight, sauntering along, pausing to examine the new foliage on the shrubs, the fading clumps of daffodils. Then he pulled out his watch, nodded to himself, and set off at a brisk walk. It was as if he had been dawdling until the time of an appointment. If so, it would be better to be ahead of him than to risk losing him in the streets to the west. Morton ran round to Great Tower Hill and concealed himself behind a hay cart, which had pulled up in the deserted cab-rank.

Corbin emerged from the gardens and looked about him perfunctorily. Then he strode across the road to the entrance of the Southwark tunnel. Morton saw him buy a ticket and disappear down the stairs. He sprinted across, and put a sovereign on the ticket counter.

'Come orf it, gov',' the clerk exclaimed. 'It only costs a ha'penny!'

'I am sorry. I have nothing smaller.'

'I'm not supposed to take anything as big as that.'

'Then keep the change,' Morton said urgently. 'Take your wife to the Empire.'

The man grinned and slapped a ticket on the counter, before Morton could change his mind. Morton launched himself down the wooden spiral stairs, then checked. The racket his feet were making might alarm Corbin. There was really no need to hurry; there was nowhere to go but forward – along the tunnel to the south bank of the Thames. The staircase wound down some fifty feet and gave on to the platform area of the old railway. In the soft gaslight, it still seemed clean and bright – after twenty-five years. But, of course, the passenger car had been drawn by cables, not a steam-engine. It was a pity, Morton thought: the concept had been brilliant, but the implementation half-hearted. As a result, the car was too small to allow the working costs to be covered. And it was too near to London Bridge to sustain much of a fare increase. So, the mechanical equipment had been removed, the track lifted and the tunnel turned into a walkway.

Morton went into the gloom of the tube. He had to keep to the centre and walk in a crouch, to avoid banging his head. In front of him, he could hear the hollow clump of footsteps. Coming towards him? He stopped . . . No, going away. As his eyes became accustomed to the diminished light, he could see the bent figure of a man, flitting ahead from one pool of light to the next. It must be Corbin. No one else had entered the tunnel between them. He closed the gap, taking care to lower his head as he approached each gas-lamp. The tunnel was dropping sharply, boring down beneath the river. Morton thought briefly of the millions of tons of water and mud above him, held at bay by interlocking cast-iron rings caulked with cement. He shook off the incipient claustrophobia. He must think . . . Corbin was going to meet someone, so much seemed clear. Someone on the south bank of the Thames. Who could it be? It was obvious that Corbin had been briefed for his mission with meticulous care. There had been no cab strike, in London, when he set out. Even so, he was aware of the existence of this tunnel. No doubt he would be reporting to a superior, another member of French intelligence. Would he be saying that he had recruited a willing tool; an anarchist named Grillon, who could be manipulated?

Now there was a jumble of echoes in the tunnel. Were they coming to the other end? No, that could not be the explanation, he had only just begun to feel the floor of the tunnel rising beneath his feet. Morton stopped and listened intently. There was another set of footfalls . . . From in front, coming towards them. Corbin was no more than fifty yards ahead of him, two gas-lamps away. Morton began to creep forward, his shoulders beginning to ache from the crouching. Then Corbin stopped in a pool of light. Morton pressed himself into the narrow recess formed by the flanges of the cast-iron lining, and listened. The new footsteps quickened. There was a booming voice uttering a greeting. Then a man emerged into the light. He shook hands with Corbin. There was a murmured conversation, a piece of paper passed between them, and the man turned back. Morton swivelled round and began a staggering half-run. Every moment he expected the sudden clatter of Corbin's feet, the numbing sting of a knife in his back . . . But no, he was drawing away. By now he would be no more than a shadow in front of Corbin. The man must be stupid! He had passed no one while walking to the centre of the tunnel; so whoever was in front of him now must have followed him. Perhaps he had paused to read the message, in the light of a lamp. Whatever it was, Morton was safe now. He crouched down as he reached the end of the tunnel, to reduce his silhouette against the brighter light of the platform area. Once there, he sprinted to the foot of the staircase and flung himself upwards.

If Grillon was Corbin's chosen instrument, Morton decided, it might be possible to push him into revealing his plans, by seeming to lose interest. If he were to continue to plot a Russian expedition with Monique, it might put pressure on Corbin. Accordingly, he went down to supper early; but she was not there. As he poured himself a glass of beer, there were footsteps on the stairs and Halder entered, followed by a newcomer.

'This is Patrick Kelly,' Halder said with a beaming smile. 'He has been seconded to McCafferty, in answer to the appeal of Eleanor Marx. Paul Grillon, here, is an experienced nihilist, who escaped to us from Russia.'

Having made the introduction, Halder withdrew. Morton observed Kelly closely. It was the first time he had met a native terrorist. He was of medium height, broad and work-hardened. He had a shaggy moustache, much like Bragg's, and a shock of grey-brown hair. One could see men like him by the dozen, in every street in the land. Kelly put his Gladstone bag in the corner and folded his overcoat on top of it.

'Do you find it cold, in the south of England?' Morton asked.

Kelly looked momentarily surprised. 'Is it the muffler you're thinking of?' he asked, in a musical Irish voice. 'Hadn't I the bad luck to get an ache in my tooth, last night? I was after going to the dentist today; instead I found myself on the train to London.'

'Is it aching now?' Morton asked in a concerned voice.

'Ah, it's a bit better now, so it is. The servant-woman upstairs put a drop of opium on it, for me.'

'I understand from Halder, that you are a Fenian, fighting for the freedom of Ireland.'

'Yes,' Kelly grunted.

'That is a great cause! But you have come from the north of England, not from Ireland?'

'Yes.'

'It cannot be easy to move freely here. You have taken a great risk in coming to London.'

'Divil a risk in it,' Kelly exclaimed irritably.

'But in the north you are with friends, who will hide you.'

'Jaysus! Do you know nothing of the country? I hide from nobody. I live in a snug, dry house with my wife and children. I go to confession regular . . .'

'But there are some things you do not confess, eh?' Morton said, with a grin.

Kelly crossed himself hastily. 'Do you think I would endanger my immortal soul?'

'Ah, you have found a priest who supports your cause!'

'There's divil a one agrees with killing,' Kelly said gloomily, 'and that's a fact. There'll be some fierce accounting at Judgement Day!'

'You fear you will find yourself in hell, my friend? Why do you concern yourself with such absurd ideas?'

'I have killed no one! And, please God, that's how it will stay.'

Morton laughed. 'And who gives you the money to live in England like a normal person? The Church?'

'What are you meaning, "like a normal person"?' Kelly

demanded wrathfully. 'I work for my living, like any proper man. Every penny that goes into my house, I have earned by my own sweat!'

'It sounds very bourgeois, for a revolutionist,' Morton said sceptically.

Kelly seemed on the point of lashing out at him, when McCafferty burst into the room.

'Jeez! This is great!' he exclaimed, grabbing Kelly by the hand and shaking it warmly. 'I guess you guys can get a move on, when you have to.'

'You'll be the American,' Kelly said shortly.

'Yep, Lee McCafferty. Halder tells me you're called Patrick Kelly.'

'I am, so.'

'Well now, Pat, I guess I should show you my credentials, so's we get off on the right foot.' He took out his pocket-book and extracted a folded paper. 'This is a letter from the Fenian Brotherhood in New York, appointing me a visitor to the Irish Republican Brotherhood over here. See, that's my signature at the bottom, so there can be no mistake.'

Kelly took the letter and looked intently at it, his lips moving as he deciphered the words. He was well above the average of working men, Morton thought. There was something wrong, when steady, estimable men like this turned against society.

'You'll be signing your name for me?' Kelly asked.

'Sure, sure! You can't take things for granted in this game.' McCafferty took up a pencil and scribbled on the border of a newspaper. Kelly compared the two signatures and grunted his acceptance.

'I guess you are wondering what this is all about, Pat!' McCafferty said effusively. 'So, let me fill you in. The FB have gotten the feeling that things have gone mighty quiet over here. The idea is to mount an operation – a big explosion – that will serve notice on the Limeys that Fenianism is not dead, and put heart into the Irish everywhere.'

'Why here? Why not in Dublin?'

'London is the centre of the world, like it or not, Pat. They wouldn't be able to ignore it here.'

'We want the bastards out of Ireland, not London.'

110

'Yeah, I guess you are right. Still, this is what the FB have decided, so we are stuck with it.'

'I'll tell you something, mister,' Kelly said pugnaciously, 'the Irish won't rise at the bidding of the Yanks, ever again. We learned our lesson last time.'

'Take it easy, Pat,' McCafferty said in an injured tone. 'We are not talking about insurrection, right now.'

Morton intervened. 'Patrick is suffering from a very bad toothache, Lee. I am sure he is not his usual self.'

'Jeez! Why didn't you get it seen to?'

Kelly's face flushed with anger. 'Wasn't I told to come down here? Didn't they tell me it was important to us?'

'Yeah, yeah,' McCafferty said in a placatory voice. 'And they were right, Pat. I'm real sorry about your tooth, I guess we gotta hope it goes away . . . Now, the plan is for one big explosion. After that, we cut and run. But it's got to be real well planned.'

'We'll be needing money,' Kelly said shortly. 'I have none. And, last time, the FB money had a way of getting stuck in France.'

'Not this time!' McCafferty said triumphantly. 'I brought it in myself.'

'What are you saying?'

'I brought over greenbacks, in my bags, and changed them into sovereigns.' He plunged his hand into his pocket and brought out a fistful. 'Here, have some.'

A look of incredulity crossed Kelly's face, as he took the coins. 'Where did you get these?' he asked.

'The Bank of England.'

'Jaysus! Is the man mad?'

'Nothing to it, Pat. Rich Americans come over here in droves, nowadays. I tell you, nobody raised an eyebrow.' He chuckled. 'My Paw used to say that deviousness got you nowheres, but plain old cheek would git you far.'

Kelly looked at him narrowly. 'Would you be related to that so-called Captain John McCafferty?'

'That was my Paw! A great Civil War hero, daring as hell – only he ended up on the losing side. After that, he came over to Europe, to lead the Fenian uprising. A great guy! Did you know him?'

'I knew of him,' Kelly said scornfully. 'He never got near enough to the action, for me to meet him.'

'Then you can't have been involved yourself, or you would have met him,' McCafferty said tolerantly.

'I was there! Your father was supposed to be leading us on the Chester Castle raid. But he decided to come down to London, to confer with the chief-of-staff, and he didn't get back in time. I'm thinking it was no accident that the police knew all about it.'

McCafferty looked thunderstruck. 'Are you saying my Paw was a government informer?' he demanded angrily.

'I'm saying he either knew enough to stay away, or he had no stomach for a fight.'

'No stomach! My Paw did his damnedest to get back. But his train was shunted into a siding, to make way for the troop trains being rushed north – he told me himself.'

'So, you don't deny we was sold?'

'Sold?' McCafferty spat contemptuously. 'Paul, just listen to the kinda guys we are dealing with. This raid was to be on a castle, near Liverpool. There was a very small garrison, only a handful of men. The plan was for the Fenians to converge on Chester from the area around, get into the castle, grab the guns from the armoury, then beat it. Sounds simple, don't it? But these Limey Irish are so goddam law-abiding, they screwed it up before it got started! The idea was that, if the garrison looked too strong, the Fenians would say that they'd just come to watch a prize-fight, and go quietly home again. But if they thought they had a chance, they would attack the castle; then, win or lose, they would make for Dublin. Do you know what these crazy bog-Irish did? When they got to Manchester station, or wherever, they booked a round-trip ticket to Chester and, in addition, a one-way ticket from Chester to Dublin. They did! Every damned one of them. Jeez! Scores of men with thick Irish brogues, buying tickets from Chester to Dublin. And they wonder why the authorities were put on enquiry! They might as well have telegraphed the Queen!'

'What were we supposed to do?' Kelly demanded. 'Line up

at Chester booking-office, with a couple of rifles under our arm?'

'My Paw would have commandeered a train, taken over the Dublin ferry, if your lot hadn't screwed it.'

Kelly snorted resentfully. 'Well, I've been sent to do a job; and do it I will, whatever happens.'

'You ain't got much fire in your belly, Pat,' McCafferty observed. 'I sure was expectin' more. These anarchist guys, like Paul here, would give their lives ten times over, just to toss one bomb at an aristocrat.'

Kelly reined in his temper. 'I wouldn't want to see young men waste their lives. There will be no revolution in England, life is too easy here. And the British are too strong, at the moment, for Ireland to win free. I'll help you with your bomb, so I will, but nothing will come of it.'

The hostile silence was broken by Schelling, who entered jubilantly with a small sack under his arm.

'I have found the answer!' he cried. 'We have been asking for potassium nitrate – we should have asked, instead, for saltpetre. That is what they call it here! Crazy Englanders!'

'Why are you wanting that stuff?' asked Kelly.

'We are making some black powder explosive. For it, you need charcoal, sulphur – and saltpetre!'

Kelly laughed incredulously. 'I can buy as much black powder as I want – dynamite too.'

'You can?'

'Am I not telling you so? I am a foreman with a demolition and construction firm, so I know the ropes.'

'Would you buy some for me?'

'To be sure I would. I'll be getting some for himself, here, I expect. I will have to be asking around, in the morning. But all the navvies are Irish; they'll be telling me where's best.'

McCafferty suddenly seemed impressed. 'That's great, Pat,' he said warmly. 'Now, how about bunking in with me and Paul? There's plenty of room.'

Catherine picked up the pre-Season copy of *Ladies' Realm*, and began to flip through the pages. Her father was up in his studio, finishing a portrait that some vain débutante wanted to hang in the drawing-room of her family's London home. Her mother stirred herself enough to take another bon-bon from the silver dish by her elbow, and went back to her novel.

The magazine was reinforcing all her worst prejudices, Catherine thought. But it really was a most appalling waste, an utterly tasteless display of wealth . . . She reminded herself that she, too, had been presented at Court, was herself part of it. But that was because she had been involved, with James and Sergeant Bragg, in a case that reflected on the royal family. It would have been moralistic in the extreme to thwart the wishes of the Prince of Wales – particularly when James had been so delighted . . . She loved the way he went all solemn and smug, when she was the centre of attraction. Well, that was all in the past; something best forgotten . . . Her glance fell on an advertisement for a temporary ballroom that could be erected on one's lawn, to save one from having to move one's furniture. The illustration depicted a polished wood floor, chandeliers, gilt mirrors, heavy curtains. Ridiculous! Now there were some suggestions for an Ascot hamper – smoked salmon, foie gras, caviare, quails, lobster salad, asparagus. The fact that she would have enjoyed it, in the right company, was totally beside the point. It might be true that this gross indulgence brought employment to lots of people; nevertheless, it was obscene! From this firm you could hire a carriage and pair, to flaunt yourself in Hyde Park . . . Confound it! Everything seemed to point backwards, to the recent past. She must look forwards . . . Anyway, James would never subscribe to this religion of self-indulgence. He was inevitably in it, but not of it . . . Yet he must be touched by it; and he, too, would be looking forwards. It was undeniable that there were scores of eligible young women who would scratch anyone's eyes out, to get him as a husband. Some of them were beautiful, a few even cultured, as well . . . Of course, there was no need for a man to rush into marriage. James could indulge his appetites for years yet. There were plenty of young, frisky matrons, who would consider it a feather in their cap to have lured him to their bed. She could not bear the thought of that! Yet, what would be acceptable to her? She sighed. If only things could have continued as they had been, if only James had not proposed. But was that fair to him? Possibly not. Could they ever go back? Almost certainly not.

'You seem somewhat agitated, dear,' her mother observed vaguely.

'Agitated? I was not aware of it.'

'Perhaps you are not getting out enough. You have been at home every evening for ages, now. It is not good for someone of your age.'

'Yes, Mamma.'

'The last time you went out was a week ago,' Mrs Marsden continued relentlessly, 'when that nice Morton boy took you to the theatre. Have you heard from him since?'

'No, Mamma.'

'I hope that you wrote to thank him.'

'As a matter of fact, I did not.'

'Catherine!' her mother said in a shocked voice. 'That is most remiss of you. Even if you have not particularly enjoyed an entertainment, you should always thank the person concerned most warmly. One can never tell how one's life will work out.'

Catherine was caught between irritation and a desire to laugh. 'I thought that you did not like him,' she said carelessly.

'Like him? As a matter of fact, I do. But that is hardly the point. Lady Lanesborough says that you could make a much better match.'

'Then, why do you chide me for not thanking him?'

'Really, Catherine! You are so obtuse, when you want to be,' Mrs Marsden said crossly. 'You should be cultivating a wide circle of acquaintances, from which to choose. You never go out of your way to meet young men. You have not accepted an invitation to a party for months. You seem to have confined yourself to seeing James, and now you behave as if you are indifferent to him.'

'I could hardly be indifferent to someone who has asked me to marry him.'

Mrs Marsden's jaw dropped in astonishment. 'Marry him?' she echoed.

'Yes, Mamma . . . I refused him.'

'You what?'

'I rejected his proposal.'

'Catherine! What were you thinking of? You should have said that you would consider his offer, then told your father so that he could make enquiries.'

'Enquiries? What possible enquiries need you make? You already know that he is well-connected, rich – and playing at being a policeman, as an erstwhile friend of mine recently remarked. Knowing that, you did not regard him as suitable. Why upbraid me now?'

Mrs Marsden sighed unhappily. 'It is just that I want the best for you, dear – and your godmother insists that nothing less than an earl would do you justice.'

'Would that everyone could achieve justice!'

'Really, Catherine! I do not know what your father will think, when I tell him. It was very remiss of you to turn him down so – so airily!'

'Airily is hardly the appropriate word, Mamma. Indeed, it was his proposal that was offhand. He treated me as if I were a shallow socialite, longing to be protected from the rigours and realities of life.'

Her mother gazed into the fire disconsolately. 'I fear that your *amour propre* will always stand in your way, child. I do not know what will happen to you, when your father and I are gone.'

Catherine was suddenly furious. 'You would not say that, if I were a son!' she cried. 'Why are daughters different? I have a responsible job, I am highly esteemed in my profession. I shall cope perfectly well, without a man to stifle me.'

Next morning, Morton awoke dull and stiff. The constant tension must be having its effect, he thought. Yet that was all the more reason for care. It would be folly to jeopardize his mission, when he was on the brink of discovering Corbin's plans. He got out of bed. Kelly had already gone. Of course – he was doing the rounds of the construction sites, on behalf of a McCafferty who was still snoring like a hog. Morton went to the back of the room, and shaved with McCafferty's razor. It was getting blunt, and needed re-setting. No amount of stropping would get the edge back. He smiled at the recollection of his father, by then a Lieutenant-General, and recently retired, solemnly showing him how it was done – insisting that he should use his left hand as well as his right. The first time he had tried, he was scraping away at his upper lip with the heel of the blade, and had practically taken off his left ear with its tip! Well, it should have taught him to keep his wits about him. He glanced in the mirror. Whatever he looked like, at least he felt more like breakfast now.

He finished dressing, and went down the back stairs to the basement. Perhaps Monique would want to begin planning their expedition into Russia! He had entered the workshop, and was making for the dim rectangle leading to the mess-room, when there was a sudden scrabble of feet behind him. A dark figure sprang at him, pinning him to the wall. He felt a heavy blow on his chest, Santo's hate-filled eyes burned into him . . . Strange, he felt no pain – just a numbness. The knife was buried up to the hilt, Santo maintaining his hold as if determined to stay with him to the point of death. It must have pierced his heart. Soon his senses would fail . . . Then Santo pulled back, with an evil chuckle.

'You see, Grillon, it is easy to surprise someone in their own surroundings.'

He was holding a flick-knife, the blade still safely retracted into the handle.

'You bloody fool!' Morton cried. 'What the hell did you do . that for?'

'I must rehearse, I must not fail.'

Morton realized that his angry outburst had been altogether English. Had it been anyone but Santo, his origins might well have been revealed. He took a deep breath.

'I suppose you must. But no more with me. Understand?'

Santo laughed happily. 'No. You will be on guard. A man alone must have surprise on his side.'

'Why are you not content to throw a bomb, like everyone else?'

'Pah! They have no courage. Bombs will never reach the leaders . . . I think I will kill King Umberto of Italy. It would be like cutting down Julius Caesar in the Senate. Come, my friend, there is cold ham for breakfast.'

They went through into the other basement, and found Bourdin picking moodily at a piece of bread. On seeing Morton, he rose pointedly and went out. It was a pity, Morton thought. Of all the anarchists, Bourdin was the only one he found congenial.

Santo filled his plate, and brought over a steaming cup of coffee. 'Monique Laloux says that *Otello* is at Covent Garden Theatre,' he announced. 'Will you come?'

'With you?'

'Yes – and perhaps Monique.'

'It would be foolish. It would not be safe!'

'Pah! Who cares about safe? *Otello* is *magnifico*! It was first at La Scala. I went six times in 'eighty-seven. Since then, never. Now I go again.'

Morton was tempted. But it would be even more foolish for him, to run the risk of being recognized.

'I do not like opera,' he said. 'It is neither singing nor drama. I saw *Die Fledermaus* in Bern, it was stupid.'

'*Fledermaus!* You call *Fledermaus* opera?' Santo banged the table with his fist. 'Some day I take you to *Figaro*, *Nabucco*, *Traviata*! Then you know what is opera!'

'Good. I look forward to it. But not now, there is too much risk. Give up the idea, and you may sing Verdi at us, all evening!'

'Hey! You guys gettin' a mite wound up?' McCafferty stumbled over the threshold, bleary-eyed and unshaven.

'We were talking about opera,' Morton said lightly.

'Oh, that.' McCafferty brought a cup of coffee to the table. 'I guess I drank too much, last night. The beer here is kinda sweet for me but, boy, does it pack a punch!' He looked at the crate of empty bottles in the corner. 'I guess I should ask Halder to get some more in.'

Then Kelly entered, two stout canvas bags in his hands. He dropped them in the corner and, sitting next to Morton, gingerly cupped his right cheek in his hand.

'Is your toothache bad?' Morton asked.

'Jaysus, the damned thing's murdering me!'

'Why not ask Halder's maid to put some more opium on it?'

'I will, when I have my breath back.'

118

'How d'you get on?' McCafferty asked dully.

'Himself has no interest except for his bloody bomb,' Kelly muttered. 'I know where I can get the stuff; and the foreman at one site gave me a couple of dynamite bags, to make it look right.'

'Great, Pat! You sure got what it takes. And when d'you aim to collect the stuff?'

'Later – when this frigging tooth quiets down.'

'Fine! I guess I'll not come with you, myself. You're the expert, and I'd rather lie low for the moment. Why not take Paul with you? He's a big guy. He'll help you carry the bags.'

Kelly grunted his assent.

'Here's some cash.' McCafferty constructed ten columns of ten sovereigns each, then pushed them over. 'Get plenty, and anything Schelling wants, as well. And be careful you don't say where we are.'

Kelly gave a scornful snort, then dropped the coins in his pockets and went out.

An hour later, a rejuvenated Kelly was striding out, with Morton, to the top of Mansell Street. Then he turned left, towards the City. Morton was intrigued to know where they were going but, as a Swiss terrorist, he must merely look bewildered. At the end of Aldgate, Kelly went down Fenchurch Street and turned into the railway station. Dear God! Surely not? Kelly bought two return tickets to Stepney East, and they climbed aboard a waiting train. Soon they were clattering along the viaduct, looking down on grimy roofs, peering into box-like bedrooms. It was like a peep-show he'd seen already – 'What the Dynamitards saw'. Their destination could only be Boland Kerr & Co; and it was little more than a week since he had been there with Bragg. Suppose he were recognized? Although he still had a black eye, the swelling from his beating had virtually disappeared. It was certainly possible. What would Kelly do, if his real identity were revealed? Could he be persuaded to change sides, become a government man? No. He was unemotional, phlegmatic, but the strength of his convictions was obvious. He had left home and family, a good job, at the bidding of the local Fenians, to strike a blow for his cause. He would never co-operate. Then why not arrest him? Get the help

119

of Boland's, and go back to Mansell Street with the explosive. But how would he account for Kelly's defection? His toothache? They would never accept that. Anyway, without Kelly, McCafferty might alter his plans, go elsewhere. What would happen then? He had not resolved his dilemma, when they arrived at the station and alighted.

'Our man was telling me that Butcher Row is behind the station,' Kelly said, 'off Ratcliff Street.'

Morton decided to be co-operative. 'There is Ratcliff Street,' he said.

'Good man, yourself!'

It seemed only moments before Kelly was leading the way into the long, whitewashed warehouse. Morton saw with dismay that the same grizzled storeman was on duty. He skulked at the back; but the space at the counter was small, he was bound to be noticed.

'I want some dynamite,' Kelly said, dumping the bags on the counter.

'Right.' The man was speaking to Kelly, but scrutinizing Morton. 'Have you got an account with us?'

'No, but Hammond's have run out. The boss thought we might give you a try. I'll be paying cash.'

'Suits me, 'specially if you stay with us.'

'I don't see why not . . . I want a hundred sticks of Nobel's number one, with blasting-caps and five hundred yards of safety fuse.'

'Got a big job on?' the storeman asked.

'Yes, driving a road through the middle of a hill. We are up against time, so the boss doesn't want to run short.'

The storeman busied himself with piling the wax-papered bundles on the counter, while Kelly stowed them into his bags. From time to time, the man would glance at Morton and wink.

'Have you any black powder?' Kelly asked.

'Sorry, mate, the last went this morning.'

'The divil it did! The rock we are tunnelling through is broken in places. You can't drill a clean hole in it. I wanted some powder for that.'

'I have some stuff called "Explosive D". That's a powder.'

'Who makes it?'

120

'Nobel's. It's new. They say it's good.'

'Give us a look at it.'

The storeman brought a small closely-woven sack to the counter. On the side was stencilled 'Ammonium Picrate'. Kelly peered at the contents.

'How much is there?' he asked.

'A stone.'

'Right, I'll give it a try. How much is all that?'

The bill was totted up, and Kelly paid from a handful of sovereigns. It seemed a ridiculously small cost for such a fearful amount of explosive power, Morton thought. He moved to the counter, to pick up one of the bags. The storeman grinned at him.

'I know you!' he said. He lifted his fists in a boxer's stance. 'You're in the fancy, aren't you? I thought I recognized you. I saw you fight the Chiswick Tiger last month, down by Barking Creek. Corker of a fight, it was. I had a few quid on you . . . Buy you a drink, some time.'

'Get away with you!' Kelly exclaimed. 'Me boy has nothing to do with fighting, with gloves or without. He's nothing but a poor foreigner, labouring for us.'

Morton beat a hasty retreat, leaving the storeman looking unconvinced. The journey back was uneventful. It was astonishing that they could carry such a lethal load through the streets of London, unchallenged. A railway policeman at Fenchurch Street even helped Kelly down with his bag! It was incredible; society was frighteningly complacent.

When they got back to Mansell Street, McCafferty was jubilant.

'You're sure some guy, Pat!' he said, thumping him heartily on the back. 'Now we can get down to some real planning! I don't rightly know how powerful this stuff is, do you? Looks like we could blow up Buckingham Palace itself!'

Schelling hurried in, smiling in wolfish anticipation.

'They had sold all their black powder,' Kelly said, 'but they offered me this stuff, instead. I thought I would bring it, as money seems to be no object.'

Schelling looked at the powder, then at the side of the sack.

'Ammonium picrate,' he murmured. 'I have heard of it, but

have never used it. Good! We shall have a small experiment. Come.'

They all trooped into the workshop, where Bourdin was aimlessly crushing lumps of charcoal in the tin bowl. Schelling brought two grenade cases to the bench, and filled them with explosive from the sack. Kelly fitted blasting caps on two short pieces of fuse, and Schelling pressed them into the bombs. He then formed a plug around each fuse with twisted newspaper, and carefully sealed the aperture with candle-wax.

'Tomorrow morning,' he said, 'as soon as it is light, we will be in Greenwich Park. No other people will be there. We will test the new bomb. We shall hear the music of the spheres!'

'May I throw one?' Bourdin cried. 'Let me go with you!'

Schelling's smile was tinged with contempt. 'Good! You shall come – and you also, Grillon. This powder may be important to you.'

'Thank you,' Morton said.

'I guess I should come too,' McCafferty asserted, 'see what my money has bought. Maybe I should report on it to the Brotherhood, back home.'

'Now, we must wake at four o'clock,' said Schelling. 'There is a ferry from the Tower pier at a quarter to five. We shall be on it.'

6

It was still dark when they left the house, next morning. Overnight the sky had cleared, and frost glinted under the gas-lamps. There were few other passengers on the steamer. The flow at this time in the morning was inwards. Street-sweepers, warehousemen, ostlers would soon be pouring in, to sustain the City's complacent pride in being the trading capital of the world. In three hours' time, trains would disgorge armies of scurrying clerks from the suburbs. But now, the only noise was the lap of water against the ferry's hull.

The others went straight into the saloon, Schelling carrying a bag with the bombs inside. Morton elected to stay on deck, hoping that the cold air would clear his head. There came the soft thud of the engine, and the swish of the paddle-wheels. Already the sky was lightening to a pearl grey. As the steamer swung into the stream, it was possible to see the jutting pinnacles of Tower Bridge, with their coronets of scaffolding. The ferry manoeuvred to avoid the contractors' barges, which had clogged the vicinity for years longer than planned. Then they were free, the paddles threshing steadily; forging on past wharves and warehouses, the dark bulk of manufactories, the cliffs of dock walls. Soon they were surging down into Lime-house Reach. Morton glimpsed the slim shape of a Thames police launch, as it chugged up-river. What would its occupants think, he wondered, if they were told what was afoot? They would probably dismiss it as fantasy – something that only happened abroad! And, until a week ago, he would have shared the same attitude. He shivered, and wondered if it was worth going down to the saloon, also. No. There were the gas-works looming up on the shore, and the lights of Greenwich pier ahead.

Bourdin came clattering up to the deck, grinning with excitement, followed by the other two. The moment the ferry touched, they were ashore, striding along the grey, empty streets. Schelling took the lead, with Bourdin at his elbow. McCafferty seemed subdued, almost dejected. He gazed at the serene elegance of Greenwich Palace and sighed.

'You know something, Paul. This place gets to you . . . America's so new, you make the rules up as you go along, everything's hustle. Here, it seems like it's been for ever; people stick in their own little rut, never break out. You feel like you'd git a whuppin', if you stepped out of line.'

'You do not wish to blow up that building?' Morton asked.

'Hell, no. Anyways it's a hospital . . . D'you know, I keep on thinking about my Paw, ending his days over here.'

'It was a glorious death.'

'Yeah, I guess so . . . But I read a book, on the ship over. It said France is full of memorials to the glorious dead. These are guys who were killed in the war they picked with the Prussians – and lost. They proclaim it's great to die for your country, when the reality was heaps of rotting corpses.'

'You should not be melancholy. We are not fighting such a war. Our aim is freedom from subjection for all peoples. Your father was a hero in that struggle.'

McCafferty brightened. 'Yeah, that's right. Y'know, Paul, in the boat, before we left, I was looking up towards London Bridge, wondering where it was that it happened. I've read back copies of newspapers, since I came over. I know when it was, what day, what time – but none of them say just where they put the bomb.'

'Does it matter? It was a splendid gesture.'

McCafferty's mood remained sombre. By now Schelling and Bourdin were far ahead. Obviously Schelling had reconnoitred the area for just such an experiment. Morton opened the gate into the park. Now it was light enough to see the trees, standing sentinel in the frosted greensward. The sky above was diffused with shadowy blue, a shimmering bloom of pink crept from the east.

'I guess I never knew my Paw real good,' McCafferty said, kicking a stone so that it hopped along the path in front of them. 'When I was born, he was away fighting the Yankees. After it, he'd no sooner settled us in Toledo, than he came over to help the Fenians. I guess the longest I saw him was after he got out of jail, and came back to us. By then, I was fourteen and acting like I was a man . . . I hate to admit it, but I was glad when he came over here with Captain Mackey.'

'It is natural,' Morton said. 'You were not to know that he would die.'

'Yeah, that's true, Paul.' McCafferty smiled gratefully. 'I guess I'll make it up to him some day.'

'Of course. You will be a hero in your turn.'

'Hey! The others are way ahead, we'd better catch them.'

Bourdin and Schelling could be clearly seen, on the top of a ridge by the shadowy bulk of the observatory. Schelling had put down his bag, and was handing a bomb to Bourdin. He was gesturing to Bourdin, urging him to throw the bomb down the slope beyond. It was a good spot, Morton thought. They would be able to observe the fall of the bomb, and the area affected by the explosion.

'We should hurry, or we shall miss it,' Morton said.

'What's to worry about? They have two of them.'

Bourdin was now holding out the bomb towards Schelling. There was the flicker of a match, a shower of sparks. Then Bourdin turned . . . and began to run along the ridge, towards the observatory! He raised his arm to throw; there was an enormous explosion, a ball of flame. Schelling was thrown flat on his back. But where was Bourdin? Morton began to run. He was a hundred yards from the crest, when the door of the observatory was flung open and several angry figures appeared. Morton checked. After the explosion, Schelling had grabbed the bag containing the other bomb, and sprinted down the slope. By now, he would be out of sight. What should he and McCafferty do? It would be dangerous to run away. At least two of the men from the observatory looked athletic enough to follow, and McCafferty was in no condition for a chase. When he came up, they both walked over to the group on the crest.

'Say! What happened?' McCafferty asked, his eyes wide with concern.

'I would have thought that you could tell us,' an elderly man said curtly. His face was cut, and there were slivers of window glass in his hair.

'No, sir! My friend and I were out for an early-morning constitutional. We were half-way up the hill, when we heard an explosion. I guess it was here.'

The grass at their feet had been torn and scorched; in a ten-foot circle around, Morton could see tatters of cloth, shreds of flesh and bone.

'Mr Mellor!' A young man was beckoning from a few yards down the slope. His face was ashen; he held a handkerchief pressed against his mouth. They went over. Bourdin's battered head had lodged against a tussock. The eyes were wide and staring, the mouth open in a snarl of hate.

'Holy Moses!' McCafferty exclaimed. 'I ain't never seen anything like this. What should we do?'

The men from the observatory were shaken and bewildered.

'I suppose we should try to find the other fragments,' Mellor said shakily.

'My friend and I will go for the police,' McCafferty said. 'I guess this is a job for them. Is there a police station in Greenwich?'

'Yes, opposite the station.'

'Fine. We'll get them up here just as soon as we can.' McCafferty grabbed Morton's arm, and they strode off down the hill.

'What in tarnation happened?' McCafferty growled.

'I think that Bourdin attempted to throw the bomb at the observatory, instead of down the slope.'

'Jeez! The guy was nuts. Lucky for us we were well behind. Where's Schelling?'

'He ran down towards the trees, with the other bomb.'

'He's got his head screwed on, then. Sorry, that sounds kinda gruesome right now, don't it?'

'That explosive must be exceedingly powerful,' Morton said. 'There was little left of Bourdin.'

'Yeah . . . This is going to be a mite tricky. Did the guy say there is a train depot here?'

'Yes.'

'I'll tell you what, Paul. I'm kinda conspicuous, and I'd rather not be seen by the cops. It might make things difficult later on. Why don't I leave you to tell them? I'll just slip off on the train – it's bound to go to London.'

'Why need either of us go to the police?' Morton asked.

'Those guys at the observatory got a real good look at us. If the cops don't show up soon, to sweep up the bits, they're going to be mighty suspicious.'

Morton realized that it would be an advantage to be rid of McCafferty for a time. 'They might not understand me,' he said tentatively.

'All the better, son.'

'But I have escaped from the police. They will be looking for me. Suppose I am recognized?'

'Then, just leg it. You can run a darned sight faster than I can.'

Morton looked doubtful. 'If you wish it,' he said.

'Right, Paul, here's the depot. Wait till I have got over to the tracks, before you go to the cops.'

Morton waited in a shop doorway for ten minutes, before going to the police station. He had heard three trains go by. At least one of them must have whisked McCafferty up to London Bridge.

The desk-sergeant was still half-asleep.

'What do you mean, explosion?' he demanded.

'*Parlez-vous Français?*'

'Stop yammering on in your bloody foreign lingo! Speak English, can't you?'

'Le bang-bang. *A l'observatoire!* A man he is . . . poof!' Morton waved his arms excitedly.

'Christ! We'd better get up there! Wait here a minute.' He disappeared through a door at the back.

Morton decided that he had done all he could for Bourdin, and slipped away. He went to a newsagent's shop, and managed to buy a writing pad and some envelopes. In the station waiting-room he wrote a note to Bragg, then caught a train back

127

to London Bridge. He prowled around the station concourse till he was sure that McCafferty had not lingered there, then he walked over the river, to the Royal Exchange. There he found a licensed messenger, and gave him a half-crown to take his letter straight to Bragg. Then he strolled back to Mansell Street.

'What happened?' McCafferty asked, as he went into their room. 'What did the cops say? Did you have to go back with them?'

Morton smiled reassuringly. 'There was no difficulty. I pretended to understand English very little. I said that there had been an explosion at the observatory, and the policeman said they would go up.'

'Did he ask your name?'

'No. I walked out, when he went away.'

'Thank Christ! I was gettin' mighty worried about you, son.'

'I thought it was yourself you wished to save,' Morton said sarcastically.

'Hey! Don't be grouchy, son. I wasn't going to let an accident spoil my operation. And it came out OK, didn't it?'

'I suppose that Halder was not pleased.'

'You can say that again! He got a mite hot under the collar. He's gone off to the West End, to talk it out with his buddies. I guess we will be lying low, for a time.'

The door opened, and Schelling burst in. His face was jubilant.

'Was it not splendid?' he cried. 'This Explosive D is magnificent! Did you see?'

'We sure did,' McCafferty said resentfully. 'There's nothing left of Bourdin but a few strips of bloody rag and his head.'

'He was a fool! I told him to throw the bomb down the slope. The fuse was not long enough for him to run to the building . . . But why were there men in it, at such a time of the morning?'

'It is an observatory,' Morton said drily. 'Astronomers work at night.'

'Ah, of course!' Schelling slapped his thigh. 'Well, I will fill the rest of the bombs with a little less explosive – and longer fuses!' He went out whistling.

'I guess we'd better tell the others,' McCafferty said morosely.

'Have you not done so?'

'No, son. You know their lingo better than I do. I reckoned you should do it.'

Morton swallowed his irritation and went downstairs. But Schelling had already broken the news. Monique sat at the table, her hands clasped, her head bowed. If there was any emotion on her face, it was resentment. Kelly was reading a newspaper, occasionally putting a hand gently to his aching jaw. Corbin was the most animated, his eyes shifting from one person to another, assessing reactions, perhaps modifying his plans.

Just before noon, Halder returned. His eternal smile was oddly shamefaced.

'I have consulted other committee members of the Autonomie Club,' he announced, 'and it has been decided – against my judgement – to acknowledge Bourdin, and give him a proper funeral.'

'But why?' Monique asked.

Halder shrugged. 'It was clearly an accident, and no one outside the anarchist movement was injured. On the broader issues, there were two views. Firstly, it was pointed out that no terrorist activities are planned for this country, so we should not forgo a propaganda opportunity.' He smiled at McCafferty. 'Naturally, I did not mention the fact that certain persons, attached to this group, were actively planning just such an outrage . . . Beyond that, there was a general feeling that the anarchist bodies in England are too fragmented, and that an occasion such as Bourdin's funeral might bring some cohesion to the movement.'

'It is absurd!'

'Perhaps, Monique. However, you should be the last person to complain. It was your obvious contempt for the philosophical revolutionist that led him to a demonstration beyond his capacity . . . Now, my friends, I will tell you the arrangements. I have consulted a funeral director. He tells me that Martial's remains will have been taken to a mortuary, in Greenwich. He will complete the necessary formalities, and bring the coffin here. The funeral will be on Saturday morning, at Finchley cemetery – I assume that Bourdin was originally a Catholic.'

'I do not wish to take part in such a farce,' Monique said coldly. 'Bourdin had abandoned his religion. He believed in nothing!'

'Unfortunately, it appears impossible in this country, to be buried without some kind of religious rite. So, you see, the Christians will have you in the end!' Then Halder's face hardened. 'As to your private objections, Monique, you may maintain them only at the expense of leaving my house and my protection.'

Monique glared at him, then dropped her head.

Halder rubbed his hands gleefully. 'At least, there is a small advantage to all this. Since I was overborne on the question of the disposal of our friend's remains, the Autonomie Club is paying all the expenses of the funeral – including the cost of mourning clothes for us all.'

'Will it not be dangerous?' Schelling asked.

'No. We will go to a Jewish tailor, in Whitechapel. The Jews understand refugees, they will say nothing. In any case, Hans, after your escapade in Greenwich Park, you will be less conspicuous in mourning than in your present clothes!'

Bragg sat at the elegant escritoire in Morton's sitting-room, and contemplated the pile of letters before him. You only had to come into this room, he thought, to realize that he must have cut loose. There were discreet signs of opulence everywhere: the thick Turkey carpet, swagged velvet curtains at the window, furniture you dared not sit on lest it collapse under you. The trouble was, Morton had come into the police because he had wanted to, not because he needed to. Once he lost interest, he could just walk away from it . . . That bloody woman! Why the hell should she set everybody at odds, because she would not accept the usual lot of women? It wasn't that she was ugly or uncouth. She could beat society dames at their own game, any day – and enjoy it! Well, she wasn't happy now, that was certain; but she would never admit it. She was like a missionary in a cannibal's cooking pot, determined to suffer for the cause. Damn her!

Bragg slit open the envelopes, and extracted their contents.

Most were invitation cards, to the first balls of the Season. Morton might show up at them with a new bride on his arm, spoiled for anything serious in life. Bragg put them all in a pigeon-hole, and turned to the real letters. Here was one from a stockbroker, recommending changes in his stocks. Another, from his bank manager, confirmed that substantial monies had been remitted, anonymously, to help the building of some alms houses in Kent. The last was from the Kent County Cricket Club, setting out the fixtures for the summer, and expressing the hope that he would be available to play. Well, that was something he would not give up lightly. As far as Bragg could gather, it was the one indulgence he had insisted on extracting from Sir William, when the Commissioner had challenged him to enlist as a flat-foot: that he must, in the normal course, be allowed to play his cricket . . . And it had served the force well. Morton had played for Kent, and then for England, too. His popularity had rubbed off on the force; more than ever, the City police were seen as a cut above the Met. They had no difficulty in attracting recruits. Was all that to end? Bragg sighed; he badly wanted a pipe, but he drew the line at stinking this place out. Anyway, the important thing was, there were no ransom letters. When he had first come in, and been reminded of the costliness of these furnishings, he'd been inclined to go along with Miss Emily's kidnap theory. He half wished it were true. Money would not have mattered. Now, there were only two alternatives; either he had eloped, or he was dead.

Bragg took his leave of Chambers, and walked sombrely back to Old Jewry.

'A letter for you, Joe,' the desk-sergeant called. 'Brought in around half-ten.'

'Thanks, Bill.' Bragg took it. It was addressed in Morton's hand! There was no doubt about it! He hurried upstairs to his room. Good God! His heart was thumping like a girl's. He composed his mind in a disapproving cast, then ripped open the envelope with his thumb. He read the letter with astonishment and growing anger. When he had digested it, he went along the corridor and tapped on the Commissioner's door.

'What is it, Bragg?' Sir William looked up from his papers reluctantly.

131

'I've had a letter from young Morton, sir. It seems he has been shanghaied by the Special Branch, for some fancy assignment of theirs.'

A cautious look came over the Commissioner's face, as he held out his hand for the letter. He read it intently.

'It would appear that he has not entirely capitulated to their high-handed methods, since he avers that he will only report to Redman through us,' he remarked.

'All the same, it's way out of line! I think we ought to complain to the Home Secretary.'

'Ah . . . Yes, Bragg . . . Hmn. I somehow do not see myself getting much support from that quarter. The Special Branch are a law unto themselves. I sometimes think that the Commissioner of the Metropolitan police has only nominal control over them.'

'Well, something should be done!'

'Undoubtedly. The question is what? I suppose it is beyond doubt that, whatever initial pressures were put upon him, Morton ultimately undertook this affair voluntarily. That being so, we can hardly thwart his efforts, however piqued we feel.'

'I feel like knocking Redman's teeth down his flaming throat! For a week, we've all been worrying – his servants, his family, me! Now we get this!'

'I suspect that we shall continue to worry. In the meantime, we cannot do anything which would undermine his mission. That means we must keep our knowledge secret, for the time being, whilst doing all we can to facilitate his task.'

'What about this letter?'

'I fear that you have no alternative but to divulge its contents to Redman. How that is done, I leave to you.' Sir William pushed the paper from him, as if glad to be rid of it.

'You don't understand, sir,' Bragg said irritably. 'Morton's my lad. But the Special Branch won't give a damn about him. He's not one of theirs. To them, he's expendable.'

The Commissioner shifted uneasily in his chair. 'I see what you mean, Bragg. Well, if Morton insists on reporting through us, to some extent you hold the aces. How you play them, I leave to you.'

'I'll have a poke around first, then.'

Sir William held up his hand. 'Within the limits of prudence and discretion, I leave you to act on your own initiative. I have no wish to become involved in internecine strife between police forces. But please keep me informed.'

Bragg left the room cursing Sir William's vacillations. He had itched to have a real bust-up with the Met. But, as his temper cooled, he realized that this outcome was by far preferable. He had the authority of the Commissioner, yet a free hand to do as he liked. Perhaps the first thing should be to draw a few more cards from the pack. Judging by the letter, Morton had made no report to Redman until this. Bragg picked up the telephone instrument. It was time he got involved himself.

'Ring me the Met station at Greenwich, will you, Bill?'

He sat drumming his fingers impatiently on the desk. Yet, a few years ago, this same query would have taken half a day to get answered. The bell on the instrument jangled, and he picked up the ear-piece.

'Greenwich Met?' he called.

'Yes, sergeant.'

'I gather that you had a bombing in the Park, this morning,' Bragg shouted. 'Has anything happened on the case?'

He listened intently. 'We know who he is,' the thin metallic voice replied. 'A bloke called Martial Bourdin, of 23 Mansell Street – that's just in your area, isn't it?'

'How did you find out?'

'Some foreign geezer came in about it.'

'Any charges?'

The man laughed a reedy cackle. 'There's not much left of him to charge! A head, an arm, and half a leg! Mind you, if the coroner gets uppity, there might be trouble.'

'Thanks, sergeant.' Bragg hung up the ear-piece; then lit his pipe and smoked it slowly, while he digested the information he had. One thing was certain, he wasn't going to let Redman throw Morton to the dogs. He was going to keep the initiative himself, from now on. He knocked out his pipe, put the letter in his pocket and went downstairs.

As he walked through the warm sunshine, he felt a lightening of his spirits, a burgeoning excitement. Morton was still a real man, after all; and this case was out of the ordinary run. It

133

could be interesting, if things went right. He went past St Paul's, down Fleet Street, and turned into the quiet courtyards of the Temple. Sir Rufus Stone QC, the coroner for the City of London, had his chambers there; no doubt making a fat living, on the side. Bragg luckily found him unengaged, and was shown to his room by the clerk, without ceremony. Sir Rufus held up his hand for silence, while he finished reading through a lengthy document. Then he grunted in satisfaction and signed his name at the foot. Only then did he look up.

'Ah, Bragg, it is you. I was not aware that I had sent for you.'

'You didn't, sir. However, I thought you might be interested in some developments.'

'Developments?' Sir Rufus narrowed his eyes suspiciously.

'Not affecting us directly, sir, but I felt you ought to know, as an important public figure.'

Sir Rufus got to his feet and took up his favourite pose, astraddle the fireplace.

'When you descend to crude flattery, Bragg,' he declaimed, 'I suspect that you are about to try to manipulate me.'

'No, sir. It would be foolish even to attempt it.'

Sir Rufus gave him a hostile glare. 'In that case, it is hardly likely to be interesting. I will not have you interrupting my peace for no good purpose, Bragg.'

'There are some who think it important, sir.'

'And who might they be?'

'Special Branch, for one.'

'Huh!' Sir Rufus threw back his mane of grey hair, and seized the edge of his coat with his right hand. 'I have always seen them as a bunch of unprincipled cut-throats, Bragg, as you well know. Nothing they could do would ever surprise or interest me.'

'You know, sir, I begin to feel that this case proves you are right.'

A wary look crossed Sir Rufus's face, but he could not resist the lure. 'Why is that?' he growled.

'You remember Constable Morton?'

'Your young cricketing chap, you mean? Out of his element in the police, I always thought.'

134

'Yes, sir. Anyway, the Special Branch have kidnapped him, and forced him to work for them.'

'Good God!' Sir Rufus's eyes bulged in disbelief.

'I don't know what pressure they brought on him, sir, but he has been compelled to infiltrate an anarchist gang, at their bidding.'

'Anarchists? Where is this?'

'In Aldgate, sir.'

'Aldgate? Damnation, Bragg! I cannot understand why we put up with them – revolutionist rubbish! If I had my way, I'd pack them all off where they came from.' He threw back his head oratorically. 'I would be the first to extol the virtues of free speech, Bragg, of liberty for the person. But that should not extend to tolerating a bunch of alien ne'er-do-wells, whose stated intention is to subvert society as we know it.'

'No, sir.'

'And what is Special Branch's interest in this matter?'

'I think their views more or less coincide with yours, sir.'

'Oh.' Sir Rufus was momentarily disconcerted. 'Then why did you come here?' he demanded. 'Not to tell me that Special Branch have come round to my way of thinking, I'll be bound!'

'My concern is with Morton, sir. I don't want Redman throwing him to the wolves, when his purpose has been served.'

'And how, pray, can you prevent it?'

'On my own, I couldn't. But, with your help, I might be able to stick my oar in.'

'What are you proposing?' Sir Rufus asked cautiously.

'This morning, there was an explosion in Greenwich Park. One of the anarchists was killed by his own bomb.'

'Very right and proper, too.'

'Yes, sir. Now, if there were a great fuss about it, the anarchists might get rattled, and a bit unpredictable. Morton might not be able to get his reports out. We'd be far worse off then.'

'You sound as if you are siding with Redman and his gang, Bragg.'

'Every right-thinking person must be against bloody revolution, sir.'

'Huh! Well, tell me what you want of me, man!'

'You can be sure that the police will keep quiet, sir. But, of course, the Greenwich coroner is separate from the police, above them. He would be within his rights to order a full enquiry into the death, perhaps even treat it as murder. Then where would we be?'

'I see.' Sir Rufus dropped his chin to his chest, in thought. 'So you wish me to intervene in some way? Were there any witnesses?' he asked.

'I know that Morton saw it. But he cannot give evidence, naturally. There were some people who came out of the observatory, immediately after the blast. In Morton's view, they will say that no one else was in the vicinity.'

'Hmn . . . suicide or accidental death, eh? Yes, I don't see why not. Anyway, for your purposes, it should be sufficient if the coroner expedites the issue of a burial order. Then things can be considered at leisure.'

'I had not looked at it that way,' Bragg said earnestly. 'I wonder, sir . . . You being the most important coroner in the country, and looked up to by all the others; I wonder if you would be prepared to have a word with the Greenwich coroner – give him a bit of guidance?'

Sir Rufus preened himself. 'Yes, Bragg, I think I could do that for you. Mind you, he is in no way bound to accept my advice – but I think I could bring him round to our way of thinking.'

That afternoon, Halder marshalled the men to go for their mourning clothes. He had presented Monique with three pounds, and advised her to take an underground train to the West End. There she would find several establishments catering for the needs of ladies. McCafferty, in a spontaneous gesture of compassion, had added ten Brotherhood sovereigns, and she had gone off in a state of anticipation tempered by apprehension. At first, Kelly had refused to come, on the grounds that he was not an anarchist and, anyway, his tooth was hurting. Certainly, the gum looked inflamed when Morton peered into his mouth. But the pain yielded to another application of opium, and Kelly was urged not to forgo the chance of acquiring a new suit. So the seven of them set out, looking a bit like a school outing, Morton thought. They walked, in a bunch, up to Aldgate and along Whitechapel High Street. Halder paused before an extensive shop, which bore the sign: 'Issy Levy. Gent's Tailoring. Mourning a Speciality.' It would save a great deal of trouble if Issy would indeed carry out their act of mourning for them, Morton thought flippantly.

The shop was empty of customers. As they went in, a stout, balding man in a frock-coat advanced on them. His shirt was immaculate, and he wore a diamond signet-ring on his finger. Evidently mourning was profitable.

'Can I be of service to you, gentlemen?' Issy said unctuously.

'I am sure that you can,' Halder replied with his innocent smile. 'We are attending a funeral, on Saturday. We need suitable attire.'

Issy clicked his fingers, and two assistants appeared. He turned back to Halder. 'May I enquire how close you were to the deceased?'

Schelling's head jerked round suspiciously.

'Does it matter?' Halder asked.

'Most certainly, sir.' If anything, Issy's tone had become even more oleaginous. 'The degree of mourning dress is quite precisely laid down. It would be a grave error of taste, to dress in a manner inappropriate to your relationship with the late lamented.'

'Then let us say that we are all members of a club to which he belonged.'

'I see, sir. And what garments do you require?'

'Everything – except, perhaps, overcoats.'

Issy pursed his lips deprecatingly. 'Would you not feel it advisable to have, say, a light vicuna Chesterfield? April is such a treacherous month. Many's the time people catch their death of cold, at a funeral.'

'No,' Halder said firmly. 'No overcoats.'

'As you please, sir. Now, I think we shall be able to fit you from stock. We have a new line in peg-top trousers, very fashionable just now. And one should always be smart at a funeral, out of respect.'

'We are in your hands. As you will have realized, none of us is British.'

'Yes.' Issy eyed the group speculatively. He was obviously not averse to making money out of fellow émigrés. 'You will need white shirts . . . I think a simple stand collar will be best. The Shakespeare is perhaps a little ostentatious. And a black tie, of course.'

'I want one like that in the window,' Corbin said. 'It looks good.'

'Which one is that, sir?' asked Issy, drawing back the curtain.

Corbin pointed to a dummy displaying a tweed lounge coat.

'Oh, no, sir!' Issy's manner became grave. 'That is a four-in-hand necktie. It would be worn only on sporting occasions. Dear me, no! I would suggest a plain black cravat, sir, with a black waistcoat and a black frock-coat without silk facings.'

'It all seems rather excessive,' Halder said. 'In Munich we respect the dead, but it is not necessary to be so particular.'

'Ah, sir,' Issy said reprovingly, 'you are in London now. May I ask where the interment is to be?'

'Finchley cemetery.'

Issy sucked in his breath. 'It's a society occasion, then . . . Oh, I wouldn't want you to go to such a one, and not be properly dressed!

Halder capitulated. 'Very well.'

'Now, for the hats, sir. Would you say that any of you gentlemen was particularly close to the deceased?'

'Why do you ask so many questions?' Schelling demanded suspiciously.

'It is important,' Issy said reverentially. 'Someone who was related, or a dear friend, would have a four-inch band of crape on the hat. For a person who was less close, it would be three, or even two-and-a-half.'

'I did not like him. Make mine one inch only!'

Issy looked up into Schelling's face and shook his head in sad rebuke. 'You should never be disrespectful of the dead, sir,' he said. 'After all, we shall go to join them one day . . . That reminds me, I have some beautiful black-edged handkerchiefs . . . No?'

He turned to his assistants and soon the shop was a hive of

138

activity – men pulling on trousers, assistants gathering the excess cloth of a coat in their hand, and proclaiming that the fit was perfect. Eventually, all were provided for, except Schelling. They had found him a coat that was just passable, though it was far too snug on his massive arms. But the trousers were impossible. Their longest pair had legs that reached only to mid-calf.

'For Saturday morning, is it?' Issy mused. 'I could make you a pair by tomorrow afternoon. I would have to charge you thirty shillings, though; my cutter would have to work overtime.'

Schelling shrugged. 'Please do that.'

'Then I'll just run my tape measure over you.'

The others strolled out of the shop with their parcels, and waited on the pavement. Soon Schelling came bursting out.

'I think they are police spies!' he said truculently. 'Why all the questions?'

'It is nothing,' Morton said, falling into step with him. 'The English are obsessed with fashion.'

'No, no! You are wrong, they were political questions. Do you know what he asked me? He said: "Do you dress by the left, or the right?". You see! The parties here wear distinctive clothes.'

Morton decided that it was not the occasion to embark on an explanation of the intricacies of male tailoring. 'What did you say?' he asked.

'I did not wish him to think that I was in any party, so I said, "I dress straight down the middle".'

Bragg was at New Scotland Yard first thing next morning. After some delay, he was shown to an impressive office on the top floor, overlooking the Thames. He was in an irritable mood. The climb had made him breathless, which would give Redman a feeling of superiority. Blast it! He really must cut down on the beer, give up Mrs Jenks's treacle puddings.

Redman looked at him dispassionately, leaving him standing in front of his desk.

'What do you want, Bragg?' he asked.

Bragg walked to the window, while he controlled his anger,

139

then seated himself in an armchair. 'You have kidnapped one of my lads,' he said in a level voice.

'What do you mean, kidnapped?'

'Shanghaied was the word he used – Constable Morton.'

'What about him?'

'Don't bloody pretend you don't know! I've just heard from him. He says that, since he acted under duress, he will only report to you through me.'

Redman regarded him coldly. 'He had no right to do that,' he said. 'I recruited him as a free agent. He is doing it of his own volition.'

'Huh! The trouble with you lot is, you think you are above the law. Well, you will find out you are wrong. From what I gather, Morton did not have much freedom to choose.'

Redman's lip curled. 'No doubt you are a great authority on freedom,' he said sarcastically. 'Let me tell you, freedom is a luxury only the secure can afford. Morton has embarked on a dangerous course, betraying our operation to you.'

'Betraying? Who the bloody hell do you think you are talking to? I am a police officer of twenty-four years' standing. I'm not going to take that from you.'

'As you will – sergeant.'

They glared at each other for some moments, then Bragg rose to leave. As he reached the door, Redman spoke.

'Do you not think you have an obligation to pass on Morton's report?' he asked.

Bragg turned and strode over to the desk, so that he towered over Redman. 'I have no obligations to you – official or otherwise. It wouldn't take much for me to bloody throttle you!'

The flint-grey eyes were watchful. 'So?'

'So my concern is with Morton's safety.'

'He is a competent officer,' Redman said coldly. 'I do not think either of us should forget that.'

'He is my bloody constable, not yours!' Bragg shouted. 'Nobody uses him, unless I agree!'

Redman pondered briefly. 'Then what are your terms?' he asked.

'I will pass on his reports, but I must be involved – part of the operation.'

'Are you asking us to co-operate with the City police?' Redman asked contemptuously.

'Not asking, demanding it! Unless you agree, I will take twenty men and arrest the whole bloody lot. You see, I know precisely where they are.'

'Would you betray the vital interests of your country?'

'So long as the likes of you decide on them, I wouldn't give a toss!'

'And what would you achieve, by frustrating our operation?'

'I would get my lad out of danger.'

Redman snorted derisively. 'There is no danger, so long as he keeps his head.'

'That's a laugh, that is! They exploded a bomb in Greenwich Park, yesterday morning. That was all that was left of the man who threw it – his head.'

'Nevertheless, risks have to be taken. Morton understands that.'

'Not without my say-so, they haven't.'

Redman sighed irritably. 'On your head be it,' he said. 'The position is that we suspect French military intelligence of trying to stir up trouble in this country. Our information is that they are proposing to incite the anarchist refugees to that end. We arrested one suspected agent and put Morton in his cell, to gain his confidence. I had already arranged to provide Corbin with a hack-saw blade and, in due course, they escaped together.'

'You must be crazy. Do you think that any half-decent agent would be taken in by that?'

Redman shrugged. 'All Frenchmen have been brought up on a diet of Alexandre Dumas. It appeals to their romantic natures.'

'And you'd risk my lad's life, so recklessly?'

'He was the only person available. What alternative had I? Britain is defenceless in these matters.'

'So, you will allow them to commit themselves to some action, then grab them all?'

'Something like that.'

'You are trying to manufacture a major international incident, aren't you?' Bragg said incredulously.

'Hardly major.'

'Let me remind you,' Bragg said emphatically, 'that the doctrine of the greater good is not known in British law.'

'Then what would you have me do?' Redman burst out angrily. 'Would you stand by, and let your country be subverted, society swept away in a bloody revolution? That is what will happen in this country – happen to you and me – unless this idiotic government can be brought to its senses!'

There was silence for a space. Then Bragg spoke in a low voice. 'I am willing to co-operate with you, and pass on Morton's reports to you. But it will be on my terms. I will act to help you to achieve your aims, but I will not take directions from you. You can rely on me not to scupper your plans without good cause but, the minute I sense danger, I shall move in. And I must be involved in the planning of the operation from now on.'

Redman gazed at him stonily. 'Very well,' he said.

'Good. Then I can tell you that Morton thinks you are right. Corbin has supported the idea of assassinating a member of our royal family – though there are no present plans to do so. Furthermore Corbin went to meet someone in the Southwark tunnel, so he has support. That's all, at the moment. I will let you know, when I hear more.'

Morton was late in going down to supper. The others were already tackling a mound of fried pork chops, and dishes of vegetables. As he took his place, the maid came down to summon Schelling to Halder. The Dutchman went reluctantly, amid jocular remarks from the company. It was almost as if they were trying to expunge from their minds the death of Bourdin, and the impending funeral. That afternoon, a hearse had brought the elaborate coffin to Halder's house. He had said that he would be honoured if Bourdin lay in his sitting-room overnight. Monique had scoffed at the proceedings, yet she was edgy, defiant.

'Paul, what d'you think of this?' McCafferty's face was pink with excitement. 'Pat and I have been turning over a few ideas. We reckon we have a great target right here, under our noses.'

'What is it?' Morton asked.

'The Royal Mint – it's just at the bottom of our street.'

'I have heard that the English are so disgusting as to eat this with lamb. Is it your plan to prevent the Queen from doing so?'

'Don't be plumb stupid, son. The Mint is where all the coins are made. If that was blown up, they couldn't make any more for a while.'

'But if in time they could begin again, what would you have achieved?'

'Don't you see? It would be symbolic. The Queen's head is on every one of those coins. We would blow hundreds of them to smithereens. And we would have destroyed an organ of the state. What does our philosopher say? Wouldn't it be a great stroke?'

Halder had entered while McCafferty was speaking, and now took a chair at the head of the table. 'It would be a splendid gesture,' he said, 'if it were successful. What precisely have you in mind?'

'We could sneak up under cover of darkness, set some dynamite, and blow a hole in the outer wall – like the Fenians did at Clerkenwell prison. Then we could toss a few sticks among the buildings, and beat it.'

'I think you would find that the walls of the Mint are much too thick for that. You would have to consult Schelling, but I imagine that, unless the dynamite were placed deep in the core of the wall, it would merely explode harmlessly.'

'I told you so,' Kelly said.

McCafferty looked crestfallen. 'We could still lob sticks of dynamite over the wall. It would make one hell of a mess in there.'

'That is undoubtedly so,' Halder said gravely. 'But the effort would be wasted, unless it were known.'

'What do you mean?' McCafferty demanded. 'You bet it would be known!'

'But would it? The success of any such operation must be measured by the extent to which ordinary people become aware of it. It is not enough that officials know about it. Unless it is common knowledge, it might just as well never have happened. There would be the noise of an explosion from the proximity of the Tower – several explosions, perhaps. But they would be

143

muffled by the walls. If anyone questioned it, the authorities could say that there had been a gun-practice at the Tower – perhaps for the Queen's homecoming. It would be absurd, of course; but the common people will swallow anything, so long as their lives are not disturbed.'

McCafferty sniffed. 'I guess you are right,' he said at length. 'We gotta start again, Pat.'

Schelling came in. He looked swiftly round the room, then sat at Halder's right. He made no attempt to resume his meal.

'My friends,' Halder said, beaming benignly on the assembled company. 'I have some information to impart to you . . . There is one among us who is not what he seems.'

It was as if Morton's heart had suddenly swelled in his chest. He could not get his breath, his pulse was racing. He glanced about him, ready to defend himself.

'Marcel Corbin, you will recall, professed to be in the wine trade,' Halder went on silkily. 'He said that he had worked in Beaune – which would not have been surprising. But our late-lamented Martial came from Gevry-Chambertin, himself; and he rapidly formed the opinion that Corbin knew very little about the Burgundy region.'

Corbin's smile seemed relaxed, but Morton could see the tension in his body.

'I was only in Burgundy for two months,' he said mildly.

Halder waved away the interruption indulgently. 'So Martial and I set him a little test,' he went on. 'You might well have thought that he was somewhat hesitant in our discussion on the wine – hesitant for so great an expert, that is. But not all of you would have realized how tenuous his knowledge really is. You will remember that we deplored the inexorable advance of phylloxera, and discussed the efficacy of the measures taken against it. Marcel did not dispute my assertion that Romanée Conti had been replanted on new, resistant vinestocks. Yet, it is well known in the wine trade that Romanée Conti has refused to follow that path. Then I suggested that the new root-stock came from Greece, and Marcel did not contradict me. In fact, the stocks are *Vitis ruparia* and *Vitis rupestris*, from the eastern United States. Strange that someone who has spent his working life in Bordeaux and Burgundy should be ignorant of that, you might think.'

Corbin managed a smile. 'I was a buyer of wine, not a grower,' he said. 'It was the taste that interested me.'

'Yes.' Halder beamed at him. 'However, being a little intrigued, I telegraphed my associates in France, and asked them to investigate the matter urgently. You will recall that Marcel said he was employed by Ginestet. Enquiries certainly elicited the information from them, that it was indeed so. But sympathizers in their office told us that Marcel Corbin was not on any payroll; nor had any of them seen, or even heard of him, until that moment. Further enquiries produced the information that he was not known in anarchist circles in Dijon – indeed, in the whole Rhône valley. It is clear, therefore, that Marcel is an impostor. Then the question arises why anyone would wish to conceal his identity among us.'

The query hung in the air. All eyes bored into Corbin. Then he shrugged. 'I assumed a new name,' he said. 'My parents are not sympathetic to the anarchist cause. I did it to preserve the family honour.'

The smile vanished from Halder's face. 'Family honour is an outdated concept,' he said harshly. 'No true anarchist would give it any weight. You are a police spy, my friend.' He glanced across at Schelling, then folded his arms across his chest.

Schelling rose, and began to walk slowly towards Corbin. He was like a wrestler, Morton thought; his huge bulk balanced on the balls of his feet, ready to take advantage of the slightest opening. Corbin watched his approach warily then, when Schelling was within two yards of him, he sprang up, overturning his chair in Schelling's path. He backed into a corner, his fists ready. Schelling smiled, brushing the chair away with his foot. Morton remembered Monique's phrase 'blood-lust'. Certainly, he seemed possessed by some atavistic compulsion. At that moment Corbin stooped and, jerking up his trouser-leg, pulled a knife from a shin-scabbard. The six-inch blade glittered in the gaslight. *'Vive la France!'* he shouted.

Schelling gave a great laugh. 'You handle it like a maiden,' he said, advancing to within a yard of Corbin. 'You should know that one seldom kills by striking down. That was how I

145

got this scar. The point of the knife glanced off the bone. It is a mistake no one makes twice.'

Corbin quickly switched the knife, so that the blade was upwards.

'That is better!' Schelling bellowed. 'I would not wish to fight with an old woman.'

Morton glanced at Monique; her eyes were glittering, her hands clenched.

Schelling was weaving and swaying now, his outstretched hands jabbing the air between them. When he got too close, Corbin would slash upwards with the blade. Once Schelling's cheek was within a whisker of being laid open again, but he only laughed. Then he feinted to the left. As Corbin's knife swept past, Schelling pivoted inside the stroke and the edge of his hand hammered into Corbin's wrist. The knife clattered to the floor, and Schelling kicked it away.

There was total silence in the room. Corbin was flattened against the wall, Schelling regarding him almost amiably. Thank God that was all, Morton thought. Then suddenly, Schelling stepped forward, arms outstretched. Corbin launched himself from the corner, slamming his fists into Schelling's body, trying to break out. Schelling laughed disdainfully; with a sudden pounce, he had him by the throat. Regardless of Corbin's blows he settled himself, feet wide apart; then began to force back the Frenchman's head, thumbs on his windpipe. Morton was paralysed from shock, unable to stir. It was like a theatre show. Any moment the protagonists would disengage, turn and bow . . . After a short, whistling gurgle, Corbin uttered no sound. His flailing arms became aimless, then drooped by his side. In a final frenzy, Schelling closed with Corbin and lifted him in the air by his neck. He shook him savagely, then dropped him in a heap on the floor. He looked down at him briefly, then turned and walked back to his seat.

'Christ!' McCafferty murmured.

'I think we would all agree,' Halder observed mildly, 'that punishment had to be meted out.'

The others still sat in wooden disbelief.

'The question now arises of how we shall dispose of the traitor's body.'

'From my window,' Schelling said, 'I have seen that there is a slaughter-house behind this building. If we chop up his body, we could throw it into the waste bins.'

Halder smiled beatifically. 'I think that we might adopt an altogether more elegant solution. Upstairs, in my sitting-room, is a most splendid coffin, with little more than a few fragments of our late friend in it. Why should we not place the traitor Corbin there? He would, at least, be given a Christian funeral – I imagine he would have wanted that.'

Kelly suddenly stirred himself. 'Would the undertaker's men not notice the difference in weight?' he asked.

'A good point.' Halder pondered. 'Then we must say that, in France, it is the custom for relatives and friends to place the coffin in the hearse, and carry it until it is lowered into the grave. They will know no better – and we will give them a generous measure of spirits, against the cold!'

7

Catherine seldom went into the office on a Saturday morning. The copy for that day's paper had been finalized by Friday night, and there was still ample time before Wednesday's edition. Once her probation was over, she had screwed herself up to asking if she might work at home on a Saturday. If the truth were known, she had felt guilty about it; because all the male journalists were expected to be in the office. She had salved her conscience with the thought that women had many disabilities laid upon them, so she was entitled to extract a small concession. And she was justified in overlooking the inconvenient fact that Mr Tranter, the editor, had agreed merely because he looked on women as the weaker sex. Most of the time she kept punctiliously to her bargain, and worked in her room. And, when she breached the arrangement, she was always able to tell herself that she worked far more hours than she was paid for.

But this morning she felt restless. She took out her notes for the article on the Honourable Artillery Company, but she could not focus her mind on it. If she had any sense, she told herself irritably, she would be working hard at this moment; laying up a store of articles to cover the inevitable interruptions that the Season would bring. She sighed. She was not looking forward to the next four months at all. And it was not merely disdain at the emptiness of it all – nor even that it formalized the debasement of women in society. If she were honest with herself, she would admit that she was cringing inside at the prospect of meeting James at some party, with his new wife on his arm. For three years, now, she had regarded him as her own property; had told herself that, were she to decide to marry, he could easily be brought to the point of a proposal. It was clear that she had miscalculated – and now he was beyond her reach. But need Sergeant Bragg have been so brutal? He was clearly upset by James's desertion, but so was she. And she had much more to lose.

Catherine mentally shook herself. She was becoming thoroughly depressed. She must get out of the house, amongst the hurly-burly of the streets. She could always pretend that she was doing research. She walked to Marble Arch, and drifted over to the omnibus stop for the City. As it was mid-morning, there were few people waiting; and, before long, she was being pushed up the stairs by an impatient conductor. She wedged herself between a clerk and a large woman with shopping bags on her lap, and pushed hard on the footboard to counteract the swaying of the vehicle. It was bitterly cold on the open top deck. The wind was not strong, but it blew up-river, straight from the frozen plains of Russia. Catherine could feel her nose beginning to glow red. She fumbled in her bag for a handerchief, and the clerk complained as she stuck her elbow in his ribs. On the spur of the moment, she ignored her usual stop at Peel's statue, and alighted at the Bank of England. There were certainly plenty of people around here: silk-hatted stockbrokers, clerks scurrying to the Bank before midday, even the odd female typewriter. She strolled along Moorgate, gazing in the shop windows. She could pop in on the Ayre's Charity almshouses, she thought. For months she had intended to write about them; it was the kind of safe, worthy subject that Mr Tranter would approve of . . . But she passed them by.

She was really quite miserable, haunted by the feeling that she had made a dreadful mistake. She paused on the edge of the pavement. A funeral was approaching up Finsbury Place. Men were holding their hats to their breasts, women checking the exuberance of their children. A solemn stillness settled on the street as the procession approached. The hearse was drawn by four black horses, with black plumes on their heads. A platoon of black plumes stood stiffly on the roof of the hearse itself. Through the glass side, the outline of an elaborate coffin appeared, masked by wreaths. Perhaps it was the funeral of

149

some respected City figure, though Catherine was not aware that anyone important had died. Her gaze lingered on the hearse as it passed her. Then she glanced at the first carriage of mourners as it followed. She caught her breath in surprise and consternation. It was James! She was sure of it – sitting on the near side at the rear. She had lost sight of him now, but she could see a youngish woman, in a black-veiled hat, sitting opposite him. So it was true! She began to walk after the carriage, bumping into respectful citizens, tripping over pavements . . . No, she had not imagined it. True, she had not seen him in mourning clothes before, but she could never be mistaken about his profile. Yet . . . If only she could get another glimpse, make absolutely certain, then she would know where she stood. The pavements were less crowded now, and she began to gain on the carriage. Would that she were wearing more comfortable shoes . . . A little more effort, and she would draw level with the door. Then she would be able to get a clear look. But, as the traffic thinned, the hearse's coachman increased his speed. She found it difficult to keep up; then the carriage was drawing away from her.

She walked on determinedly, her feet tingling: now the head of the horse pulling the second carriage was at her shoulder. She was losing ground all the time. What was the point of it? Why bother? No! She must be certain, whatever the cost. There was nothing more important than this. She was becoming short of breath now. She unbuttoned the coat of her tailor-made . . . That was better. Now she was looking into the second coach. There were only three men in it; she recognized none of them. They were smoking cigarettes and talking. So none of them was particularly grief-stricken. Now they were past. If only she could keep with the cortège, she would be all right. She would know James even at a distance. Catherine glanced over her shoulder for the next carriage, but there was none. She began to run, but her skirt hampered her and her shoe was rubbing her heel. She resumed a dogged walk but, all the time, the procession was drawing away. She strained every sinew to close the gap. At that moment, it was the most important thing in her life, the only thing that mattered. Now they were coming to a group of new shops. They must be close to Islington. But the nearest cemetery was at Highgate. That was two miles further . . . Catherine stifled an impulse to weep. She was not going to give up.

Propped at the edge of the pavement was a delivery bicycle. Its sign proclaimed that it belonged to Jas Long & Co, Provision Merchants . . . Dare she? There was no doubt that she could ride it, and her gored skirt was not excessively full. But the top bar of the frame was higher than on the women's bicycles she had ridden. It would hardly be modest. She glanced at the rapidly disappearing cortège. What did modesty matter? She looked around. No one was watching. She hitched up her skirt, straddled the bicycle and was off.

At first, she found it difficult to balance. The huge basket, over the front wheel, seemed to make the steering stiff and awkward. But the road was smooth, and she was catching up every second. Now they were approaching Holloway village, with Saturday morning shoppers thick on the pavements. She ran into a barrage of whistles and ribald comments. She could feel the colour rising in her cheeks. She didn't care, she told herself. She was within a hundred yards of the funeral procession. Highgate cemetery was a mere quarter-mile away. Then the road narrowed, the jeering faces were closer to her.

'Which are you, love?' a man shouted.

'A bit o' crumpet like that don't need no advert,' called another.

She tried to shut out their jeers. What did it matter that they could see her ankles? Stupid people! She stood on the pedals in her haste to get away from them. She felt her skirt billow out. There was a jerk, a wild wobble and she was flat on her face in the dust. She gave a whimper and tried to get to her hands and knees, but her skirt was trapped in the chain. She managed to get her hand to the pedal and freed it, then scrambled to her feet. Thank goodness her face had not been scratched! But she could feel a painful scrape on her elbow, and her knee was sore. Then she became indignant. No one was coming to help her. It was as if she were taking part in a side-show, or a circus. She stooped to right her bicycle – and saw the other side of the sign-board. It bore the legend: 'High-class Tarts and Faggots'.

She did not know whether to cry or laugh, as she tucked her

151

skirt safely under her, and set off again. She was now well behind the funeral procession, but she knew her way from here. She was about to tackle Highgate Hill, when she glanced to her right and glimpsed the last carriage disappearing up Archway Road. Catherine's heart sank. That meant Finchley. Another three miles away. She wobbled across the road and took up pursuit again. She had lost considerable ground, but there was no hurry. The road stretched wide and straight in front; there was no danger that she would lose it again.

As they neared Finchley Village, Catherine saw that there was a crowd lining the street – a hostile crowd by the sound of it. A knot of men dashed towards the hearse, and the coachman raised his whip. But the demonstrators were headed off by policemen, and the cortège got through. There was a considerable police presence, Catherine realized. Trouble of some sort must have been expected. Perhaps it was the corpse of some mass murderer or child molester. In the main street, the pavements were lined shoulder-to-shoulder by straining police; the crowd was even more hostile. As the hearse passed through, four other carriages of mourners attached themselves to the rear of the procession. The police thereupon gave up their efforts, and the crowd closed in behind, shouting abuse.

Catherine abandoned her machine in a side-street, and hobbled after them on foot.

'I'd watch out for myself, if I was you, young lady.' A large fatherly man took station by her side. 'Things could get a bit nasty, from what I hear.'

'I am a newspaper reporter,' Catherine said. 'What is going on?'

'They say it's an anarchist's funeral. Shouldn't be allowed, if you ask me.'

'Anarchist?'

'S'right. We can do without the likes of them, in our area. It's bad enough having to put up with cemeteries for half of London.'

The police were now having to clear a way through the jeering crowd. There were more police at the cemetery gates, fighting to make a path for the barely moving procession. Catherine forsook her protector and began to work her way through the demonstrators. If only she could reach the first carriage, she would have succeeded. She indulged in a fantasy of wrenching open the carriage door, confronting him . . . Then the way was cleared, and the carriages moved into the cemetery. No sooner was the last one through, than the heavy iron gates were closed, and a phalanx of policemen stationed themselves outside. Catherine pushed her way through the disappointed crowd, and approached the sergeant in charge.

'I am a reporter for the *City Press*,' she said. 'I have been sent to cover this funeral.'

The sergeant shook his head firmly. 'I won't open these gates again for anybody, miss. Not even the Archangel Gabriel.'

'But I shall miss my story!'

'Look, miss, I've got three constables injured; one of them looks real bad. And we are only half-way through.'

An onlooker overheard the conversation and set up a chant of: 'We'll get them coming out!'

Catherine peered through the stout railings. The hearse had drawn up by the chapel, the mourners were inside. She heard the brief strains of the organ; shortly afterwards the coffin emerged, borne by six shuffling men. They carried it awkwardly to a grave two hundred yards from the gates. There was some confusion as the undertaker's men replaced them, then lowered the coffin to its resting place. A short fat man appeared to say a few words, and they all began to put on their hats and turn away. Then they stopped, irresolute, as one of the mourners broke into a wailing dirge. From where Catherine stood, it sounded like the song of the Hebrew slaves, from *Nabucco*. What relevance that had, she could not possibly conceive. But the band of mourners stood till it was finished, then quickly got into their carriages.

An excited hum rose round her, as the crowd whipped itself up into a frenzy of hate again. The policemen stood alert. Then there came a shout from the railings.

'The bastards! They are going out the other way!'

There was a sudden movement in the crowd, as men dashed down the road to cut the carriages off. But the vehicles were moving briskly towards a gate at the far corner of the cemetery. There was no danger that they would be caught.

153

'May I go in now?' Catherine asked the sergeant.

He looked round at the sullen demonstrators, then nodded to a policeman.

Moments later, Catherine was walking up the avenue to the chapel. The priest was packing his robes into a bag.

'I am a newspaper reporter,' Catherine announced. 'I wonder if you can give me some information about the funeral you have just conducted.'

He looked up, with an expression of distaste. 'Information?' he asked.

'Could you tell me the name of the deceased?'

'I would have thought that you knew it already.'

'No. I was merely told to cover a funeral here.'

'We have had quite enough unpleasantness already,' he began.

'I can see no possible reason for your withholding the information,' Catherine said sharply. 'It is not secret. It is in the public domain!'

The priest pursed his lips unhappily, then put his hand in his pocket and gave her a piece of paper. It was a burial order for one Martial Bourdin, of 23 Mansell St, London E.

'They were saying, in the crowd, that he was an anarchist,' Catherine observed.

'It may be so,' the priest said, 'but he was still a child of God.'

Catherine turned away from the empty platitude. She had learned all she needed. She wondered idly whether to leave the bicycle, or return it to its rightful owner. How would she explain herself, she wondered . . . It was of no consequence. She had achieved what she had set out to do. One of the men who had borne the coffin to the grave was, without a shadow of doubt, James Morton.

When they arrived back at Mansell Street, Halder went to his own quarters, while the rest gathered in the basement messroom. Kelly's tooth had been affected by the cold wind; he had wrapped a scarf around his head, and was sipping from a large glass of whiskey.

'What is this?' Schelling asked, picking up the bottle.

154

'Bushmills' Irish,' Kelly mumbled.

'May I try it?'

Kelly nodded, and Schelling half-filled a tumbler. 'To the health of your tooth!' he said, and tossed it back. 'Ah! This is good!' He filled his glass again, and topped up Kelly's.

'Jaysus, the divil is murdering me!' Kelly moaned. 'I'll have to get it to a dentist.'

'It is Saturday evening,' Morton pointed out. 'You will have to wait till Monday now.'

'Holy Mother of God! Is there no Jewish dentist around at all?'

'I will pull it out for you, my friend,' Schelling said. 'In the past I have pulled out the teeth of horses.'

'Holy God, no! You'd have me destroyed.' Kelly took another swig of his whiskey.

A silence fell on the group. It was extraordinary, Morton thought. From the time that they had unscrewed the lid of Bourdin's coffin and placed Corbin's body inside, no one had mentioned him. In a purely physical sense, it had been more his funeral than Bourdin's; yet he had vanished into the earth, unrecorded and unmourned. Then McCafferty stirred uneasily.

'Well, I guess Martial had a great funeral,' he said. 'I would like to think my Paw got one as good.'

'Do not be stupid!' Monique exclaimed angrily. She had taken off the close-fitting jacket of her mourning costume, to reveal a purple blouse beneath. 'I do not understand why we had to be involved in such a farce.'

'The Autonomie people wished it,' Santo said.

'Pah! Why should anarchists promote a religious funeral? I would rather be thrown in a ditch than have that happen to me! Remember that, Paul.'

'You heard Halder say that it was good propaganda,' Morton reminded her gently.

'What's wrong with religion, anyway?' McCafferty asked defensively. 'The guy was born a Catholic, he was entitled to a Catholic funeral.'

'Entitled?' Monique sneered. 'Do you not see that this is how they keep you in subjection? So long as you fear that there might be a next world, you will ultimately come to heel. Only

155

when mankind realizes that God does not exist, will they be free of oppression.'

'Hey! Take it easy, ma'am. Religion does no harm, and a deal of good, I reckon.'

'You people are so blind, so cowed!' Monique cried shrilly. 'Your faith prescribes poverty and humility in the clergy; yet its churches are stuffed with treasures, while millions starve! There you are, Santo! There is a fitting target for your glorious sacrifice. The Pope of Rome!'

'His Holiness?' Santo looked dumbfounded.

'Why not? He colludes in the subjection of the people. It should not be difficult, Santo. With care, you might survive to strike another blow at the oppressors.'

McCafferty crossed himself. 'I want no part of that,' he said.

'What is it, Lee?' Monique asked scornfully. 'Are you afraid? What will you do when you have made your great explosion – possibly killed many ordinary people? Will you go to your confessor and seek absolution? How many Aves and Paternosters will he set you to recite?'

'Children, children! You must not quarrel.' Halder had appeared at the doorway. He crossed to Kelly. 'How is the bad tooth?'

'It's killing me, so it is.'

'I have offered to pull it out,' Schelling said cheerfully. 'Will you now allow me?'

Kelly turned his woebegone face. 'What with?' he asked.

'I have pincers and pliers in the workshop.'

'Jaysus, Mary and Joseph! The man's a bloody butcher.'

'Drink deep from your bottle, my friend. You will feel nothing.' Schelling topped up Kelly's glass, and filled his own.

'Let us speak of something more cheerful.' Halder's beaming smile embraced them all. 'Paul, tell us something of your childhood home, in Switzerland. Where was it, did you say?'

Morton felt a cold worm of fear crawling up his spine. Suddenly, everyone's eyes were fixed on him. Schelling's face bore a sadistic grin.

'Vernier, near Geneva,' he said casually.

'Is it on the lake?'

'No. Indeed, from our house it was not possible to see the

lake, though it was only a kilometre away. But we had a glorious view of the mountains.'

'Your father was the innkeeper, was he not?'

'No, the local schoolmaster. He has now realized his life's ambition, for they have recently built him a new school.'

Morton had a flash of gratitude for Redman and his meticulous preparation. But he must keep it conversational, seem relaxed.

'I thought you mentioned an inn,' Halder persisted.

'No! You forget that it was a predominantly Calvinist village. The nearest we got to having an inn was the *Café de l'Etoile*, at the crossroads.'

'But, am I not right in thinking that there is a Catholic church there, also? I seem to remember a picture of the village, with a church tower outlined against the sky.'

Morton was tempted to take the initiative, pour out his knowledge and rid himself of this inquisition. But that could be courting disaster.

'The Catholic church has a spire,' he said, 'above a somewhat Italianate bell chamber.'

'Ah, yes, you are right. But the interior is gothic, I believe.'

Morton laughed. 'I have to admit that I did once peep inside it! Had my father known, he would have thrashed me. He taught us that the Catholic church was the abode of the devil himself!'

Halder looked at him narrowly. 'And was it gothic?' he asked.

Morton considered for a moment. 'I would not say that it was. There were lancet windows, certainly, but there were no pillars inside. Nor was there a chancel. The east end was in the form of an apse, with decorative ribs running to a boss in the roof. I remember thinking how open and light it seemed – presumably, because the organ was in the gallery over the west window.'

'Interesting . . . And were you an only child?'

Morton smiled. 'I had a younger sister, Simone. Now, she could twist our father round her little finger! I suppose it is often the way of things.'

'You attended your church, as a boy?'

157

'Yes. I was compelled to do so. It was the main reason why I broke with my parents.'

'That you had to go to church?'

'That the religion they expected me to embrace was so literalistic and bigoted.'

'I see. Who was the pastor, in your youth?'

'It was a man called Louis Choisy. Indeed, he is still pastor, so far as I know.'

Halder seemed to relax. Morton gave an inward gasp of relief; then he remembered the parallel inquisition of Corbin, the way Halder had become casual when he knew he had trapped him. Had he made a mistake? He was sure it was Choisy . . . or was it Chouilly? It was certainly the name of a village in France. Halder was speaking again, quietly. He must concentrate.

'One of my numerous interests has been the finials of church steeples,' Halder murmured.

'Then you ought to go to Vernier,' Morton interrupted. 'The steeple of the Catholic church is surmounted by a cross, upon which perches a fat cockerel – a French revolutionary cockerel!'

Halder laughed. 'I am sorry for these questions. As you realize, it is important that we should have confidence. I am happy to accept that you are, indeed, Paul Grillon.'

There was a collective sigh, as the others relaxed. Schelling had a peevish look of disappointment on his face. He emptied his glass and refilled it. As an afterthought, he topped up Kelly's and nudged him to drink.

McCafferty broke in, to dispel the charged atmosphere.

'Pat and I reckon we've got our target,' he announced. 'I saw the thing when I was walking from the railway station, the other day. A darned great column; says it's the Monument, though I ain't clear what it's a monument to.'

'It was built to commemorate the conflagration which destroyed the old London,' Halder said.

'Great! Then if we knock it down, it could signal the start of new things for Ireland.' He looked for support from Kelly, but he was sitting, eyes glazed, clutching his whiskey glass.

'Excellent!' Halder said. 'It is positively poetic. Perhaps your example will stir the ambitions of the rest of us. I came back from the funeral of our late friend, in the same carriage as

Andreas Scheu and Kropotkin. We were discussing the hostility and derision of the crowd. It concerned Scheu greatly. He complained that anarchists were being seduced by soft living. Here they are safe, can go about openly, publish newspapers, even proselytize. They preach, but do nothing. This feather-bedded image evokes only scorn from the proletariat. I must say that Kropotkin was lukewarm. But I agreed with Scheu that the time has come for the anarchists, and all who fight for freedom, to strike a blow which will kindle the imaginations of the masses, rouse them from their lethargy.'

'Excellent!' Monique cried, her eyes shining. 'When shall it be?'

'Wait a minute,' McCafferty objected. 'I thought that you guys could only stay in England if you kept quiet.'

'That is the fallacy we have all fallen into,' Halder said. 'We will only be tolerated by the authorities on those terms. But, if we continue to abide by them, we might as well be in prison. May I point out that the unfortunate Kelly, who is a Fenian, lives openly in England with his family? Yet he is prepared to assist you in demolishing the Monument.'

'That's different,' McCafferty said. 'I know about these things. He's a British citizen, we're not.'

'I cannot think that it would exempt him from the consequences of his crime.' Halder looked around the room, his face beaming. 'My friends, the time for action has arrived. We must prepare a plan!'

'My Paw was going to kidnap the Prince of Wales,' McCafferty said thoughtfully. 'I guess Captain Mackey must have talked him out of it. He explained it all to me, once. I can't remember it now, but he made it sound real easy.'

'That sounds promising,' Halder said. 'He is frequently seen in public places, and it is said that he is given to making indiscreet journeys, at night. What do you think, Monique?'

'I say yes!'

'Schelling?'

'It seems dull. But we would have to forcibly take him from his guards . . . Yes, why not?'

'Grillon?'

'I agree.'

159

Santo got to his feet. 'I would not wish to have my name soiled by such an unimportant deed,' he said, and stalked out of the room.

'Who shall be charged to plan the operation?' Halder asked.

'I shall need Hans to help me, with blowing up the Monument,' McCafferty said.

'Then that leaves Monique and Paul. An excellent team! I am sure that the project will be crowned with success.' He beamed around once more, and went out. As he did so, Kelly slowly keeled over, and fell to the floor.

Schelling licked his lips in anticipation. 'Now we can proceed,' he said. 'Who knows which is the bad tooth?'

No one could tell him, so Halder's maid was summomed. She said that it was one of the two molars in the right jaw, she was not sure which. They rolled Kelly on to his back and held open his mouth. With the aid of a candle, they inspected the area. Certainly, the gum was even more inflamed. When they poked it, Kelly stirred and groaned.

'I think it must be the first one,' Schelling said. 'Let me get some tools.'

In a few moments, he was back with a small pair of pincers, and some broad-nosed pliers. He pulled Kelly's jaw down, and tried to manoeuvre the pincers inside his mouth. He could just get the closed pincers in, but could not then open them.

'Have you any smaller ones?' Morton asked.

'No. It will have to be the pliers. That is a pity. They will slip off the tooth more easily. Perhaps I should loosen it first, with a hammer and chisel.'

'Hell, no! I need the guy,' McCafferty protested. 'You'll break his jaw!'

Schelling snorted in contempt, then got the pliers on to the front molar. 'Hold his head,' he said to McCafferty.

'No, siree! I ain't no good with blood.'

'Grillon, you do so.'

Morton crouched beside Kelly, and grasped either side of his head. Schelling hooked his thumb behind Kelly's bottom teeth and pulled. The pliers slipped off the tooth, and trapped Schelling's finger. He cursed violently, and sucked at the rapidly-forming blood-blister.

'Hold him again,' he ordered.

This time, he tried to lever the tooth from side to side, but it remained rock solid. Now Kelly was groaning in his drunken stupor. This seemed to enrage Schelling. He wedged a small piece of wood in Kelly's cheek, to keep the jaw open. Then, putting his foot on Kelly's shoulder, began to pull at the tooth. Again the pliers slipped, this time cutting a weal on Kelly's upper lip. Schelling swore.

'He is not a man, he is a hippopotamus!' he said. 'Grillon, brace your feet against the table and hold his feet.'

With the inert body thus anchored, Schelling knelt at Kelly's head and took hold of the tooth once more. Morton could feel the tug of the pliers. Thank God that Kelly was insensible! Certain that he had got a firm hold, Schelling was yanking the tooth from side to side. Blood dribbled from Kelly's mouth.

'He will suffocate,' Morton warned.

Schelling took no notice. He got into a crouching position, both hands on the pliers, and pulled. Kelly's whole body was lifted from the ground. It hung there for a long second; then there was a crack, Schelling was catapulted against the wall, the tooth in his pliers.

'You see!' he shouted triumphantly. 'I said I could do it!' He turned the tooth over in his fingers. 'It does not seem rotten to me. Do you think we should take out the other one, also?'

The bells of scores of churches, it seemed, were clashing and clamouring for morning service, as Catherine walked through the narrow streets towards Bragg's lodgings in Tan House Lane. She half hoped that he would not be at home. Her battered self-esteem had suffered enough recently. When she had finally got the delivery boy's bicycle back to the shop, the previous afternoon, Mr Long had been really quite abusive. Her assertion that she was a reporter had not been believed. Even when she had produced her *City Press* card, he had declined to accept her plea of *force majeure*. No funeral, even that of an anarchist – particularly that of an anarchist – could justify the mischief caused to his business by her purloining the vehicle. Nevertheless, he had been somewhat mollified when she pressed two pounds on him, as compensation. And he had been positively mortified when she pointed out the salacious interpretation that could be placed on his advertisement. All in all, she felt the honours in the conflict lay with her.

She rang the bell, and Mrs Jenks took her through to the back garden, where Bragg was cutting the patch of lawn with hedging shears.

'I am sorry to disturb you on a Sunday, sergeant,' she said brightly.

'That's all right, miss. I could do with a pipe.' He fumbled in a jacket hanging on the wall, and found his pipe and tobacco pouch.

'I was wondering if you knew anything about anarchists,' Catherine began.

'That's a bit out of your usual field, isn't it?' he asked in a neutral voice.

'It is a matter of personal interest to me.'

'Not thinking of joining them, are you?'

'Of course not!'

Was there a constraint in his manner, she wondered? He was certainly abnormally preoccupied with his pipe; peering into the bowl and poking at the half-consumed contents with his finger. But, last time they had met, he had been very short with her. Perhaps he was embarrassed by her visit.

'I followed a funeral, yesterday,' she said, 'from the City to Finchley cemetery.'

'Did you, now?'

'The man being buried was named Martia Bourdin. The crowd were very hostile, saying that he had been an anarchist.'

'Were they? Still, I expect even anarchists have to be buried.'

He was defensive, holding her off. Not at all the Sergeant Bragg she had come to know.

'I am certain that I saw James there,' she said.

'Morton? Where?'

There was no real surprise in the response. Why not?

'In one of the carriages, and also in the cemetery.'

'And what did he have to say for himself?'

'I could not speak to him. The crowd was kept well away from the graveside, by the police.'

162

Bragg eyed her sceptically. 'Are you sure it was Morton?'

'Of course I am! How could I be mistaken?'

'I see.' Bragg stuck the pipe in his mouth and, cupping the flame with his hands, applied a match to it.

'You do not believe me!'

He flicked the spent match into the grass. 'Well, I thought of several things he might have done, but I never imagined him joining the anarchists.'

'I assure you, sergeant, that I am not imagining it.'

'So, why have you come to me?'

'After the funeral was over, I spoke to the priest who had officiated. He told me that the address on the burial order was 23 Mansell Street.'

Bragg appeared to ponder the information. 'Even if you are right,' he said at length, 'it is obvious that Morton was there voluntarily. I take it you are not suggesting that he was under any kind of duress.'

'No.' Catherine recalled the face of the young woman under the veil. Well, she would not humble herself to the extent of telling Sergeant Bragg about her!

'Then what do you want me to do?'

'I want you to answer me a question honestly, without evasion.'

'Oh?' Bragg was watching her warily.

'Are you and James conducting any kind of covert operation, similar to the one concerning the counterfeit notes?'

'No, we are not.'

The answer was unequivocal enough, but had there been the faintest pause, before he gave it?

'I see.'

'I cannot understand your interest,' Bragg said. 'After all, you have refused his offer of marriage. I would have thought that was an end of it.'

'We are still friends.'

'I suppose that is your business.' Bragg knocked his pipe out, and made to resume work.

Catherine felt the familiar stirrings of dejection and helplessness. 'Could you go to meet him?' she asked. 'I wish to be sure that he is all right.'

163

'Whatever reason would I have? No one has broken the law.'

'At the very least, he is missing from the police force,' Catherine declared spiritedly.

'Not any more, he isn't. Inspector Cotton has had him removed from the roster.'

Catherine fought against her growing despondency. These two had formed so great a part of her life, over the last two years. She had to hold on to them. She could not start afresh.

'Then, if you will not look for him, I will!' she said.

'You don't want to get mixed up with that sort of riff-raff,' Bragg said in a fatherly tone. 'These anarchists are erratic, unbalanced people. You could easily come to harm.'

'What would that matter?' The phrase seemed to have been haunting her for days. 'In any case, the funeral was public enough. The anarchists might welcome some additional publicity.'

Bragg sighed. 'You are a headstrong young woman,' he said. 'All right, leave it to me. I will see what I can do.'

Morton woke early, the following morning. He decided that he ought to get a report to Redman, through Bragg, as soon as possible. It could be that Special Branch's interest would continue despite Corbin's death, if they took the threat to kidnap the Prince of Wales seriously. And, of course, there was always the shadowy figure in the tunnel to consider . . . What if he were to leave the cell, make a final report to Redman and return to normal life? He would be able to say that the Monument was to be blown up, but not when; that there was a plan to kidnap the Prince of Wales, but neither where nor when. That would be useless. And, once he had defected, the cell could move on, seek other targets. The only sensible action would be to surround the houses and arrest everyone. But there were no charges that could be brought . . . What about the murder of Corbin? That might be stretched, with incitement and complicity charges, to cover them all. But Redman was sure to oppose it, his Branch's involvement would become all too clear. No, he would have to stick to his task until he knew every detail of their plans.

He got up. Kelly was snoring loudly; he did not even stir as Morton washed and dressed. He had stayed in bed for most of Sunday, nursing a thick head and a swollen jaw. But he had had to admit that Schelling's rough surgery had cured his toothache. McCafferty was dreaming, muttering and turning his head from side to side. Morton opened the door quietly and went into the street. A light rain was falling, driven into his face by the strong east wind. He had a sudden impulse to nip up to his rooms, and get his overcoat. He could always say that he had bought it at a second-hand clothes stall . . . At this time in the morning? Ridiculous! He contented himself with a quick stroll, round the Tower and back again.

When he returned he found breakfast laid in the mess-room. Ugh! Cheese and cold ham again! He was longing for some crispy bacon and fried eggs, perhaps some devilled kidneys or kedgeree . . . Damn Redman to hell!

Before long, the others drifted down, Kelly the last of them. He had not yet shaved, and looked old and spent.

'Is your mouth still sore?' Morton asked.

'It's as tender as a boil on a baby's arse, so it is.'

'Soon it will be better,' Schelling said genially. 'You will be able to blow up your Monument a happy man!'

'I went over there yesterday afternoon, Pat,' McCafferty said. 'There's a room in the plinth, and steps up inside the column. I hung around till they closed down. There's only a wooden door on the east side, held with a padlock. It should be a cinch.'

Kelly was drinking some milky tea, sluicing it audibly through the gap left by the molar. 'Good,' he grunted.

'But we shall have to take care. I've been giving thought to what the little lady said. We don't want to hurt any civilians. So I guess we shouldn't use more dynamite than we need.'

'It is an interesting problem,' Schelling said thoughtfully. 'Not that I would worry about a few score of the bourgeoisie, but technically it is a challenge.' He paused, considering. 'I have it!' He slapped his thigh. 'When Bourdin and I were searching for quarries from which to steal explosives, we stumbled on an abandoned brick-works. It had a tall chimney, much like your Monument. Why do we not take some dynamite and use it for a practice?'

165

'What d'you think, Pat?' McCafferty asked.

'That's not a bad idea.' Kelly seemed to be reviving. He was even gingerly chewing some cheese and bread.

'I shall have to look at the map. I have forgotten where it was, but I will find it. Shall we go tomorrow?'

'Great!' McCafferty said excitedly. 'You want to come too, Paul?'

'If Monique will release me from plotting the capture of the Prince of Wales.'

'We shall have to find the occasion first,' Monique said. 'Yesterday, in the afternoon, I went to the Tower Bridge. It is said that the Prince of Wales will declare it open. I spoke to the watchman, but he said it will not be finished for two months.' She put down her coffee cup and lit a Caporal.

'Then we will all four go, at first light,' Schelling said.

'I think the best plan is for me to seduce him,' Monique said reflectively.

'Who?' Kelly asked.

'The Prince of Wales, of course! I could stand at the gate of his palace, he would notice me, *et voilà*! When he took me to his bed, I would stab him.'

'Hold on, little lady,' McCafferty said. 'The guy is an old man, he's not going to fall for that.'

'He is also a satyr.'

'He can have any woman,' Santo declared. 'You are not beautiful.'

Monique shot him a venomous look.

'Good morning! I see that you are hard at work.' Halder beamed all around, then took a chair.

'We are considering the best way to carry off the Prince of Wales,' Morton said diplomatically.

'Yes . . . He is less well guarded than the Queen, of course. But it would be well to avoid a ceremonial occasion.'

'Have we any spies in his palace?' Monique demanded brusquely.

'None, I think,' Halder said.

'Then we need information about where he is to be.'

'Why don't you read the newspapers?' Kelly asked. 'Sure it'll all be there, in the Court circular.'

'Do you have any newspapers, Halder?' Morton asked.

'No. Only out-of-date German ones, I fear.'

'They have newspapers in the libraries,' McCafferty chipped in. 'I read scores of them, when I was looking up about my Paw. And sometimes they have a news report about the movements of the royal family, weeks ahead.'

'Excellent,' Morton said. 'Monique, you could go to White-chapel library. It is not far – next to the tailor's shop. I will try to find another, to make more speed.'

'Your zeal is most gratifying,' Halder said, his glance drifting towards Kelly. 'And how is it that you know about things like the Court circular, Kelly?'

'Just because you are downtrodden, you don't have to be ignorant as well. My wife's had schooling, she reads the paper to me.'

Halder laughed expansively. 'You Irish are a most unfathom-able race. You seek to expel the English in the name of Catholicism and the Pope; yet it was Pope Adrian IV who persuaded Henry Plantagenet to subdue the unruly Irish, and bring their church to heel.'

'That was a long time ago,' Kelly muttered.

'And you claim to be a downtrodden Irishman, who are a trusted employee of the English, with a home, a wife, children?'

'My family in Ireland are kept down, all right,' Kelly said. 'They're peasants because that's the way the British want it. How would you like to bring up a family on a labourer's wage of twelve shillings a week?'

'But not everyone is a labourer,' Halder murmured.

'No. The landlords are comfortable all right. They are worse than the British, so they are – forcing their tenants to fortify their houses against eviction. And for nothing more because they are refusing to pay their rent!'

'As I said, it is a strange country!' Halder's smile faded. 'But there are many strange things, not least in the New World.'

At the change of tone, McCafferty jerked alert.

'You will know,' Halder went on smoothly, 'that for the sake of our security, I enquire into the background of everyone who is sent to us. After all, Corbin could have destroyed us, had he remained undetected. It is a matter of regret that, even with the

167

magnetic telegraph, the results of enquiries made in America take a long time to reach us.'

'Hey! What is this?' McCafferty blustered. 'You've seen the letter the Brotherhood gave me.'

'Of course,' Halder said soothingly. 'But these things can be forged.'

'Hell! I've been keeping this two-bit dump going with my money! You weren't slow in getting hold of that.'

Halder raised his hand. 'Our enquiries have confirmed the truth of your story, so far as it goes. But it is beyond doubt that you have been accepted by us – and perhaps the Fenian Brotherhood also – because you are your father's son.'

'So?' McCafferty said belligerently.

'It is when we come to look into the father, that we find he is not what he seems.'

McCafferty sprang to his feet, his fists clenched. 'What in hell do you mean?' he bellowed.

'Calm yourself, my friend. None of us can choose his parents; nor can one alter fact, however inconvenient . . . The so-called Captain John McCafferty was not a Southern gentleman, as he claimed. He was born in Ohio. In fact, he was a bartender on the Detroit to Milwaukee railway, at a place called Atwater East. Far from being a hero in the Confederate army, he does not appear to have figured in any recorded actions. There is no trace of his being in Morgan's guerrillas, nor of that unit's exploit with the steamboats. It seems that all these matters existed in John McCafferty's imagination only.'

McCafferty slumped to his chair, white-faced.

'After the American Civil War, in which he probably did take some small part, he resumed his bartending. It seems that he was an expert in an illegal game called Three-Card Monte, and he returned to this, also. There are several convictions on record against him. He persisted in it, however, and it was his fear of imminent arrest that drove him to Europe, with Mackey Lomasney.'

'That's all of a piece with your man being late at Chester,' Kelly observed bitterly.

McCafferty looked across angrily. 'No one can say he wasn't

168

killed, with Captain Mackey, trying to blow up London bridge! It's in the newspapers!'

'That is so,' Halder said. 'And that is why you will continue to be accepted here. But it was necessary to put the facts before your comrades.'

'It sounds as if your father was born to be a loser,' Schelling said, with a sadistic smile.

'That's a lie!' McCafferty yelled. 'I'll show you!' He sprang up, overturning his chair, and marched out.

8

Morton strolled up to the entrance of the Guildhall library and paused. He looked around him, as if admiring the building. No one was tailing him. He felt a sense of profound relief. Ever since the murder of Corbin, he had lived with the image of Schelling's great hands clamping themselves round his own throat. Not that he need worry this morning. He was playing the part of a perfectly ordinary terrorist, planning a world-shattering outrage.

He went into the library, and took down recent copies of *The Times*. His immediate aim was to work out a comprehensive plan. He was reasonably sure of being able to gain Monique's acceptance – if only because she was unlikely to evolve a coherent scheme by herself. But any plan he proposed must be convincing. The others would weigh every factor critically, test it against their experience. His only advantages were a knowledge of the terrain, and of the Prince's habits, neither of which he dared reveal. Further, the plan must have elements beyond an intrinsic probability of success. It must draw all the members of the cell into participating, one way or another. And it must take place where the conspirators could be apprehended. He would then have discharged all the obligations he felt were on him, for no one could say that conspiring to kidnap the Prince of Wales was not a crime. And, although Monique was the only French citizen left among them, Redman would have his stick to beat the French government with. Above all, Morton himself would be able to get back to a normal life.

He started with a paper dated one month earlier, and began

to read forwards, skipping through the columns, seeking inspiration. What was he looking for? Halder had been right, a ceremonial occasion would be useless for their purposes, if not for Redman's. Yet Monique's scenario – capturing the Prince on some nocturnal visit to a lady-love – while all too likely to succeed, was too unpredictable to allow the arrest of the anarchists to be planned. There would be plenty of opportunities, once the Season began. It ought to be possible to work something out. The Prince would have to be there, of course, or no offence could be proved. Morton wondered if he would be told. That course had advantages and disadvantages. It was a situation that the man might relish – a spark of excitement in a meaningless social round. But, if he knew, he could hardly be expected to act normally. He was not an actor. And if the conspirators became suspicious . . . Morton toyed briefly with the idea of getting an actor to play the Prince, then dismissed it. No one else would act naturally, then.

So he was left with an informal occasion, something like a ball. It was hardly ideal. For a start, no one could gain entrance without a ticket. That meant the kidnap attempt would have to be staged in the street – a night-time street cluttered with carriages. It was hardly attractive from either viewpoint. The same would be true of a garden-party, though apprehension of the criminals would be easier in daylight. A drum would be more satisfactory. It was much less formal. Hundreds of people might pass through the house in an evening – dropping in to see and be seen, squeezing through the crush to find friends, or a glass of champagne, then off to another party. One could introduce the conspirators easily enough, throw a police cordon round the house and . . . and have a complete shambles on one's hands! Even if it were successful, the host and hostess would be scandalized to learn that the police had deliberately planned to wreck their party! Perhaps a race meeting would be better. Everyone knew of the Prince's passion for racing; the conspirators would not be suspicious. And there would be no difficulty in their getting access to the course. But there were problems associated with an open rural, wooded area, like Goodwood. Anyway, the race meetings that Society attended were still weeks away. If he were to remain in control of the operation, he must come up with a plan soon. He scanned issue after issue of the newspaper, without finding anything. Then his eye fell on an item in the Court circular. Was this what he was looking for? It was not an occasion as such, which was to the good. The location was less than ideal, but it was contain- able . . . Yes, it would suffice. Glancing around him, to ascertain that he was not overlooked, Morton began to scribble a long note to Bragg.

Morton got back to Mansell Street in mid-afternoon. The house was quiet, innocuous-seeming. McCafferty and Kelly had gone out. Morton lay down on his bed to think, and soon drifted into a doze. He started awake, to find that Monique was standing over him, smiling coquettishly. She was wearing her purple blouse, her hair was freshly washed, and a pleasant perfume overlay the smell of cigarettes. She sat beside him on the bed, and gazed into his face. The purple blouse made her complexion less sallow, the trace of lip-salve gave her teeth a new whiteness . . . She was really rather attractive.

'I am so lonely, Paul, and a little afraid,' she said softly. 'Will you come and sleep with me in my room?'

She leaned forward, and Morton could see the heaviness of her breasts through the thin silk.

'I . . . I would have to ask the others,' he said idiotically.

'I know they would not mind.' She was almost crooning now. 'After all, soon we will be in Russia, living together as if we were married.'

Morton could feel a tumescence growing in his trousers.

'I suppose so,' he mumbled.

'It will not all be a pretence . . . I long to look at you naked, to see your strong body, to press my breasts against the hardness of your chest.'

Morton tried to control his clamouring concupiscence. 'Soon, Monique, it will be soon,' he said.

'Hold me, Paul. Tell me I have no need to be afraid.'

He took her by the shoulders. As he did so, she dropped her hand to his crotch.

172

'See!' she cried delightedly. 'You desire me, you wish to possess my body. Why should not the Prince of Wales, also?'

Morton thrust her away, suddenly angry. 'We are not here to play games, Monique,' he said.

'I was not playing with you.' There was something of the old contempt in her tone. 'I was showing you what I believe – that any woman can entice any man. They are so gross.'

Morton sat up and forced a shamefaced laugh. 'You must remember that our aim is to kidnap the Prince, and carry him away as a hostage. We are not trying to kill him.' He expected Monique to denounce the pusillanimity of his remark, but she did not. Instead, she gave an inward smile and walked to the window, where her figure was outlined against the light.

'So you have a plan?' she said.

'I have discovered that the Prince and Princess of Wales will travel by train to Sandringham, on Friday.'

'Where is that?'

'In the east of the country. He has a château there.'

'Ah.'

'The railway station he will depart from is Liverpool Street, a little to the north of us. I have looked at the map. To the east of the station is a warren of old, tumbledown alleys. If we could get him across Bishopsgate Street, we could hide him there. I think that we should put this forward as the basis for our plan; see what the others think about it.'

She walked towards him, hands outstretched.

'And, if I agree, will you kiss me?'

'Yes.'

'Then I do agree.'

Morton put up his face to her, as she came close. She smiled provocatively and bent over him, their lips almost touching. Then she straightened, smacked him lightly on the cheek, and skipped out laughing.

Catherine laid down her pen and looked critically at what she had written. It was a mere recital of dead facts, there was no life in it, nothing to catch the attention of the reader. If she were honest, she had to admit that she had not written anything

173

interesting for ages. She seemed to have lost her enjoyment of life, and a sour gloom had settled on her work. Well, she was doing no good here. She might as well go home . . . Five o'clock. For the next hour the omnibuses would be crammed with odoriferous, irritable people. She could not face that. But she must get out into the air. She put on her coat and crept downstairs.

It was absurd, she thought, to be sneaking away early. What on earth was the matter with her? She ought to be on top of the world. And Sergeant Bragg had promised to find James, so there was nothing to worry about . . . But he had only promised because she had threatened to go there herself. He had been very sceptical and scathing, when she had told him that she'd seen James. But then, he had been hostile ever since she had admitted to rejecting James's proposal of marriage. Well, Bragg was not going to run her life. She had taken her destiny in her own hands from the moment she left school, and that was how it would stay.

She looked about her. She was at the Bank crossing, already a surging tangle of omnibuses and carts. She might as well continue eastwards. It would not be worth trying to struggle home yet. She followed a bowler-hatted man through the traffic, and began to walk up Cornhill . . . Whatever Bragg might say, she was convinced that James was a mere half-mile away. She wondered whether to go to his rooms, in Alderman's Walk, and enquire from Chambers if he had returned. Suddenly she knew, without any doubt, that he would not be there, that Bragg had done nothing. How ridiculous men were! Afraid of interfering in each other's precious freedom to do exactly as they liked. Well, she had no such inhibitions. It was inconsiderate in the extreme for James to behave in this way. She had a good mind to go and tell him so. But could she endure to meet his new wife? She checked in her walk. How idiotic she was! She had been so . . . so perplexed to see the woman in the carriage that she had not been thinking clearly. Bragg's hypothesis was that, having been rejected, James would seek solace in the arms of someone in Society. But this was no Society girl. She was positively middle-aged! And her hat could have been bought at any corner-shop milliner's. Catherine felt relief flooding through her. Perhaps the woman was no more than another mourner – she might even be the widow. She resumed her walk towards Aldgate, her pace quickening. There was really no reason why she should not call at the Mansell Street house . . . She heard her mother's voice enjoining modesty, decorous passivity. What of it? They were still friends . . . at the very least, she could enquire after his health.

Within a few minutes she found herself in Aldgate. It was a striking contrast to the City streets. The pavements were encumbered by butchers' stalls, with carcasses of lamb and geese in feather brushing her shoulder, as she sidled by. The buildings were old, their frontages irregular. They were tall and narrow, their gables jutting anarchically into the sky, like dirty broken teeth. Catherine shivered. She was letting her excitement run away with her. Even if the woman had nothing to do with James, there was no certainty that he would be in Mansell Street. Why on earth should he consort with anarchists, anyway? Yet he had been at the funeral; that she was certain of . . . She stood at the corner irresolute. But what had she to lose? She could at least probe the situation there. She turned and began to look for number 23.

Her ring on the bell was answered by a smartly-dressed maid.

'I should be pleased if your master could spare me a few moments,' Catherine said, passing over her card.

'Please wait.'

The reply was in a heavy German accent, but her face had been friendly and respectful. Catherine turned to gaze at the dreary houses of the street. How on earth could James bear to live in such a place?

'Please follow me.' The maid was standing back, holding the door for her. Catherine furtively straightened her jabot, and followed the maid into a long high-ceilinged room. From her rapid glance, it was over-furnished but comfortable; very much a working place.

'My dear Miss Marsden, how can I be of assistance?' A plump middle-aged man was bearing down on her, exuding *bonhomie*.

'I am preparing an article on *émigrés* in the City. I wondered if you would consent to be interviewed.'

175

The man smiled tolerantly. 'Then why come to me?'

'Believe it or not, this section of Mansell Street is actually within the Portsoken ward of the City.'

'I see. I shall be able to boast of that to my grandchildren!' He looked reflectively at her. 'Why not?' he said. 'Please take a seat.'

He gestured to an armchair beside his desk.

'I am afraid that I do not know your name, sir.'

'Do you not?'

He was fencing with her, Catherine thought. Was that significant? Or was it the natural caution of a foreigner being questioned by the press?

'I can assure you,' she said, 'that my article will be purely factual and objective. I am not concerned to take sides . . . But I am particularly interested in the anarchists.'

Another benign smile.

'Again, why come to me?' he asked.

'I am aware that a man called Martial Bourdin was buried in Finchley cemetery, last Saturday. It seems that he was a well-known anarchist. The burial order gave this address as his residence.'

'I see!' He laughed gleefully. 'An amusing, if inaccurate, piece of detection! I am afraid that any foreigner is likely to be regarded as an anarchist, because of the hysteria whipped up by the Continental governments for their own ends.'

'What ends are they?' Catherine asked, opening her pad.

'The maintenance of the *status quo* – which means keeping their peoples disenfranchised and powerless.'

'You have come here from Germany?'

'I can see that I shall have to confess all!' he said with a delighted laugh. 'My name is Franz Halder. I am a Social Democrat, and was a prominent politician in Bavaria. When I was a boy it was a relaxed, tolerant, Catholic state. But, after the Franco-Prussian war, the iron hand of Protestant Prussia was laid on us. Ludwig II of Bavaria was graciously allowed to proclaim the foundation of the new German Reich – it was the last meaningful act of his life.'

'But I thought all Germans welcomed the consolidation of the states,' Catherine said.

176

'By no means. We find ourselves in a militaristic society, where might rides rough-shod over the will of the people. It is worse under Wilhelm II than it was under Bismarck. Almost his first act, on assuming the imperial purple, was to propose a large increase in the army. My party, with the progressives and the centre party, succeeded in blocking this in the Reichstag. What happened? The Reichstag was dissolved, and the army increased anyway.'

Catherine dutifully recorded his words. The important thing was to get him talking freely. She could work around to what she wanted to know later.

'Why did you flee from Germany?' she asked.

Halder beamed at her. 'I must be careful not to incriminate myself!' he said. 'It was put about that I was implicated in an attempt to assassinate the Kaiser. It was a slander, of course, disseminated by my enemies. Nevertheless, I did not stay to debate the point!'

'But why come to Britain? After all, our royal family originated in Germany.'

'Fortunately, Britain and its empire are ruled by Parliament; the will of the sovereign holds little sway . . . It is strange that Britain and Germany are moving in opposite directions, is it not?'

'You seem to be gambling on the interests of Britain and Germany never coinciding.'

Halder smiled. 'You think very deeply, young lady . . . No. I think there is no danger there. Britain has a proud record of supporting oppressed peoples; and not only because it has been to her advantage.'

Catherine changed tack. 'Is it not correct that anarchists want to destroy society as it is?'

Halder gave a somewhat theatrical sigh. 'That is a gross over-simplification,' he said. 'In Britain, for instance, you tend to think of Russia as a country under constant terrorist attack by anarchists. It is a fact, however, that there is a constitutional party in Russia, the Narodniki, which openly advocates anarchist principles.'

'Then, why are other governments afraid of anarchists?'

'Because they advocate change, and any change is anathema to a ruling élite.'

'Was Martial Bourdin an anarchist?' Catherine asked.

'Indeed, no! I would say that he was a-political.'

'I gather that he was killed by a bomb, which he was throwing.'

'Is that what is being said? How absurd!' Halder exclaimed deprecatingly. 'Martial was a talented marine engineer from Nantes. He had come to London to carry out research. He was trying to develop a small rocket which could fire a line out to a vessel in distress. You will appreciate that the existing apparatus is cumbersome, and can only be used from a fixed point. Bourdin had designed a rocket which could be discharged from a tube held over the shoulder. Had he been successful, it would have saved untold numbers of lives. Unfortunately, there was some malfunction in the prototype. It appears that the rocket was not released from the tube, but exploded in his hands . . . A great tragedy. And now, young lady, I must deny myself the pleasure of your company. I have a pamphlet to finish.'

Catherine took her leave. It had all been very pat and good-tempered. Halder had succeeded in telling her absolutely nothing. But one thing she was convinced of – he had been lying his head off.

At ten o'clock next morning, Morton found himself tramping the countryside of his native Kent. Kelly and Schelling, as the experts, were striding ahead, deep in technical discussion. A morose McCafferty walked at Morton's elbow. Inexplicably, Morton's own mood had lightened. Perhaps the sense that he would have some control over events was contributing. Or it might simply be that the wind had swung to the south, and the skies had cleared. Whatever the reason, there was a spring in his step, a pervasive feeling of optimism. That could be danger-ous, he told himself; he must curb his exuberance, lest it betray him.

They followed a vestigial cart-track into a wooded area. The sun was thrusting through the lime-green canopy of new leaves, the birds fluttered and sang. It was good to be back in the country, with the crackle of dead bracken beneath his feet. Perhaps his future did lie at the Priory, Morton thought. He might be able to find a role for himself there, without being so insensitive as to upset the family convention that his invalid brother was running the estates . . . No. That would never be possible. Even on a weekend visit, he had to watch his tongue. An incautious remark about the crops would cause his mother to snap at him. It must have been agonizing for his parents. It was over nine years, now, since his elder brother had been wounded in a colonial skirmish; shot in the back and paralysed from the waist down. For nine years, Edwin had fought resentfully against his incapacity, plagued by minor illnesses, confined to his rooms on all but the balmiest days. It was tragic. Yet Morton had only to set foot there – to see the lack of tight control over the farming, the uneconomic policies still being pursued – and exasperation would well up inside him. It was obvious to everyone that he would inherit the estates, that the Morton line could only survive through him. But no one would acknowledge it. He was still treated as a younger son, kept at arm's length. No, he could not go back, while Edwin lived. At the beginning of the year, it had seemed as if a resolution of the impasse was at hand. Edwin had contracted bronchitis, which turned to pneumonia. He had not been expected to live; Morton had seen it in his mother's eyes. He had gone down whenever he could, sat with his brother through long wakeful nights, felt his bitter stare. It was only the force of Edwin's resentment that had kept him alive, it seemed. Now he had recovered again, and things were back to their irksome norm; which meant that James's place was still in the police force.

Schelling and Kelly had halted, and were beckoning impatiently. Over the brow of a low hill, Morton could see a stout brick chimney towering above a ramshackle huddle of buildings.

'This is it,' Schelling shouted exultantly. 'It is just as I remembered it.'

'I guess it's a mite different from the Monument,' McCafferty said sourly.

'But it will be perfect for our rehearsal. Come and see!'

Schelling led them down the slope. Everything seemed

179

dejected and desolate. A monument to failure, a casualty of the economic strife which had depopulated the countryside. Brambles had invaded the yard, ash plants taken hold on the mossy roofs. Schelling had gone into the kiln, and was crouching at the base of the chimney.

'The kiln walls are not strong,' he said. 'But look at the thickness of the chimney!'

Morton crawled through the flue, until he could see a circle of blue far above him. 'It must be at least two metres,' he said.

Kelly was peering at the brickwork, scratching his nose.

'Now, if I was to bring that down,' he said, 'I would drill some holes on this side, then shove the dynamite in. But, sure, we can't do that.'

'Anyways, the plinth of the Monument is stone,' McCafferty objected peevishly.

'I did not say that this was identical,' Schelling replied, 'but it will help us to decide what we should do. It was you who said that there were to be no casualties.'

McCafferty shrugged. 'I guess so.'

'It should be possible to so fire the explosive that the column will fall westwards, along Arthur Street. I suggest that we place it as we would a mine to bring down a fortification.'

'And how's that?'

'Instead of blowing up the column, we should destroy the western wall of the chamber. Once the Monument is not supported on that side, it will topple over.'

'I guess that makes sense.'

'But half the force will go back into the chamber, and up the stairway,' Kelly said.

'That is why we are here. We have brought only twenty sticks of dynamite. Four times that number are remaining. For our rehearsal, I think that we should place the dynamite in the flue aperture of the chimney. So part of the force will be wasted here, also. Will you prepare the charges, Patrick?'

Kelly opened the canvas bag he had brought, and took out four bundles of dynamite. He inserted the blasting caps, then spliced the individual fuses to a master fuse, which he ran out of the kiln and over the hill. They all lay prone beside him, below the crest.

180

'Would you want to light the thing yourself, Lee?' he asked.

McCafferty's face brightened. 'Yeah, I guess I ought.' He fished in his pocket for a box of matches.

'Remember,' Schelling warned, 'you must keep your heads down.'

McCafferty propped the end of the fuse on a piece of wood, then struck a match. He cupped the flame till it burned steadily, then eased it towards the fuse. There was a sudden hissing spurt. A trail of sparks leapt to the crest and was gone. There was an eerie silence. Even the birds seemed to have stopped singing. It was incredible how quickly the fuse had burned, Morton thought, far faster than he had expected. But why had nothing happened? It should have reached the dynamite long ago. He levered himself on to his elbows to look, then felt a powerful shove between the shoulder blades.

'Fool!' Schelling hissed.

At that moment, there was an enormous detonation; the ground shook, a wave of dust-laden air rushed over them. Debris had been hurled skywards, and was crashing down around them . . . Then there was stillness.

Morton raised his head. The chimney still poked skywards above the shattered saplings.

'Hey! You guys!' McCafferty was sitting up, holding a piece of brick. 'This thing missed me – by six inches! I guess that's some kind of omen. Let's go see!'

They scrambled down the slope. The kiln had been blown to smithereens, only a few jagged remnants stuck up from the foundations. A great hole had been torn in the side of the chimney.

'Glory be to God!' Kelly exclaimed. 'It will never stay up now. Will we put it out of its misery, so?'

'No! We must escape. It will have been heard.' Schelling was shaking the dust from his clothes. 'Come!'

They ran back down the cart-track and took the road to the station. They were laughing and joking like a bunch of naughty schoolboys, Morton thought. It was evident that Kelly and Schelling were satisfied with the results of their exploit. Well might they be. That four times such terrifying power should be detonated in a London street was unimaginable. But there was no doubt that they intended it to happen. The only question remaining was when.

Bragg paused on the top landing of New Scotland Yard, and mopped his brow. The sudden warm spell had caught him in two minds, as usual. It had been tempting to shed his thick winter clothes, wear something lighter. But there was no heat in the soil yet, the nights would still be cold. Anyway, in a couple of days it could be hailing again. Meanwhile he sweltered. He went up the final flight of stairs, and knocked on Redman's door.

'Ah, Bragg. Sit down, will you? Have you something for me?'

He was amiable, almost effusive, Bragg thought. But, for a ruthless devil like Redman, it could not be easy to surrender the initiative, sit around waiting for crumbs of information. Bragg had the uneasy feeling that he would pay for humiliating him, some day.

'I have another report from Morton.' Bragg took the letter from his pocket, and tossed it on Redman's desk.

He read it carefully, nodding to himself from time to time, then looked up.

'Morton is living up to my expectations,' he remarked. 'Have you shown this to Sir William?'

Bragg was not going to parade the Commissioner's weak-kneed vacillations before Special Branch. 'No,' he said. 'He was not in his room, and I thought this was too important to wait.'

'Good, good! Now, let us see how we can exploit the situation.'

'You would not let it go ahead, surely to God?' Bragg exclaimed.

'Why not?'

'But, suppose the Prince were hurt? He might even be killed!'

'Would that be much of a loss? He is excessively pro-French; and he has a dangerous gift for rubbing his nephew, the Kaiser, up the wrong way.'

'I will not stand for your needlessly risking his life,' Bragg said firmly.

'They are only planning to take him hostage! Anyway, the

decision is out of our hands. This is a matter for the politicians. Let us walk round to the Home Office, and see what Asquith has to say about it.'

They waited for half an hour in a lofty stone corridor, with busy clerks brushing past them. Then they were ushered into the Home Secretary's office. He greeted Redman abstractedly, and gestured them to chairs.

'What is troubling you now, Major?' he asked in a carefully modulated voice.

'We have uncovered a plot to kidnap the Prince of Wales, sir.'

An indulgent smile formed on Asquith's lips. 'I see. And, what credence can we give to this information?'

'The highest possible degree, sir.'

'Hmn . . . Might one enquire as to the identity of your informant?'

'He is a detective constable of the City of London force, on temporary secondment to Special Branch, sir.'

'Ah! A detective constable, no less.'

Bragg felt like knocking the supercilious look from the man's face.

'He is an educated man,' he said gruffly. 'He has a Cambridge degree and, what's more, he is nobody's fool.'

'You must he speaking of General Morton's son, then.'

'Yes, sir.'

'And does your information go further than a bald statement of intent, as it were?'

Redman passed Morton's letter over. 'He has infiltrated an anarchist cell, sir,' he said, 'been accepted as one of them. It seems that he has been given responsibility for planning the operation, which is just how we would want it.'

'I see.' Asquith skimmed through the letter quickly, then reread it in visible concern. He put it down and gazed out of the window, his brow furrowed.

'This is clearly a matter for the Prime Minister,' he said at length. 'It is fortunate that he is in Downing Street today . . . If you would wait for me outside, I will sign a few letters while the carriage is coming.' He rang a bell on his desk, then folded Morton's letter and put it in his pocket.

Bragg and Redman kicked their heels together, for twenty

183

minutes. It was like a truce in a long war, Bragg thought. They were co-operating because they had to; but he could never bring himself to accept Redman's methods. Yet their aims ought to have been the same – to ensure that ordinary law-abiding citizens could live their lives in peace and safety.

At length Asquith emerged, and a brougham whisked them round the corner into Downing Street. They could have walked it in five minutes, Bragg decided; but the Home Secretary had no doubt been consulting his officials, working out how to handle the affair.

Once in number ten, Bragg and Redman were kept waiting in an ante-room, while Asquith saw the Prime Minister. Although Lord Rosebery had held that office for only a few weeks, Bragg had dealt with him some two years earlier, when he was Foreign Secretary. He knew that the urbane horse-racing image concealed an incisive brain and a masterful will. Then a clerk hurried out, returning, after what seemed an age, with a tall, distinguished-looking man. Redman nudged Bragg.

'That's Lord Kimberley, the Foreign Secretary,' he said with satisfaction. 'There'll be fur flying before long!'

After ten minutes – just time enough for Kimberley to absorb the letter – Redman and Bragg were ushered into the Prime Minister's room. Rosebery nodded at Bragg.

'Good afternoon, sergeant,' he said. 'You and Constable Morton seem to have a flair for provoking international discord, though it is a new departure for you to be acting in concert with Major Redman!'

'I would hardly say "provoking", sir.'

'No . . . Of course not. Well, this is so serious a matter, that I felt everyone with responsibility – both political and executive – ought to consider it together. I must say that I face the problem in considerable perplexity. It is clear that Constable Morton is in favour of allowing the, er, project to go forward; on the basis that, if it is properly controlled, the Prince of Wales would be in no danger and the nest of conspirators could be eliminated. On the face of it, that is an attractive proposition, though perhaps a trifle simplistic.'

'As the minister most directly concerned,' Asquith broke in, 'I have grave doubts about such an approach. If the public became aware that we had used the heir to the throne in such a way, it might bring down the government – certainly would, if harm came to him.'

Rosebery pursed his lips. 'Well then, Major, why do you not simply arrest them all?'

'To begin with, sir,' Redman glanced warningly at Bragg, 'I do not know precisely where they are. Even if I did, there is not a lot we can do. We just have not the powers. These anarchists have a club of their own in Great Windmill Street – the Autonomie Club. As soon as we got a whiff of this plot, we raided it. We quietly took possession of the premises in the early evening. Whenever a member arrived, we admitted and detained him. But what else could we do? They all sat around, talking in German and laughing at us, till midnight. Then we had to let them go. There was no legal basis for holding them.'

'But now they are plotting to abduct the Prince. That, surely, is a crime?'

'I doubt if we could prove it, sir. We only have the word of a policeman for that. And you know the public don't care for *agents provocateurs*.'

'I suppose we could rush through a bill . . .'

'No, Prime Minister!' Asquith exclaimed. 'It would be electoral suicide. Even to propose such a measure would be to play into the hands of the Tories. We have always stood for freedom of speech, we have opened our arms to the oppressed of less fortunate lands. It would be inconceivable for a Liberal government to reverse that stance. Consider, also, how a future Tory government could apply such legislation. They could use it to suppress free speech, to portray liberal ideas as seditious. We might never get back into power again!'

'Yet, as I well know,' Rosebery said musingly, 'we are under constant pressure from foreign governments to expel their disaffected nationals. Might we not have something to gain in that area? It might be possible to enact legislation which merely curbed the activities of foreigners.' He picked up Morton's letter. 'This particular cell contains a Dutchman, a German, a Frenchwoman, an Italian, and a citizen of the United States. Surely there might be political advantage to be gained with those countries! What do you think, Kimberley?'

185

The Foreign Secretary cleared his throat. 'That is not a question I can answer simply, Prime Minister,' he said in a dry voice. 'We are in an exceedingly complicated and volatile situation. I would feel it extremely unwise to allow minor matters to influence policy-making.'

'I would hardly have thought the Prince of Wales would sympathize with such a view!'

Kimberley sniffed. 'Nevertheless, it is one that I would maintain,' he said pedantically. 'At the present time, France is striving to create a new sphere of influence, after the *débâcle* of the war with Prussia. I have, this morning, received a report of secret negotiations between France and Russia. It is said that France will make large loans to the Tsar, to help him re-build Russian industry and agriculture. No doubt the Tsar is attracted to this *entente* with France as a means of quelling the unrest amongst his subjects. But what will be the effect of such a policy? The Russian peasant has no money to buy grain or manufactures. So they will be unloaded on the world markets, to the detriment of our own producers.'

'Hmn . . .' Rosebery pondered. 'That would seem to suggest that our interests lie in a closer relationship with Germany – which would please the Queen. There are very many German refugees here; we could use this incident to pack them all off home.'

Kimberley leaned back in his chair, and fixed his eyes on the gasolier. 'You have, of course, great experience in foreign affairs, Prime Minister, yet I do not find myself taking your benign view of German intentions. Let me remind you of what the present Kaiser said, when he claimed a place in the sun for Germany: "A global policy the task, world-wide power the aim, the navy the means".'

'Surely, we need not begrudge them the odd slice of Africa?' Rosebery asked. 'Anyway, von Breberstein, the head of their Foreign Office, is hardly enthusiastic about the policy.'

'Perhaps not. But I am told that the head of the political section, von Holstein, is staking his career on supporting the Kaiser. And I would point out, Prime Minister, that "world-wide power" means dominance in Europe also.'

'Bismarck used to assure us that the alliance with Austria and

Italy was purely defensive,' Rosebery objected. 'And I, for one, believed him.'

'I am sure you are right. But the Kaiser is his own man now, and keen to demonstrate that his tutelage under Bismarck is over. It was not without significance, that Germany failed to renew its defensive alliance with Russia.'

'Perhaps, after defeating France, they now feel secure.'

'I am afraid that I place an altogether more serious interpretation on it,' Kimberley said gravely. 'Germany is not furiously building battleships to convey supplies to her colonies. Once her fleet begins to rival ours, can there be any doubt what the Kaiser's next move will be?'

'Hmn . . . Then it seems that you are advocating a continuance of our policy of splendid isolation.'

'It has served us well in the past, Prime Minister.'

'Very well . . . We seem to have strayed rather far from our original problem but, by our somewhat circuitous route, we seem to be approaching a solution. The question seems to have clarified itself into whether or not we are prepared to accept the domestic political consequences inherent in the plan put forward by Constable Morton. Before we take a decision as to what we will recommend to the Prince, perhaps we should have the views of the experts as to its feasibility.' He looked across at Redman.

'It is my belief that it could not be bettered, sir. I would arrange with the railway police for my officers to be present. So His Royal Highness could feel perfectly secure.'

Rosebery looked at his colleagues. 'Then, we are agreed. I will go to Marlborough House immediately. Obviously, I can only advise; but I am sure that the Prince would not submit to having his activities curtailed for the rest of his life. Constable Morton has asked that an advertisement be placed in the personal columns of *The Times*, should we decide to proceed. If His Royal Highness agrees, I will place it there myself.'

That evening found McCafferty sauntering moodily along Lower Thames Street. This would certainly be the best route, he decided; it was quiet, away from the traffic. Now what he needed was to find an alley leading up to the Monument itself. From here, all he could see was the golden urn at its top, poking up above the warehouses. He glanced at the river thronged with barges and steamers; and beyond them the dark bulwark of London Bridge. That was where his daddy's life had ended . . . Grillon had said that the attempt was a splendid gesture, that he had died a hero. The praise had made him feel warm inside. His father's example had given him something to live up to: a deed he must equal – or even surpass . . . But Halder's revelations had spoiled all that; made his Paw out to be a no-good sharper, freeloading his way to Europe to escape the law. Three-Card Monte! Up to that point he'd been prepared to call Halder a liar. But that was the clincher. It explained too many things in his childhood, for him to doubt it.

All those years he had believed his father's yarns as gospel truth; disregarded the sceptical twist of his mother's lip; ignored her angry outbursts over her husband's card playing. Three-Card Monte . . . When she had been widowed, he had interpreted her calm acceptance as reflecting her pride in his father's heroic death. The truth was that she was glad to be free . . . But why had she kept him in ignorance, all these years? Just the wry smile when he talked of his father's deeds. Maybe she thought it was best . . . Maybe it was, at the time. But now he felt cheated and betrayed. He'd had to come all this way, to find out that his father was a bum. Hell! There was no way he would have gotten involved in this Fenian business, if he'd known. He could have made something of his own life; stayed with the insurance company, married and had kids . . .

No. It would never have happened. He was his father's son, after all. That was why he had known Halder's story was true. He, too, had never put down any roots. He, too, was plausible, or he would not have been so good at selling insurance. In his turn, he had come to Europe on FB money, just for the hell of it. Well . . . So what?

He turned up Fish Street Hill and gazed sourly at the Monument. In twelve hours it would be a mass of rubble, strewn down the middle of the street. Then he snorted with self-contempt. That proved he was a phoney – worrying that someone might get hurt. Guys like Schelling relished the thought of gutters running with blood. They would willingly die, if they could take enough of their enemies with them . . . But that didn't make them heroes; in truth they were more like savage animals. Anyway, the Fenian Brotherhood hadn't asked for mass slaughter; they wanted to make a political point. His explosion was to be a symbolic gesture, to show the English that they could not hold Ireland in subjection for ever. Even Kelly had gone along with the idea . . . And a message could be honourable, even if the messenger was a mite shop-soiled.

His father had died a hero – that was what Grillon had said; and he must hold on to it. All this business about Three-Card Monte couldn't take that away . . . And yet his father and Captain Mackey had failed in their mission. He had read the reports in the newspapers; they had scarcely scratched the bridge. In a curious way, their failure had reinforced the authorities' smug feeling of invincibility. So how could that be heroic? It couldn't be enough just to die bravely; the action itself had to suceed . . . Well, it was too late for his father now, but he would make the Limeys sweat! He had ample explosive, the right expert help. Nothing could stop him now! And he was a McCafferty, too. Perhaps his success would validate his father's attempt, rehabilitate his honour among the Fenians. Yes, that was it – their names would be linked as heroes, they would go down in history together.

McCafferty took a lingering glance at the Monument towering above him, then turned and began to walk upstream.

Either everyone was inordinately fractious, Morton thought, or he was beginning to feel the effects of the prolonged tension.

After supper, that evening, Halder and Santo had begun a dispute in the mess-room, which developed into a prolonged argument. When Morton went upstairs to his bedroom, Kelly and Schelling were wrangling about the effects of various explosives. If only he could get away for an evening, to a theatre perhaps, he would come back to this bizarre situation refreshed. He went into the hallway. Monique was coming down the stairs. She stopped.

'Why is it, Paul, that everyone is quarrelling?' she asked. 'I wanted you to explain the kidnap plans to me. Franz said that they were excellent.'

She was wearing a pale lilac-grey blouse with her black skirt, and her hair was piled up on her head.

'I have clarified them since we spoke,' Morton said. 'I went to Liverpool Street station, this afternoon. I am sure that we could succeed.'

'Good! Then come up, and you shall tell me all about them.' She turned and held out her hand. 'Do not worry, I will not tease you again!'

Morton followed her up the stairs and into her bedroom. She seated herself elegantly on the only chair, so Morton perched on the edge of the bed.

'The Prince drives to the station,' she prompted. 'What will happen then?'

'I have discovered that his train will be at the furthest of the platforms from the entrance, where it will not interfere with ordinary traffic. That is good for us. They will feel the more secure. However, there is a stairway in the middle of the platform, which leads out to Bishopsgate Street. Once we have him there, we can spirit the Prince away.'

'But there will be guards,' Monique pointed out.

'No more than a single personal detective, it seems. Once I have my revolver to the Prince's head, he will be powerless. It is arranged that Halder and McCafferty will loiter on the platform, and hinder any attempt to rescue him. I shall force him to walk to the stairway with me. As we go up it, to the street, Santo and Schelling will be at the bottom to prevent pursuit.'

'Where will you take him?'

'That will be decided tomorrow. But Halder has arranged for a carriage to be in the street outside. It will not be difficult to drive him away.'

'And what must I do?'

'Well,' Morton hesitated. 'I would prefer you to do no more than stand in the crowd, at the head of the platform.'

'Poor Paul,' she said caressingly. 'You will never believe that a woman can fight beside a man.'

She got to her feet and walked across to him, hands on hips.

190

'You regard a woman as fit for bed only. You think a woman should be concerned about running a house, organizing the servants.'

She sat by him, and ruffled his hair.

'But I think of bed also . . . Sometimes my body aches to feel the hard thrust of a man, the spurt of his seed inside me.'

She lifted his hand and pressed it against her breast.

'Paul, I want you to be with me tonight.' She undid his shirt and slipped her hand to his chest. 'Soon, soon we shall be together . . . together till the end. We shall share our last months, share our minds, share our bodies . . .'

Morton could feel her straining against him, his own lust rising. What did it matter? To Monique, it was just an animal act; there could be no question of betrayal. For her, it would no more than confirm their supposed partnership . . . But perhaps that was important. She had to be convinced that she could trust him, over the next few days . . . And he had no ties, no need to feel guilty.

She put both her arms round his neck, and smiled. Then, as he fumbled for the button of her skirt, she began to kiss him.

9

Schelling went downstairs at five o'clock, next morning. He
roused McCafferty and Kelly, without remarking on Morton's
empty bed, and hustled them downstairs for breakfast.

After the experiment with the chimney, McCafferty had spent
the rest of that day in London, alone. He had come back late,
and announced that the demolition of the Monument must take
place next morning. Kelly would have preferred to postpone it
till Sunday, when there would have been fewer people about.
But McCafferty had pointed out that, with the kidnap of the
Prince of Wales scheduled for Friday, the cell might be dis-
persed by then. So Kelly had worked till midnight, priming and
fusing the dynamite charges. The plan was for him and Schelling to go singly to the Monument, as if they were workmen,
and conceal themselves in the narrow streets. McCafferty would
follow, with the dynamite hidden in a handcart which he had
obtained.

By six o'clock, Kelly had joined Schelling in an alley off
Pudding Lane, where they waited until the beat constable had
gone by. According to McCafferty, they had a little over half an
hour before he would come round again.

'Now!' Schelling hissed, and they ran towards Monument
Yard, hugging the silent buildings. Kelly could feel an unaccustomed excitement rising in him. In all his years of supporting
the Fenian cause, he had never actually struck a blow for
freedom. The idea itself was intoxicating. His name would go
down in the annals of the movement as a hero. When freedom
came, all Ireland would murmur his name with reverence . . .
But not his wife. Maureen cared more for her home and the

192

children than for causes. She scoffed at his Fenianism because she feared for the consequences, said he was foolish. He had not been prepared to argue the point, when the call came. He had waited till she went out to the shops, then absconded leaving a note. Now his moment had come. He hoped, without much conviction, that she would be proud of him.

They reached the Monument. A quick search of the area confirmed that it was deserted. Schelling jemmied open the door, and they went into the chamber. It was just as McCafferty had described it.

'Good!' Schelling whispered. 'The bottom of the staircase will stop too much of the force escaping. Now we must wait for the dynamite.'

They went outside and wedged the door closed with a folded piece of paper; then placed the broken hasp so that it still appeared to be locked. They concealed themselves in the entrance of a warehouse in Fish Street Hill, where they would be able to see McCafferty and his barrow coming down from Eastcheap. Ten minutes gone, Kelly thought. It would take a good five minutes to place the charges, ten if the fuses had been disturbed . . . He could run the master fuse up here. It was well concealed and out of the wind. Once the fuse was lit, nothing could stop it.

'We can run towards the Bank, when it goes up,' he remarked.

'No, my friend.' Schelling gave a fierce grin. 'No, we shall walk to the scene as if we were appalled. The police would be suspicious of anyone running away. But we must keep apart.' He pulled out his watch. 'Where is McCafferty? He should have been here, by now.'

They waited, in growing impatience, for another ten minutes. McCafferty had planned to take advantage of the police's six o'clock shift change, when the constable would be up at King William's statue. If they missed this, they would have a new constable, fresh from his night's sleep, and coming round every twenty minutes.

'Where is the imbecile?' Schelling said angrily.

'Perhaps he has been stopped.'

Schelling swore violently and peered out. 'Come,' he said, 'we will look for him. Do not hurry, and talk as we go.'

They strolled along McCafferty's route, as far as Great Tower Street. There was no sign of him.

'Perhaps he saw the police, and came a different way, to dodge them,' Kelly suggested.

'Then, where would he go?'

'Along a street nearer the river, I expect.'

'Let us see.'

They went down a steep street, and found themselves near Billingsgate Market. At this hour it was thronged with traders. Porters with strange padded hats carried baskets of fish on their heads. The street was clogged with customers' traps and barrows.

'This would be a good way to come,' Schelling observed. 'He would not be conspicuous.'

They worked their way through the press, looking for signs of McCafferty, but there were none. As they moved away from Billingsgate, they could see that he was not in Lower Thames Street.

'Maybe we have missed him, and he's waiting for us,' Kelly said.

They sprinted along till Monument Yard was in sight again. McCafferty was not there, either.

'He might have been taken,' said Kelly, feeling a mixture of trepidation and relief.

'There may be another street, closer to the river. Come!'

They went down the hill, and found themselves on London Bridge Wharf.

'There is no street along here,' Kelly said. Then a movement upstream beyond the bridge, caught his eye.

'Jaysus!' he exclaimed. 'The divil is in a boat, casting off from the pier.'

'What is the fool doing?'

They ran to the upstream end of the wharf, and waved frantically. McCafferty was in a small rowing boat only two hundred yards away, bobbing slowly down the river towards the bridge.

'Will we shout to him?' Kelly asked.

'No! He has gone mad!'

It was almost high water, the tide neutralizing the river's

194

current. The surface was a smooth grey, with scarcely a ripple. McCafferty had shipped his oars and was standing in the stern. As the dinghy drifted under the arch of the bridge, they saw him whirl a grappling hook around his head. He let go, and the line snaked out. The grapple dragged across the surface of the stone, then lodged. McCafferty pulled the boat to the pier of the bridge, and began piling the bundles of dynamite on to its downstream shoulder.

Kelly could restrain himself no longer. He sprang to his feet.

'McCafferty!' he shouted.

The figure in the boat turned and gave a triumphant grin. There came the spurt of a match, and McCafferty was frantically casting off. He got to the oars and began to row towards them. But there was no pull of the river to help him. Kelly saw a look of horror on his face, then Schelling dragged him down. There came an immense explosion, the shock wave shattering the glass in the warehouses, tearing away roof tiles. Then there was silence . . .

Kelly raised his head above the river wall. There was nothing to be seen. A few splinters of wood floated lazily by, a faint spray of water still hung in the air. Of McCafferty nothing remained.

Schelling swore violently. 'Come, we must save ourselves. Walk quickly, but do not run!'

They went back up the hill, past the Monument – the sun golden on the flaming urn at its top – and trudged home. It was all for nothing, Kelly thought dejectedly. He had screwed himself up for it, persuaded himself that it would help to liberate his nation, and now this . . . He had got away unscathed, it was true, but there was nothing he could be proud of. And what was he going to say to Maureen now?

Morton awoke to see the sun colouring the chimneys of the houses opposite. Beside him, Monique was sleeping quietly. He could hear the sound of horses' hoofs from Aldgate. It must be nearly six o'clock, he thought. Surely it would not be long before he could resume his normal life; shake off this nightmare? It would be good to go for a run around the streets in the cool morning air; to feel free and wholesome again. But first the gang had to be captured. Well, Bragg would have received his proposals by now; nothing more could be done. When he consulted the personal columns of *The Times* later on, he would know if his plans had been approved . . . There was, of course, McCafferty and his scheme to blow up the Monument. The only missing piece of that jigsaw was when the attempt was to be made. Presumably it would be before the kidnap operation. If not, McCafferty would have to find a new base. But Halder would, no doubt, have worked it all out.

Morton wondered idly why such a cultured, well-bred man should become involved with dangerous fanatics like Schelling and Santo. Despite his background of persecution and exile, he did not belong with them. And the toast to anarchy, on the evening when he'd quizzed Corbin about wine, had jarred with the anarchists. True, it had led smoothly to the catechism, but it had been a false note . . . What was the essence of the relationship between Halder and the people under his roof, Morton wondered. On the surface, he was merely a fellow *émigré*; of a different political persuasion, but nevertheless willing to shelter this disparate band of cut-throats. Why should he do it? If his involvement in their plots were discovered, his nest would be fouled with a vengeance. Why would he knowingly take such a risk?

But his conduct went far beyond merely giving them food and shelter. This generosity enabled him to exert a great measure of control over them. True, he had not objected to Schelling's explosions – in the manhole, the park, at the brickworks. But it was doubtful if anyone could control Schelling; and he had been useful in eliminating Corbin. Yet Halder had compelled Monique to attend Bourdin's funeral, despite her fierce objections. This naked exercise of power had been forced on him by Monique's irrational prejudices. But, looking back, it was obvious that Halder had always been able to persuade the anarchists to accept his ideas. Why should he bother? If he were what he pretended to be, surely he would have no truck with such murderous fanatics . . . Yet, against that must be set the fact that he had given shelter to McCafferty and tacit support to his bomb plot – long before he gave his consent to the kidnapping of the Prince of Wales. But, in a sense, he had not been able to control McCafferty and his bags of sovereigns. Even so, he had sought to influence him. The proposed attack on the Royal Mint would have served McCafferty's purpose just as well as one on the Monument. Of course, that proposal had arisen at the time when Halder had vetoed an attempt on Queen Victoria's life; before the leaders of the anarchists had decided to show their true colours.

Halder's occasional consultations with the members of the anarchist Autonomie Club were a strange business, Morton thought. A German social democrat could hardly have much standing in that company. And why should they employ Halder as their agent? It could be dangerous for them, to take into their inner councils someone who was not committed to their cause. It was inexplicable. Yet the demonstration at Bourdin's funeral had been real enough, so perhaps it was fruitless to search for logic and consistency among these people. But that had been a peaceful affair, perhaps designed to test the sentiments of the English public towards their movement. It was a far cry from that to the plot to kidnap the Prince of Wales. What were their real motives, Morton wondered. The business about the *émigrés* having been made soft by their sojourn in England was pure claptrap. They were playing right into Redman's hands.

Morton stopped the flow of his thoughts. Of course . . . He might not be the only card in Redman's hand. Suppose that Halder were also one of his agents. Or suppose that Redman had inserted one of his men into the ruling body of the Autonomie Club. Then it would all make more sense. The public display by the anarchists, at Bourdin's funeral, would have served to discredit them in the eyes of the ordinary Londoner . . . Yes, Halder was certainly taking his orders from someone else, making the members of the cell dance to their tune. If Redman were behind it all, then the Prince of Wales should be safe. And some way would be found to neutralize the efforts of McCafferty and Kelly to wreak havoc in the capital.

In that case, what was his own function? A second string to Redman's bow? Well, he had no objection to that. Then Morton thought back to his inquisition at Halder's hands, the near panic it had induced in him. That had not been play-acting . . . Come to think of it, how could Halder, an *émigré* ex-professor of philosophy, initiate enquiries into McCafferty's antecedents half a world away? The anarchists were not strong enough in America to provide such detailed information so quickly. Then Morton remembered that the request for it had been telegraphed by Halder before he himself had been shanghaied by Redman. So Halder was not working for British intelligence . . .

There came a sudden explosion echoing from the buildings, a shock that rattled the window. The Monument! It must be! Morton leapt out of bed, grabbed his shirt and trousers and sprinted downstairs.

Twenty minutes later, Santo opened the door to Schelling and Kelly. 'We heard the explosion,' he cried. 'It was *magnifico*!'

They went to the mess-room in silence. The others were met there expectantly.

'Where is McCafferty?' Halder asked.

'Dead,' Schelling said curtly.

'Dead? What happened?'

'Instead of attacking the Monument, he decided to try to blow up London Bridge. The fool blew himself up.'

'Why did you not stop him? You are the experts.'

'He deceived us. He sent us to the Monument, then went himself to Old Swan Pier, where he had prepared a small boat. He drifted down to the bridge and put the dynamite on the shoulder of a pier. It was suicidal. Had he confided in us, we would have told him so. He must have planned it yesterday evening. With the tide at the full, it was just possible for him to reach the top of the pier. But, at that time, the river was not flowing strongly enough to help him escape.'

'A pity,' Morton said, to break the ensuing silence.

'I think that he had some notion of rehabilitating his father, through his own efforts,' Halder said. 'Frankly, I begin to regret supporting him in his enterprise. It has been a failure; and I fear that it will be regarded by the populace as an anarchist outrage.'

'No!' Santo exclaimed. 'Anarchists do not fail!'

'I had almost made up my mind that it was time to move on,' Halder said. 'Two days ago, a female reporter named Miss Marsden called on me. She had been ingenious enough to discover this address from Bourdin's burial order. She specifically came to obtain information about anarchists. I told her there were no anarchists here, that Martial had been an altruistic scientist, who had lost his life testing a life-saving device. But she is clever. She heard what I had to say, but she did not believe it. She will pursue the matter further.'

Morton listened with a mixture of pride and anxiety, which was quickly blotted out by guilt at having shared Monique's bed. He would make amends, he vowed – if Catherine would let him. Once out of this morass, he would try again, see if he could woo her from her precious career.

'I think that we should withdraw from London, perhaps even seek another country,' Halder went on. 'What are your views?'

'I'll be going home, so,' Kelly said emphatically. 'There's nothing for me here, now – and I will take the rest of the Brotherhood money with me.'

Halder shrugged his assent.

'As for me,' Santo declared, 'I do not wish to waste myself on taking prisoner an English prince. I have made up my mind. I shall assassinate President Carnot, of France. Tonight I shall go to Dover.'

'As you will, Caserio,' Halder said. 'However, I feel that we should make our one and only operation here as spectacular as possible. I suggest that we should carry out Grillon's plans to the letter – except that he will shoot the Prince dead!'

'Magnificent!' Monique cried. 'I agree!'

Schelling was grinning sadistically.

'Have we enough people, though?' Morton asked.

'Of course!' Schelling said. 'Now that we only need to cover your escape, it will be simple.'

'Then we will go to Russia, Paul,' Monique said warmly. 'You will be a hero amongst heroes!'

Morton smiled. 'Well, if I am to kill the Prince of Wales, I had better make sure that there have been no alterations to his plans. This afternoon I will check at the library.'

Catherine had taken an early omnibus, to avoid the crowds, and so was the first reporter to hear of the explosion at London

Bridge. With evident misgivings, Mr Tranter had agreed that she could cover the story. She hurried to Old Jewry, where she was passed on to Inspector Cotton. He looked at her card with distaste.

'You are Bragg's tame journalist, are you not?' he asked.

'I am no one's tame journalist,' she said, nettled. 'I hear that there was an explosion at London Bridge, early this morning. Can you tell me about it?'

'What?'

'Everything there is to know. Obviously, it is a matter of great public concern.'

Cotton pondered for a moment, then stood up. 'I do not think that there was anything great about it,' he said with faintly lubricious geniality.

'The sound was heard as far away as Euston!'

'Maybe. These modern boilers work at high pressure.'

'Boilers? I do not understand.'

'As far as we can make out, a vessel was passing under the northernmost arch of the bridge, when its boiler exploded. The Thames police fished a quantity of wreckage out of the river, downstream.'

'Were there any casualties?'

'Not so far as we know. There are very few people about, at that time of the morning.'

'Surely, someone must have been on board?'

'I have no information on that. You had best ask the river police.'

'Was the bridge damaged?'

'A few chips out, here and there, but nothing of any great consequence. The City Engineer is down there now.'

Catherine tried a new tack. 'Is there any truth in the rumour that anarchists filled a boat with explosive, and floated it down to the bridge?' she asked.

Cotton grinned. 'Whoever thought that one up had an overheated imagination,' he said. 'The anarchists in this country never do anything more dangerous than spouting from soap-boxes, on a Sunday afternoon.'

'So, in your view, there is no public safety aspect to this?'

'No, miss. After all, accidents will happen.'

200

Dissatisfied, Catherine went to London Bridge. Traffic was tangled up at the approaches, solid on the bridge itself. Horses staled, drivers swore; everything seemed as normal. She pushed her way on to the downstream pavement. A self-important group of men were clustered around the lamp-standard at the centre of the second arch. She peered over the balustrade, and saw that a cradle was suspended from it. A man on the bank was pulling on a line, to drag it over the first pier. A frock-coated silk-hatted man was in it, examining the stonework. She could see a large discoloured patch, and some light grey areas, where the soot-stained surface had been chipped away. After a time, he waved his arm and was gently pulled upwards. He grasped the balustrade and stiffly manoeuvred one leg over. His associates then grabbed him, and pulled him over like a sack of flour. In the process, his splendid hat fell off and rolled into the gutter. For a moment his omniscience had slipped, he looked vulnerable and old.

'Miss Marsden, *City Press*,' Catherine said crisply. 'Have you a statement to make concerning the safety of the bridge, after this morning's explosion?'

For a moment he looked surprised, even disconcerted. Then a mask of composure settled over his features. 'I shall be making my report to the Court of Common Council, in due course,' he said.

'But, this is important to the public,' Catherine protested. 'Hundreds of thousands use this bridge every week. They have a right to know whether it is safe or not.'

The engineer gave a prim smile. 'Paramount among my duties is the ensuring of public safety,' he said pompously. 'You may assume that I have not neglected it.' He gestured towards the crawling traffic, and turned away.

Everyone was being very tight-lipped, Catherine thought. She knew nothing about explosions, but even she could see that it had been considerable. And Inspector Cotton's reticence about casualties had been absurd. But she had exhausted her sources of information – unless she went to the Thames police station, at Wapping. She groaned inwardly. But for the cab strike, it would have been easy. Now she would have to walk to the fringe of the City, where she could get a tram to Stepney

201

town hall. Then there would be the long walk down Wapping Lane. Even though she was wearing old, comfortable shoes, her feet were still tender from her Finchley expedition . . . But a man would think nothing of it, and she would have no one insinuating that she was not up to the job.

She set out defiantly, past Billingsgate Market and the Tower. Soon she found herself waiting for the tram, just opposite the top of Mansell Street. She wondered if James really was there. Halder had been lying, of that she was sure. Which led her to a presumption that anarchists were, indeed, in the Mansell Street house. So, why would James be there? He would never have become an anarchist himself, she knew him well enough for that. Sergeant Bragg had been convinced that he had run off with another woman. Even now, the thought gave her a pang of jealousy – and Bragg had been genuine enough then . . . But the last time she had seen him, he had been evasive. Instead of berating her for rejecting James, he had blocked her questions, said as little as possible. So he too was a part of this conspiracy of silence. The tram came. Her thoughts beat at her with the relentlessness of the horses' hoofs. Everyone was lying to her, excluding her – something was terribly wrong.

She alighted, and walked quickly down the mean, disquieting street. She picked her way past a woman mopping the granite steps of the police station, and went inside. A well-built young man was sitting behind a desk, writing a report. She summoned up what she hoped was a beguiling smile.

'*City Press*,' she said. 'I was wanting some information about the explosion at London Bridge, this morning.'

The man looked at her stolidly, then got to his feet.

'Inspector Dyson is dealing with that,' he said. 'Just a minute.'

He soon returned, and ushered her to a room at the back of the building. Inspector Dyson was tall and slender, with a trim moustache and balding head. He came towards her, hand outstretched.

'It is not often that we have a reporter down here,' he said effusively, 'particularly one so charming.'

Catherine took the proffered chair, trying to stifle her irritation. Why was it, she wondered, that men treated one like a cross between a half-wit child and a wanton?

202

'You are interested in the explosion at London Bridge this morning?'

'Yes.'

'Well, there is very little that I can tell you about that,' he said. 'You should go to see the City police. After all, it is their bridge!'

'I have been to see them. They said they thought that the boiler of a boat had exploded, while going under the arch. Having seen the damage, I would have thought that something much more violent was involved.'

'Such as?'

'An anarchist bomb.'

Dyson sucked in his breath. 'If you'll forgive me for saying so, miss, you sound more like the *Reynold's News* than the *City Press*.'

'I am not interested in dredging for scandal,' Catherine said sharply. 'But the people who live and work in the City are entitled to know if their lives are at risk.'

'I am only a humble policeman,' Dyson said with a placatory smile. 'I have nothing to do with such great issues.'

'Then, what can you tell me as a humble policeman?'

He considered for a moment. 'Not much,' he said. 'None of our launches was in the vicinity. One was approximately half a mile downstream, and proceeded to the site of the explosion. On the way it encountered certain flotsam, which might, or might not, have been the remains of a boat – and which might, or might not, have been connected with the explosion.'

'Was there any sign of casualties?'

'No.'

'What is your opinion of the idea that the bridge might have been damaged by the explosion of a boiler?'

Dyson gave a twisted smile. 'Since I have not seen the damage,' he said, 'you will forgive me for not having an opinion.'

Catherine took her leave, with as good a grace as she could muster. At least, she thought, this time the lack of co-operation was not because she was a woman. There was something decidedly odd going on. All she could now do was to retrace her steps and report to Mr Tranter. And she knew full well what that would mean. At the slightest whiff of irregularity or scandal, he would retreat into his den, murmuring: 'The *City Press* is concerned with the ebb and flow of the economic tides that govern the destiny of nations.' Not that it need inhibit her completely. Mr Tranter had consented to her becoming an occasional correspondent for the *Star*, as a means of deflecting her crusading zeal. Since that was a radical daily, it might welcome a story involving misrepresentation in high places. But they would not be content with vague assertions on her part. So, what could she honestly say she knew?

She reached the Aldgate terminus in a doleful state of mind. Anyone looking dispassionately at her material would put it down as the ramblings of a discontented, jealous woman. That was certainly the impression Sergeant Bragg gave. But he was one of the conspirators. More and more, she was convinced that James held the key to it all. If only she could speak to him about it. Catherine's gaze drifted towards Mansell Street, and there he was! Walking up the street, turning towards the City. She concealed herself behind the tram, until he was a hundred yards ahead of her, then went after him. He was not hurrying, thank goodness; but occasionally he would glance behind, as if afraid of being followed. She dropped back, and almost lost him at the Bank crossing; but he seemed to loiter and she closed the gap in King Street. Then he increased his pace again and went to the Guildhall buildings. After a pause, she followed him into the library. He was in the reading room, poring over the personal columns of that day's *Times*. He seemed exhilarated by what he found. Catherine refused to speculate as to its nature; she had tortured herself enough of late. James folded the paper and went into the reference section. He found an empty table in the corner, and Catherine saw him take a couple of books from the shelves. He opened them, apparently at random, then produced a writing pad from his pocket. She watched him scribble for some time, apparently absorbed in his work. Then he began to draw. The action awoke fearful memories of a case involving counterfeit notes, and James drawing the faces of the conspirators in a gas-lit crypt. On an impulse, Catherine took a book from the stack and went to sit opposite him. He did not stir.

'You still draw well, James,' she whispered, then pretended to read her book.

He did not immediately respond, concentrating on finishing the likeness of a villainous-looking man. Then he folded the sheets of paper and put them into an envelope, which he sealed.

'Take these to Bragg,' he whispered. 'It is very important . . . Insist on four men for Schelling . . . Thank you for following me.'

He pushed the envelope under the cover of her book, returned his own to the stack and strolled out. And he had not once looked at her, Catherine thought in disquiet.

When he had gone she slipped the envelope into her handbag and hurried out. She went straight to Old Jewry, and was told to go up to Bragg's room. She found him with a dismembered pipe on his blotter, poking at the stem with a pipe-cleaner. 'You lied to me, on Sunday,' she said severely, placing James's letter in front of him.

'Did I, miss?'

'Yes, you did. I have brought that from James.'

He looked at her quizzically. 'Well, if I did, it was a white lie.'

'That is hardly the point,' she said crossly. 'You had no right to do it.'

Bragg put down the pipe-stem. 'Before we go into what rights people have, or don't have, I had better have a quick look at this!'

He slit open the envelope with his tobacco-stained knife, and read the contents intently. Catherine watched him in growing impatience. Was he still going to shut her out? Eventually he put down the letter and leaned back in his chair, deep in thought. Then he spoke, addressing the ceiling.

'I wanted to keep you out of this, miss. It's a very dangerous business.'

'That is what you always say, when there is something newsworthy going on,' Catherine said sharply.

'Can I trust you?' he asked.

'Of course you can! Have I ever breached your confidence?'

'No. But we have never had anything quite like this.'

205

'Well, it would appear that, like it or not, I am already involved.'

Bragg grunted and sat forward to look at her. 'Young Morton was shanghaied by Special Branch for an operation of theirs. I have known this for only a week.' He put up a hand to still her protests. 'He was infiltrated into a cell of anarchists, in Mansell Street.'

'Number twenty-three. I know.'

Bragg raised his eyebrows, and a smile crept from under his moustache.

'Then perhaps you can tell me what it's all about.'

'No, no. Please go on.'

'He let us know, yesterday, that these revolutionists were plotting to kidnap the Prince of Wales at Liverpool Street station, when he goes to Sandringham tomorrow.'

'Good heavens!'

'Morton is the one in charge of their planning. He suggested that we should let it go ahead, and arrest the conspirators in the act. It seemed to have a good chance of success to Redman and me, and the Prime Minister agreed. It all turned on what the Prince thought. Knowing him, there was never a chance that he would veto it. He seemed almost to welcome it, I gather – but I doubt if he will any more.' Bragg tossed the papers to Catherine. 'Read that,' he said. 'Somebody has now got to tell the Prince that they intend to murder him.'

Bragg damned the striking cab-drivers to hell! By the time he had walked to New Scotland Yard, it was seven o'clock and Redman had disappeared, none knew where. Perhaps he ought to have rung on the telephone, after all, Bragg reflected. But he would have had to explain to some underling in the Met. And his own top floor would have heard all about it, as he'd bellowed to make himself heard. Blast it! He went to seek an audience with the Prime Minister, but Lord Rosebery had spent the day at the races, and his whereabouts were unknown. What next? Bragg asked himself. Lord Kimberley seemed too dry and scholarly for urgent action, and he frankly distrusted Asquith.

Anyway, there was no time to debate the matter. The only way was to consult the man most closely concerned.

It was fortunate that the flunkey on duty at Marlborough House recognized Bragg from the year before, and he soon found himself in an ante-room in the Prince of Wales's private quarters. He strolled over to the window, to watch the carriage lights streaming along the Mall. Then he heard a noise behind him. Francis Knollys, the Prince's private secretary, stood there, a worried look on his face.

'Ah, Sergeant Bragg,' he said. 'I am afraid that His Royal Highness is dressing for dinner. I have informed him that you have called.'

'Thank you, sir.'

'Is it, by any chance, related to the terrible business that the Prime Minister acquainted him of, last evening?'

'I am afraid it is, sir.'

'Very well. I am sure that he will not keep you long. Pray, have a cigar while you are waiting.'

'No, thank you, sir; but I will smoke my pipe if I may.'

'Of course.'

Bragg kicked his heels for almost half an hour; then the concealed door in the panelling opened again, and Bragg was beckoned through into the Prince's study. He was standing with his back to a log fire, short, despite his built-up shoes, corpulent and balding. Bragg wondered why he should be such a success with the women – but he did have certain advantages . . .

'Well, Bragg, I gather that I am to entrust my person to you and your worthy Morton tomorrow!' His voice was unmusical, the accent heavily Germanic.

'I regret that I have had to come tonight, on my own initiative, sir. The Prime Minister and Major Redman are not available, and it is very urgent.'

'I see.' His heavy-lidded eyes narrowed.

'No doubt, they explained the problem to you, sir, and our proposed course of action.'

'Indeed, they did, Bragg!'

'And I gather that you decided to fall in with it.'

'That is true.'

'I am afraid Morton has just let me know that the anarchists have changed their plans – er, slightly. Instead of kidnapping you, they now intend to assassinate you.'

The Prince stiffened, his blue eyes widened momentarily. 'It is not a slight change so far as I am concerned sergeant,' he said with a wry smile.

'No, sir. The question is whether you want to change your mind about tomorrow. I should say that I do not foresee any added danger. Constable Morton is the man who will be pulling the trigger. You can rely on him to be careful.'

'Careful! You speak as if he will be clipping my toe-nails! Is he accustomed to the use of firearms?'

'Oh, yes, sir. He's a first-class shot.'

'I do not know, Bragg. Princess Alexandra will be with me. I would not wish to put her at risk.'

'I appreciate that, sir, and no one will blame you if you decide not to go through with it.'

The Prince of Wales sat down, stroking his greying beard thoughtfully. Then he looked up.

'As you appreciate, Bragg, I value your opinions highly. You have already been of great service to me and my family. Will you answer one question honestly for me?'

'Of course, sir.'

'When he came, last evening, Lord Rosebery made some play with the opinion that, should I decline to fall in with this scheme to capture the conspirators, it would not be the end of the matter. They would be expected to try again and again. I would have to go around my own country, surrounded by detectives and bodyguards. Is that also your opinion?'

'From all that Constable Morton has reported, sir, I can only agree that it would be so.'

'I'll be damned if I will put up with that, Bragg! I might just as well be dead . . . So it looks as if we shall proceed, tomorrow, as previously arranged.'

'Not quite, sir. Can you tell me a bit more about the arrangements? I gather that the train will be waiting at the far platform.'

'As usual, yes. You must understand that it is not the royal train. Mamma keeps that very much to herself. It is an ordinary train – though, of course, no members of the public will travel on it.'

'Where will your compartment be, sir?'

'In the middle. You will know which one, by the strip of red carpet to the door – a silly business, but it pleases the station-master.'

'And what will happen when you arrive at the station?'

'It will be much as normal. As I believe you insisted, no one outside the police and myself will have any inkling of the plot. Not even Princess Alexandra will know. I have, however, contrived that the staff and our guests will go to the train well in advance. They should, therefore, be in no danger.'

'Good. You will appreciate, sir, that Morton will have to pretend to shoot you, so that the rest of the conspirators will move to ensure his escape. Special Branch men will be in the crowd, ready to pick them up. Constable Morton has provided us with likenesses of them.'

'I must confess,' the Prince said petulantly, 'that I resent having to submit to this imposition, merely because the government has not the will to take powers to arrest these people.'

'I quite understand that, sir. As I was saying, Morton will have to discharge his revolver. But he will shoot into the roof, so you will come to no harm.'

'I have ordered that Her Royal Highness and I shall be alone in our compartment. I regret the necessity of even her presence, but I accept that we cannot arouse suspicion among my would-be murderers. I suppose that, after the first shots, I would be expected to perhaps stumble . . . Yes, what I will do is fall on Princess Alexandra, so that, whatever happens, she will be safe.'

'That's a good idea, sir.'

'Is there anything else you can suggest, Bragg?'

'No, sir. Just act naturally, and leave the rest to us.'

'Believe you me, sergeant, that is going to be far from easy. I am damned if I even feel like dinner tonight, after what you have told me.' He took a cigar from the humidor. 'Would you like to join us in a game of baccarat, Bragg, to pass the time?'

'No, thank you, sir,' Bragg said stolidly. 'I am not acquainted with any illegal games.'

The Prince laughed. 'Very well, then. *A demain!*'

Bragg took his leave, and tramped to the West End studio of Aubrey Rivington, the society photographer. They would be using Special Branch men to arrest the conspirators, and they could show Morton's drawings to them. But he had just realized that he had no likeness of Morton himself. Nor had he seen one in Morton's rooms. Rivington seemed the best bet; but it was nine o'clock by now, so he hadn't really much hope. He turned into the narrow street behind Park Lane, and saw a gleam of light through the curtains at the back of the studio. Good! He was working late . . . At least, it was to be hoped that he was working late; Bragg didn't want to walk into a nest of nancy-boys. He turned the doorknob, and pushed; the door was locked. He banged at the knocker furiously. After a few moments, he saw the curtain drawn back and a figure come into the studio.

'Who is it?' a mincing voice cried. 'I am closed.'

'Police! Open up!'

There came the squeak of the lock, and the door was opened a crack.

'What is it?'

'Just a social call,' Bragg said amiably. 'Are you going to let me in?'

'Why, it's Sergeant Bragg. How nice!' Rivington stood back and Bragg strode into the studio. He noted that the curtain had been pulled across the passage again.

'Working late, are you?' he asked stolidly.

'You know how it is, sergeant. In this profession you are at everyone's beck and call.' His long fair hair was tousled, his floppy bow-tie awry.

'I expect you are,' Bragg said. 'Well, I'm sure you have better things to do than talk to me. What I want is a photograph of James Morton. Nothing elaborate, just something to show to some men.'

'Oh! I say! How lovely! When can he come?'

'Don't be daft! I am not wanting one taken; I just hope you have one already.'

'Oh, no,' Rivington said wistfully. 'I've never taken a portrait

210

of James. The best I could do is an enlargement from a group, taken at Lady Empringham's garden party, last summer.'

'All right then, that will have to do. How long will it take? Half an hour?'

Rivington's face flushed pink to his sketchy beard. 'Oh, I couldn't do it now,' he said. 'Anyway, my enlarger is broken.'

'I bet if we went into the dark-room,' Bragg said helpfully, 'we could find the plate. I could take it to another photographer then. I only need the print for nine o'clock tomorrow.'

'No, no! I have just remembered. I lent the plate to Mrs Humphrey Stukeley, and never got it back. I imagine she has it at her home in Shropshire.'

'So, what do I do?' Bragg asked irritably. 'It is vital that I should get Morton's likeness. There could be a life at stake.'

'Ooh! I say! Well, you could try Miss Marsden. They are very close, you know.'

'That's true,' Bragg said thoughtfully. 'Right, thank you for your help. Don't work too hard!'

He walked round to Park Lane, and found the Marsdens' imposing villa. His ring was answered by a smart, uniformed maid.

'I would like to have a quick word with Miss Marsden,' he said. 'I know it is late, but I won't keep her long.'

The maid cocked her head appraisingly. 'Who shall I say has called?' she asked.

'Sergeant Bragg, of the City police.'

'I see, sir. Would you like to wait in the hall?'

He took off his hat, and watched her skip lightly up the stairs. What it was to be young, he thought. Moments later, Catherine came down, a look of concern on her face. She led him into the drawing-room. 'I hope that a visit at this hour does not mean bad news,' she said anxiously.

'No, miss. Everything is going to plan. I should have thought of this earlier. You see, we shall be using Special Branch officers, tomorrow morning, when we arrest the conspirators. I have just realized that none of them will know what young Morton looks like. I've tried Aubrey Rivington, but he cannot help me.'

'And he sent you to me?' Catherine asked happily. 'Well, I have only a snap. It was taken by his sister, when I was

211

languishing at the Priory with a sprained ankle, a couple of years ago. I am afraid that I am in the photograph also, but I am sure that the Special Branch men will overlook that! It is really a very good likeness of James.'

'May I see it, miss?'

Catherine picked up her handbag from the settee, and took out the snap. It was dog-eared at the corners, but it was a very good likeness of them both. He had his arm round her waist, no doubt keeping the weight off her injured foot; they both looked very gay and happy. Blast it! They were a perfect couple. Why the devil didn't Morton marry her, before some society clown beat him to it?

'Is it not good enough?' Catherine asked, misinterpreting his frown.

'Yes, miss. It will do very well.'

'Then you may borrow it. But please guard it with your life! It is my most treasured possession.'

10

Bragg followed Redman to the platform of the lecture-room, and gazed at the ten men seated in front of them. They were all well built, naturally enough, but they would not stick out in a crowd as being policemen. That was the advantage of using Special Branch men; they were used to hanging about inconspicuously, melting into the background. Among the crowd at Liverpool Street station, no one would notice them.

Redman stood up. 'Good morning, gentlemen,' he said breezily. 'The reason that we are meeting in such unaccustomed splendour is that the University has an experimental machine for projecting pictures, in this lecture-room. They have been persuaded to let us play with it. You will see why, in a moment. As you are aware, this operation concerns an attack on the Prince of Wales, when he leaves London this morning to go to Sandringham. When you were originally briefed, the object of the terrorists was to be the kidnapping of His Royal Highness; now it is his assassination. So there is no room for mistakes. Understood?'

There was a general murmur of assent.

'Now, this is Detective Sergeant Bragg, of the City police. Since the location of the attempt is to be in his patch, and as he knows the station like the back of his hand, I have deputed him to work out the arrangements on the ground. Listen carefully to what he has to say. In two hours, the life of the heir to the throne may depend on it. The only thing I want to add is that the Prince has volunteered to be our stalking horse.'

'Good old Edward!' a voice cried.

'Yes,' Redman said. 'And we are not going to let him down.

Now, I will go to the back, and see if I can find out how to work this amazing new machine of theirs.' He went down from the platform to subdued cheers.

At least the men were relaxed about it all, Bragg thought. But this was their life's work, preserving the *status quo*, keeping watch on aliens and other undesirables. He stood up and went to the rostrum.

'I am sure that we would all have preferred to go round the station on foot,' he began. 'But Major Redman was afraid that the conspirators might already have someone there, looking for signs of unexpected activity. So, instead, you will have to manage with a plan I've drawn.' He tapped twice on the desk with his pencil, like a missionary at a lantern-lecture. In response, a beam of light shot out from the back of the hall and fell on a screen behind him.

'I will get it right, in a moment,' Redman called. 'I cannot seem to find the focusing device . . . Ah, this must be it.'

Gradually an image formed on the screen, gaining definition every moment. It became a series of lines and squares – a plan of the railway station. It was upside down! There was a sardonic murmur, a round of applause, then the paper was turned round and Bragg's plan was on the screen, stark and clear. He took the pointer.

'The Prince's train will be at the furthest platform from the main entrance, here,' he said. 'So your field of operations will be the area around it. There will be the usual scattering of uniformed constables around the entrance to the station, but nothing more. And I have arranged with the railway police that they will keep away from the departure platform, so you won't be falling over each other. In addition, I shall have two detective constables on the stairs leading from the station concourse to the Great Eastern Hotel, here. So you need not worry about that.

'The Prince's guests and household will already have boarded the train, before he arrives; so they will be out of the way. But we shall make no attempt to regulate the number of people who come to see them off – members of the public, railway staff and so on. To do so might create suspicion in the minds of the conspirators, and spoil the operation. So there will be quite a

214

crowd at that end of the concourse, when the Prince and Princess arrive in their carriage. They will drive down the ramp to the main entrance of the station, here, where they will be met by the station-master. He will then walk with them for the whole length of the station, to the departure platform and down the train to their compartment, here. Any questions so far?'

'What about the foot-bridge to the other platforms, sergeant?' someone asked.

'A constable from the railway police will be on it. That is normal procedure, and shouldn't alarm the conspirators . . . Right. Now, our man, Constable Morton, has been accepted by the gang as a Swiss anarchist. He has devised the attempt on the life of the Prince of Wales, and has ensured that he will be the one to pull the trigger. We know precisely what he will do. The Prince and Princess will be allowed to board, as usual. The station-master will close the train door and step back. Everyone will relax. It is at that moment that Morton will dash forward, wrench open the door and fire his revolver into the compartment. He will, in fact, shoot into the roof; but the conspirators will believe that he has shot the Prince. Naturally, the focus of attention will be the door to the compartment; so it will be necessary for two of you to grab Morton and subdue him. Who will deal with that?'

Half a dozen hands shot up.

'Right. You . . . and you. Work out how you will set about it; but make out that you have been taken unawares. Now we come to the tricky part. Originally, as you know, this was going to be a kidnap attempt. Morton was going to put his revolver to the Prince's head, and hustle him to the stairway leading to Bishopsgate, here. The other conspirators would have moved towards them, to hamper pursuit. Clearly, that won't apply any more. The general notion among them is that they will try to ensure that Morton escapes up those same stairs. But it could be a bit unpredictable; the more so since we cannot let Morton go very far without grabbing him. So you are going to have to identify the conspirators in the crowd, and jump on them as soon as they move. Is that clear? . . . Good.'

Bragg tapped on the desk with his pencil, and Catherine's prized snap appeared on the screen.

'Bags me the pretty one,' someone called amidst the whistles.

'She won't be there,' Bragg said with a grin. 'The man is Detective Constable Morton, who will carry out the supposed assassination. He's Jim Morton, the Kent and England cricketer, so don't damage him too much!' He tapped again. Morton's drawing of Schelling appeared on the screen. 'Yes, he is an ugly bugger, isn't he? Morton said, very forcibly, that we were to detail four men to take him. I know it sounds a lot, but Morton saw him pick up a grown man like a doll, and strangle him. So we will do as he says. Any volunteers?'

Three hands shot up, followed hesitantly by a fourth.

'Worried about not drawing your pensions, are you?' Bragg quipped. 'All right. I leave you to work out how you will grab him – but don't underestimate him . . . One further thing; you need not be over-gentle with him. All we have to do is dig up a coffin, and we have a murder conviction.'

Bragg tapped again, and Halder's face appeared. 'This man should be easy,' he said. 'He's the intellectual of the bunch. That probably means you should handle him gently; the fewer bruises the better. One man for him, then? . . . Right.'

Another tap, and Monique's face appeared, to general groans of protest from the men who had already volunteered. 'Yes,' Bragg said with a grin. 'She must be the least of our problems; but, all the same, she will need to be watched. She is quite prepared to go and murder archdukes in Russia, so she'd knock off an English copper as soon as blink. Who will take care of her?'

The remaining three men shot up their hands as one. 'The man in the middle,' Bragg said. 'You other two will not be in the station itself. I want you in Bishopsgate, outside the stairway to the station. That is their escape route, and you must grab any of the gang who manage to get away. As soon as you hear the pandemonium inside, be on the alert . . . Any questions? Right. The train is scheduled to leave at eleven o'clock, and the Prince will be at the station ten minutes before that time. You will make your own way there, and infiltrate the crowd as only Special Branch men know how. I shall be walking down the concourse behind the Prince; but shall have to draw back once they are in the train. So I shall be a spectator on this

216

occasion. Is everything clear? . . . Good. I am sure that you will do a quick, clean job.'

The Prince of Wales raised his Homburg to the waving bystanders. It was a beautiful morning, and he had decided on an open carriage. For one thing, it would indicate confidence, normality. And, if this was to be his last morning on earth, it would be good to be reminded of the people's affection for him and the Princess.

Alexandra was enjoying it too. With her growing deafness, she would not be hearing their cheers, but she could certainly see the warmth of their regard. Men were raising their hats, women holding up their children to see them pass. He glanced at his wife. It was a pity, he thought, that they had never been really close. For her age, she was still handsome, with her long aristocratic face and dark hair. Somehow, she had never made the transition from giggling girl, fond of pranks and party games, to a warm and loving woman. He had overheard people gossiping, saying it was her deafness; but he did not think so. She had done her wifely duty – as witness their children – but a duty it had been. And his own nature was so warm that the outcome had been inevitable.

He mentally shook himself. He was rambling on as if it really were his last day on earth. He was only playing a part! After this, he would deserve a little recreation. Perhaps he would steal off to Paris with Daisy Warwick. Or, better still, go there *en garçon*, inspect the new crop of girls at Le Chabanais. He only had to get through today, and he could feel free again, go where he wanted, when he wanted. It was worth it. He raised his hat to the crowds at Holborn Circus, and they shouted in approval. He could carry it off, all right. The reality was that he had always been acting a part; whether he was attending state occasions dressed up as a Field Marshal, or opening hospitals as a scion of a benevolent royal family. But why did everyone think of him as a brave man? It had been assumed by everyone connected with this enterprise, that he would jump at the opportunity of an adventure. Just because he was interested in military matters, in uniforms and etiquette. But, at this moment, he did not feel at all brave. He had only consented because he could not bear to have a private guard constantly with him, like some Ruritanian princeling.

St Paul's, and more crowds to acknowledge. Alexandra was revelling in their adulation . . . It was intolerable that she was being exposed to this, but politicians would exploit anyone. The truth of it was that their lives were being risked to get the government out of a hole; to allow it to preserve its liberal principles, while thumbing its collective nose at the French government. That would please Mamma, no doubt. She saw Franco-Russian friendship as being directed against Germany, the land of her beloved Albert. But any fool could see that Germany was the real threat to peace – particularly now that his nephew, Willy, was at the helm. How could such an arrogant, unstable autocrat be the son of a courtly liberal like Frederick? It was a tragedy that Frederick had not lived . . . If he himself became king of England, he would try to persuade the politicians towards a *rapprochement* with France, an *entente cordiale*. He had tried to point the way, when he coined the phrase, years ago; but that was all it had remained – empty words.

Would he ever have the chance, he wondered. The Queen was still healthy, despite her years – traipsing around Europe, dressing down her Ministers if they crossed her. She could well outlast him; certainly would, if anything went wrong today. He wondered if she had been acquainted with this master-stroke of policy. It hardly mattered. She had always been disappointed by his failure to measure up to the image she had of his dead father. She had seen him as a threat to her position, rather than a dutiful son . . . The Bank of England, and more cheering crowds. Would they cheer, he wondered, if they knew what was afoot? Probably. Whatever happened, they would have their excitement in tomorrow's papers. And, with the imminent birth of Prince George's child, the succession would be secure for as far as anyone cared to look. In truth, he himself was expendable . . . It was a pity. He would like to have had a go at being King – wielding real influence, instead of the empty routine of opening schools and entertaining buffoons like the King of Portugal . . . But he was becoming maudlin! Today was a charade, and he a mere actor. Liverpool Street station was ahead, he must screw himself up to play his part.

As they turned down the ramp, he made a remark to Alexandra, and she smiled the vague smile that meant she had not heard. Then the carriage was drawing up, the footman sliding off the box to open the door and pull down the steps. He suddenly felt as if a giant hand was twisting his entrails. Dear God! Let him not beshit himself. That would be worse than death! He felt a laugh rising at the absurdity of it all; his stage fright was gone, it was time for his big entrance.

Bragg was standing by the station-master, to receive them. He smiled reassuringly, then fell in behind them. Alexandra was quite excited, acknowledging the railway officials they had come to know over the years. He had manoeuvred her to his left side, away from the spectators, where she would be screened by him. Apart from that, everything must have seemed normal. He was tempted to look into the crowd, search for the faces of his would-be assassins. But that would be foolish. He must not show even a hint of recognition, if he saw Morton near the train. A score more steps and there it was, just as usual. They turned on to the platform. A small group of people was by the strip of red carpet. He slowed his pace, so that the station-master could overtake them and open the compartment door, as protocol demanded. Alexandra was handed up, then he followed. The door was closed behind them. His wife busied herself, settling into the corner seat. He stood irresolute, waiting . . . The fool had missed his cue! It was all to be for nothing. Then the door was wrenched open, a wild figure leaned inside, there was a fusillade of shots. He knew that he was supposed to fall on to his wife – yet here he was, still erect, fumbling for a non-existent sword. He saw Morton seized, dragged away. Suddenly a swarthy young woman dashed to take Morton's place. She drew a revolver from her handbag, and levelled it at him; he could see her finger tightening on the trigger. Then, just as the gun went off, another woman launched herself at the assassin. There was the crack of the shot, he felt a sudden blow on the side of his head and blackness swallowed him.

*

219

Catherine's sudden onslaught had felled Monique, and Bragg sprang to secure the thrashing Frenchwoman. He thrust her into the care of the Special Branch men who had been pinioning Morton, and dashed into the Prince's compartment. He was slumped in the corner, the Princess staring at him in frozen disbelief and horror. Blood was oozing from a wound above the Prince's right ear. Bragg slipped his hand inside his coat – his heart was beating strongly.

'It's all right, ma'am,' he said reassuringly. 'He was hit by a spent bullet. It isn't serious.'

A cordon of railway police held off a rapidly growing crowd, as the now conscious Prince was whisked off to the police hospital in Bishopsgate. Then Major Redman appeared and took Morton to New Scotland Yard, away from newspaper reporters.

'Well, Miss Marsden,' Bragg said heavily, 'it looks as if we fell into the usual male trap of underestimating the importance of the feminine element. Morton had told that woman to keep out of the way. I don't believe that he even knew she had a gun. But for you, this business would have had a very different outcome.'

Catherine smiled. 'Thank you, sergeant,' she said. 'I will take that as a very handsome apology! Now, unless you have very serious objections, I will go and play at being a journalist.'

'Objections! Not me! I will escort you there myself.'

They hurried to the office of the *Star*, where Catherine wrote a first-hand account of how she, merely intending to cover the royal departure, had been instrumental in foiling an assassination attempt. It could in no way be an exclusive, but it hardly mattered. The next morning, stories of her bravery were in all the papers. Her fellow-journalists had done her proud.

That night, James took Catherine to dinner at the Savoy. As he showed them to their usual table, the head waiter murmured that he had read all about her exploit. It made her feel quite a celebrity! Some of the other diners raised their glasses in salute. It was delicious! She glanced across the table.

'Stop smirking so, James,' Catherine said.

'How can I fail to smirk, when I am with so admired a young lady?'

'Admired?'

'So admired and beautiful a young lady!'

Catherine smiled. 'That is much better, James.'

Morton lifted his glass. 'I owe you a great debt,' he said. 'Without your intervention, La Laloux would have turned her gun on me. The stupid Special Branch men were holding me as if I were a real assassin. I could not move! And I saw from her look that she would save one for me.'

'You had come to know her so well?' Catherine asked lightly.

'To have come to know her at all was more than I would have wished.'

Catherine gave him an appraising glance, then raised her glass also. 'To our future professional co-operation,' she said.

'To a great deal more than that!' Morton exclaimed. 'I have the temerity to feel that my continued existence has created a liability it will take the rest of my life to discharge.'

Catherine laughed happily. 'At this moment, I can imagine that I might exact the very last iota of interest on the debt!'

'Miss Marsden,' Morton said in a rallying tone, 'without attempting to define it, dare I believe that we are back in our old relationship?'

'One could never define something so perplexing, yet so cherished,' she said softly.

'Then, may I repay the first instalment? During my period of enforced secondment, I have been thrust into a certain familiarity with the operas of Verdi. It is the opening night of his *Falstaff* on Tuesday. Will you come?'

Her face dropped. 'Oh, James, I would have loved to. But I know that it has been booked up for weeks.'

He smiled conspiratorially. 'I know,' he said. 'But I have heard a whisper that there will be room for us – in the royal box!'

Bragg was gazing out of the window of Marlborough House, having been summoned by a convalescent Prince of Wales. No doubt, he would want to talk over the events of the previous day. Bragg was not at all sure that he welcomed the honour. The request had been conveyed to him via the Commissioner and Inspector Cotton. His colleagues had been ragging him about having a special relationship with the royal family, but there was always a suspicious, grudging note in it. It was something he could well do without.

The only good thing to come out of it, to his mind, was having Morton back with him. Bragg still felt a lingering sense of guilt at the uncharitable things he had thought and said about him. He sometimes wondered if he wasn't too close to the lad; looking on him as the son he might have had. Well, there was time enough to worry about that. In the meantime there was a pile of work waiting. He pondered; perhaps the alleged abduction of the governess should come first . . .

'Sergeant Bragg!'

Francis Knollys had appeared like a pantomime king.

'Good evening, sir.'

'His Royal Highness has returned from dinner,' Knollys said. 'He wonders if you would care to join him.'

He turned, without waiting for an answer, and led Bragg into the Prince of Wales's study. The Prince was sitting by the fire, smoking a cigar and holding a large glass of brandy. Around his head was a neat white bandage. Opposite him was a young man with a long nose and waxed, military moustache.

'Ah, Bragg!' the Prince said. 'Let me introduce you to my nephew, Kaiser Wilhelm of Germany. He has just come over to observe the manoeuvres of the First Royal Dragoons, of which he is Colonel-in-Chief. Willy, this is the detective sergeant I have told you of.'

The Kaiser nodded stiffly at Bragg.

'Now the doctors have pronounced that I shall live, sergeant,' the Prince said in a rallying tone, 'I wanted, as my first act, to congratulate you personally. Though it was too much of a near-run thing, for my comfort!'

'Has Her Royal Highness recovered, sir?' Bragg asked.

'Oh, yes. She was terrified at the blood, of course. But, once she knew it was only a superficial wound, she took it all in her stride . . . Women are remarkable, Willy. I would have liked you to meet the young lady who saved my life.'

The Kaiser gave a knowing smile. 'She is pretty, then?' he asked.

'Why, yes. She is a beautiful and talented girl, who prefers being a newspaper reporter to enjoying my friendship.'

'Remarkable, indeed! But being a reporter could prove to be the more permanent position, Uncle Bertie – especially if you acquire a taste for courting danger, instead of handsome women.'

'There is no chance of that!' The Prince turned back to Bragg. 'And was the exercise a complete success?' he asked.

'Almost complete, sir.'

'Oh?' The Prince's smile faded. 'In what way was it unsuccessful?'

Bragg dropped his eyes. 'I really think you would be better leaving it till Lord Rosebery can explain it to you, sir,' he said.

'Nonsense, Bragg! Out with it! In my present euphoria, I am hardly likely to hold it against you.'

'Well, sir,' Bragg said slowly. 'We didn't manage to capture all the gang. One got away.'

'Who?'

'A man called Halder. He was what you might call the mentor of the anarchists.'

'Has he fled abroad?'

'Not exactly, sir, though I am told that he is out of our reach.'

'Stop talking in riddles,' the Prince said irritably. 'Where has he got to?'

'I do think it would be advisable . . .'

'I insist on knowing,' the Prince interrupted. 'It was my life at stake, after all!'

Bragg took a deep breath. 'Well, sir. He had a carriage outside. Once he saw that you had arrived at the station, he ran to the carriage and was driven off. The two Special Branch men watching him gave chase. They commandeered a greengrocer's trap and followed him, but they never quite caught up.'

'Did they see where he went?'

'Yes, sir.'

'Well, then?'

'He ran up the steps of the German Embassy, and they slammed the door after him . . . I am told that he has some kind of diplomatic status there.'

The Prince stared in disbelief, then swung round angrily.

223

'Willy, what the devil are you up to?'

The Kaiser shrugged his shoulders deprecatingly. 'I will look into it,' he said. 'I know that there are some stupid people in my Foreign Ministry – though what they thought would be gained by assassinating you, Uncle, is difficult to conceive. Please accept my assurance that it would not be my wish.' He smiled blandly. 'After all, if I could no longer race my yacht Meteor II against your Britannia – and beat her – my life would be immeasurably the poorer!'

HISTORICAL NOTE
On 24 June 1894, Caserio Santo stabbed President
Carnot of France to death, when he was on his way
to the opera in Lyon.